# REBELS AND PATRIOTS
## Book One

AG Claymore

## Also by A.G. Claymore:

*Beyond the Rim – Rebels and Patriots #2*
*The Gray Matter – Rebels and Patriots #3*

*The Black Ships – Black Ships #1*
*The Dark Defiance – Black Ships #2*
*The Orphan Alliance – Black Ships #3*
*Counterweight – Black Ships #4*

*Terra Cryptica – Firebringer #1*
*Prometheus Bound – Firebringer#2*

# REBELS AND PATRIOTS
**By A.G. Claymore**
**Edited by B.H. MacFadyen & C. Nuttall**
Copyright © 2014 A.G. Claymore

Andrew Claymore asserts the moral right to be identified as the author of this work.

This is a work of fiction. Names, characters, places, incidents and brands are either products of the author's imagination or are used fictitiously. The author acknowledges the trademark status and trademark owners of any products referenced in this work of fiction which have been used without permission. The publication/use of these trademarks is not authorized, associated with or sponsored by the trademark owners.

All rights reserved in all media. No part of this book may be used or reproduced without written permission, except in the case of brief quotations for use in articles or in reviews.

ISBN: 9781729266182

## free stories

When you sign up for my new-release mail list!

**Click this link to get started:**

# http://eepurl.com/ZCP-z

# TABLE OF CONTENTS

Under Attack ........................................................................ 7

Reconnaissance ................................................................. 37

Enemy Contact .................................................................. 67

Escalation ........................................................................ 169

Consolidation ...................................................................251

From the Author .............................................................. 281

# UNDER ATTACK

## *Terrorist Incident*

The middle-aged man dragged a hand across his forehead, scraping the sweat away before it could run down into his eyes. Even after six months he doubted he'd ever get used to the long hair, especially now that his assignment routinely exposed him to the heat of Irricana's three suns.

Despite the heat, he liked the view just fine. Having been born on a binary system, any world with only one sun just felt... wrong.

He leaned against the hood of the large ground-car and closed his eyes, enjoying the dry, rattling croak of the local avians. The jungles here were filled with some of the strangest life forms he'd ever seen and he'd fought on dozens of worlds throughout the Imperium. Harsh environments always seemed to bring out nature's creative side.

Those sounds were definitely starting to diminish and he opened his eyes, knowing what it meant. If they didn't manage to...

"I think we found it!" one of the younger men shouted. The older man walked across the maintenance road, stopping at the concrete barrier to look down the slope.

Six men, stripped to the waist, had hacked the exuberant foliage away from an airlock hatch and they stood looking up to him for orders, severed leaves twitching spasmodically around their feet as the rudimentary nerve conduits began reacting to a heightened electrical potential in the atmosphere.

He nodded up at the jungle canopy.

## Rebels and Patriots

The reddish orange foliage, dominant in the permanent twilight latitudes of Irricana, was slowly retracting into the dense wooden trunks. "Get it open and place the charge," he ordered. "Storm's coming and we want to be far from here when it hits."

Fourth in the Gliese system, Irricana was a tidally locked planet, one side eternally facing toward the three suns. It made the presence of indigenous life something of a minor miracle and many Imperial terracologists insisted the world had to have been developed by an unknown alien race.

Terraformed or not, the constant condensing of the atmosphere on the night side combined with the malevolent convection currents generated on the day side resulted in a planet lashed by storms of incredible violence.

As the men struggled with the hatch, a dense cloud cover quickly formed. A cascade of flashes lit the brooding vapor from deep within, followed by the rumbling crashes of thunder.

The sounds of wildlife were fading fast as the animals sensed the change in air pressure and sought cover. A large, scaled avian landed on the slope just beneath him and began burrowing into the hillside with its wide, flat beak.

He frowned up at the treetops. The jungle was almost completely barren now. "We've got less than ten minutes," he shouted down at his men.

They were manhandling an unconscious form in through the upper airlock hatch.

"That'll do," the younger man asserted, waving them up toward the access road. He followed them up the slope, scrambling over the barrier as the first drops of rain came pelting down.

The older man held out his hand to catch a few drops. He licked the water from his palm. It wasn't gritty so he figured they could get all the way back to the city without having to stop and take cover.

He looked up at the muted *crump* sound from down-slope.

A howl of rushing air grew in volume, suddenly deadened as the unconscious body plugged the hole and then resumed as their unfortunate victim was spewed through the rough opening.

"Alright," the older man shouted over the noise, "mount up, we need to get…"

His sentence was cut off as a rumble beneath their feet preceded a jet of plasma up through the shattered airlock. They dropped, scrambling over to shelter behind the concrete barrier.

"Shit!" one of the younger men exclaimed, flinching as a small piece of debris struck his shoulder. "That wasn't in the projections. Who do you think…"

"Never you mind who it was," the older man snarled. "Get in. We need to get moving."

The shriek of rushing air was already diminishing as the safety shields started to cut in. The High Speed Vacuum Line was the life blood of Irricana and, for once, the Imperial Engineering Corps hadn't skimped on the design.

The HSVL was a tunnel system that ran around the doughnut-shaped habitable zone of the planet. There was wide band of territory circling the day side of Irricana at just the right distance from its three suns to allow liquid water. The planet's North Pole continually pointed in the direction of its suns, resulting in a world with no seasonal change.

The shape of the zone made for inefficient ground transport and so the HSVL was built with a near-total vacuum inside. It allowed vehicles to move at incredible velocities, reaching cities on the other side in a matter of hours.

Unfortunately, some poor bastard had come along just after the inner airlock hatch had been blown, but before the safety protocols could kick in, seal off the section and halt all traffic. Whoever it was, they'd slammed into the intruding air like an orbital tender hitting atmo, but without any shielding.

The older man climbed into the front passenger seat, leaning forward to look up at the fast-moving clouds above as the vehicle started accelerating along the maintenance road.

If not for the damned storm making them rush, someone would simply be sitting down there, facing a containment shield and cursing the delay.

The man they'd put in the airlock had been a real piece of Human garbage and he didn't regret his role in killing him, but that might have been a family down there…

The pounding of the rain on their roof suddenly ended as their ground-car floated into one of the hundreds of mountain tunnels between their objective and Vermillion, the planetary capital.

"Thirty klicks to the end of this one," the young man behind the controls advised.

The older man nodded, releasing a tired sigh. "If the wind reads negative for particulates, we'll keep moving."

The repair crew would arrive within the half hour, after all. They didn't want to be seen anywhere near the mess they'd just made.

A.G. Claymore

# *Portal to Hell*

"**D**avai," the crew chief shouted at his thruster team. The recovered diplomatic shuttle was slowly easing through the forward nav-shielding of the CVN *Manifest Destiny* and you'd think it was the first time they'd pulled in a drifter.

"Come on!" a loud voice exclaimed behind him. "I don't have all morning!"

The chief closed his eyes, taking in a deep, calming breath. This was why he conversed with his crew in Rushto, their ancient language. If their clueless, high-born officer was going to insist on trying to do the chief's job, then he at least had to come up with his own orders.

The thruster team always took the Rushto orders anyway.

They were through the shielding now and coming down on the quarantine pad. "*Smirno... smirno,*" the chief urged as the last few inches disappeared between deck and shuttle.

"Easy now..." the aristocratic officer growled authoritatively.

Though the chief wasn't rolling his eyes at this, he somehow managed to convey the impression that he *was*.

"We'll need to get the containment shielding in place before we cut into her," the officer advised the chief.

"*Spasibo za informatsiyu,*" he replied politely, noticing his plasma specialist had turned away to hide his expression. The phrase was usually said in a drier tone, indicating the uselessness of the offered information.

It was an odd little game that had sprung up when the young aristocrat had rotated aboard the *Manifest Destiny* six months ago. The chief was free to poke fun at his officer in Rushto and the officer, in turn, was free to pretend an understanding of their enigmatic language.

The crew got stress relief and the young noble got a little respect from his fellow officers.

With the shielding up, the plasma specialist moved his boom-lift forward, leaning over the railing of his basket as he ignited his cutter.

The instant his torch began emitting a pilot-arc of plasma, every helmet inside the containment field snapped into place. The visors darkened, protecting their retinas from the torch flare and the helmets would stay closed to protect against any bio-hazards that might be lurking inside the stricken shuttle.

The boom pulled back, taking a door-shaped section of hull with it and the chief was shouldered aside. Their *brave* officer marched to the opening as a crewman extended a boarding ladder.

This time, the chief actually did roll his eyes. His officer's 'first through the breach' attitude was almost certainly a symptom of the shame he must be feeling at his safe posting.

If an aristocrat intended to hold public office, he first had to serve in the military. Most took the requirement as a chance to seek combat on the frontiers, burnishing their reputations against the day they would need to seek votes.

Some, like this pompous young fool, sought out the safest postings. The *Manifest Destiny* cruised the deepest heart of the empire, never seeing a hostile vessel.

The officer disappeared inside and the chief caught the raised eyebrows of his plasma tech. He shook his head and shrugged. "*Chto delyat?*" he asked pragmatically – *What are you gonna do?* If they managed to arrange an 'accident', the next guy might actually be worse.

His gaze darted back over to the opening in the hull, his knees flexing as if to propel him toward or away from the mysterious shuttle as the comms system picked up a strangled scream of pure

## A.G. Claymore

terror. He heard a crashing noise through his ear-piece and then the young officer came scrambling out the opening, tumbling down the boarding ladder to slam onto the carrier's deck.

"Se... security!" the young officer blurted frantically as he crabbed away from the shuttle, waving a warding hand in front of his face. He convulsed, eyes wild, his hand scratching at the front of his visor, and then he vomited all over the inside of the glazing.

"*Bozhe moi!*" The plasma tech looked back at the opening, drawing his sidearm.

The chief backed away from his panicked officer and drew his own weapon, pointing it up at the rough portal. He waved the security team forward through the shielding.

Bio-hazard or not, there was something terrible going on in that shuttle and it wasn't his job to deal with it.

## A visit from the Eye

The desk sergeant looked up as the shadow fell across his counter. He gave Paul a quick once-over before turning his chair toward the back wall to continue his conversation, touching his right hand to his ear-piece as if to accentuate where his priorities lay.

Paul's lips twitched up at the corners. Nobody of any importance would be standing at this counter. His expensive clothing, combined with his being here would have told the desk sergeant he was dealing with some prosperous merchant from one of the non-voting classes. Some disenfranchised plebeian come to bribe his son's way out of trouble.

If there was one thing a flatfoot like this loved, it was putting prosperous merchants in their place. Cops were usually just barely on the right side of the poverty line and the system of *baksheesh* had been an accepted form of income for so long it was no longer considered to be even remotely illegal.

He'd start by making Paul cool his heels on the sidewalk while he finished his conversation. The more a citizen felt like a supplicant, the bigger the bribes.

Paul understood the tactic. A rush of warm stink blew past him as a cargo carrier roared past, forcing poorly-circulated air down a passageway that was miles from real sunlight. Nobody stood out here for long if they didn't have to.

Whatever Paul's 'son' had done, it would require hefty payments, first to the desk sergeant and then to the investigating officer. From there, the money flowed up the chain. If a death was involved, it could take a cop's annual salary to make it go away.

Except Paul wasn't a prosperous merchant. He slammed his palm against the secur-shield, square in the middle of the area marked for identification.

The sergeant, hearing the hum of the resisting shield energy, turned a bored face back to Paul, his mouth opening to issue a reprimand that died as his eyes widened in shock at the orange haze around the palm.

Paul Grimm, much to the sergeant's dismay, was an equestrian-knight, an Imperial rank that indicated friends in very high places. He was also an inspector and, to make matters even worse, Paul wasn't just a local city or planetary inspector.

He was from the Imperial Corps of Inspectors – the ICI, the 'Icy Eye' or, most commonly…

"Sir…" The sergeant jumped out of his chair. "My apologies, Inspector. I didn't realize the 'Eye' was sending anybody down here to…"

"The door, Sergeant," Paul cut him off.

"Sir?" The terrified officer gaped at him like an idiot.

Paul pointed at the shutter, just to the left of the shielded window. "The door. It stinks out here."

A moment of stunned silence and then the man seemed to lurch back into action. "Yes, sir. Of course. My apologies for any…"

His words were lost in the grinding of metal on metal as the ancient grille rolled up into its housing. Paul stepped through and the portal snapped shut with a crash behind him.

The station was laid out in accordance with standard police architectural guidelines. If you were a cop, you could walk into any station in the empire and know exactly where you were going.

Paul headed for the inspectors' bullpen. A knot of plainclothes cops were huddled around one desk and he headed straight for them.

They turned at his approach, their faces showing that amusing blend of hostility & curiosity common to those who find their inner sanctum breached by a stranger.

He looked down at the inspector behind the desk, the one who'd been the center of attention until he'd walked in. "Inspector Mallas, I presume."

It was a safe bet. The attention from his co-workers was almost undoubtedly due to his newest case.

"I am," the man replied cautiously. "And you are?"

Paul smiled. "Inspector Paul Grimm, ICI. You've been assigned a hand-over case from the military," he explained, "and the senate has asked me to conduct a jurisdictional review."

Inspector Mallas nodded. "Hardly surprising, given the connections involved." He waved a hand at the one man who hadn't melted away when Paul announced his credentials. "This is Captain McElroy, our boss."

"Captain." Paul nodded politely. He turned back to find Mallas rooting through a desk drawer. The home-world cop held out a handful of green and white plastic bags. "Bag of joe?"

"Thank you, no," Paul smiled. "I've had too much already this morning and I'm dangerously close to seeing through the fabric of space-time."

With a shrug, Mallas handed one to his captain and each gave their bag a twist to release the heating catalyst. Mallas gave the bag a good shake and set it down while he brought up a holo-screen.

"Pretty much cut and dried," he declared. "The CVN *Manifest Destiny* found a drifting diplomatic shuttle and, when they cut her open, they found the entire crew and two couriers stabbed to death." He brought up the evidence holo, putting them in the cockpit, though the effect was marred somewhat by the furniture of the bullpen.

Paul suppressed the shudder of horror crawling beneath his skin, tickling at his muscles. "Where's the pilot's skin?"

Mallas put his hands above a point on his desk and dragged them back toward his abdomen. The shuttle slid past them, putting them in the passenger area. More bodies and at the back, draped in the pilot's skin, was the closest thing to a friend Paul had ever had.

And the reason Paul enjoyed the patronage of the powerful Nathaniel family.

"Julius Nathaniel," Mallas announced, "son of Senator Hadrian Nathaniel and the current magistrate of Kepler62e. He killed three flight crew and two Imperial couriers before helping himself to a nice new suit."

Paul cut him off. "It's only cut and dried if we understand the motive."

A nod. Mallas brought up a new scene and the other inspectors cheered. The holo showed Julius in bed with two young women. "They're not on any retinal register," he said with a shrug. "Big surprise, right? But the tattoos are clearly visible, showing them to be from a courtesan guild on TC-465."

"The 'happy ending' virus," Captain McElroy explained. "Carried only by the guild members of Temporary Colony-465. It's sexually transmitted, spreads quickly and dies out within forty-eight standard hours."

"Giving the client a delightful, eight-hour burst of endorphins as the infection dies out," Mallas explained. He nodded to where Julius lay. "A very small percentage of clients are genetically predisposed toward a psychotic break."

Paul looked away from the holo of his old friend. "Well, I suppose that covers motive, doesn't it?"

"So are you taking the case off our hands?" McElroy opened the nozzle on the corner of his coffee bag and took a sip.

Paul shook his head. "Like Mallas said, it's cut and dried. You don't need me interfering."

McElroy's brows lowered a few millimeters, but it was the closest he came to showing his true feelings to an inspector from the

*Eye*. He obviously assumed Paul didn't want to get tangled up in the prosecution of an aristocrat.

In most cases, he'd be correct. Most inspectors knew better than to make powerful enemies and putting a senator's son in a 'silk scarf' was a sure way to end a promising career with the *Eye*.

It was an assumption Paul was relying on. "Thanks for your time, Officers." He waved toward the hallway. "I'll see myself out."

He left the building, crossed the street and stepped into a waiting passenger mover he'd requisitioned that morning.

"Un-mute Senator Nathaniel," he sub-vocalized.

"… so get back in there and tell them you're going to take over the case, dammit!" an angry voice insisted.

"Senator," Paul replied, firmly but politely, "I don't tell you how to do your job; don't tell me how to do mine. When have I ever let your family down?" He neglected to point out that he'd only heard the last few seconds of Senator Nathaniel's angry demands.

"But we have to get him…"

"Out?" Paul cut him off. "Julius is in a holding complex, surrounded by hardcore killers. The second our enemies think we're going to get our hands on him, they'll arrange for a 'gate-glitch' or 'administrative prisoner movement error' and Julius will find himself in the same cell with some very unfriendly roommates."

"You're convinced this is a setup?"

"Absolutely. There's no way he'd be involved with courtesans and certainly not a guild from TC-465." Paul waited, wanting to see how much Hadrian Nathaniel knew about his son's service on TC-465.

"Why not them, in particular?" Nathaniel asked. "He spent five years there when he commanded 488 MEF. He would have heard about them…"

"He heard about them before he brought his troops down from orbit," Paul agreed. "You know that's how we met – he came in to ask for a BPS threat briefing."

The BPS or biological/physical/societal threat briefing was maintained by the military police on each frontier world in the Empire. It was a meticulous description of all the possible sources of danger to the Imperial Marines assigned to garrison duty on the frontier, but it was rarely accessed by incoming forces.

Julian could have relied on the overwhelming strength of his Marine Expeditionary Force to get through his five-year hitch but that almost always resulted in the loss of a few troops due to sickness, wild animals or social mistakes.

Paul had been a military policeman on TC-465 when Julius arrived and he'd been the one to give the young colonel his briefing. Paul had realized he was taking the threat to his troops seriously, that Julius was one of the few nobles who understood the concept of reciprocal duty.

"I warned him about the risk from the 'Happy Ending' virus. He got his troops tested before he let them off the ship and he was the first to hand over a blood sample." Paul took a final glance at the station house.

"Random course," he ordered his vehicle.

"You noticed," he asked the senator, "there was no evidence Julius was conscious while he was with the two courtesans?"

"I did."

"So someone grabbed him, drugged him and had those two courtesans infect him." Paul let that sink in for a few seconds. "He's an operational objective, but you're probably the strategic target in all this."

The Nathaniels often treated crime and intrigue as open combat. Every member of the family spent their obligatory term of service in the family unit. The 488 Marine Expeditionary Force descended from a unit raised by Constantine Nathaniel. He'd presented it to the Emperor's service five centuries ago using private funds. The Nathaniels had supported the unit ever since.

Paul's military service had been as a policeman, but he'd quickly learned to apply a military template to the endless machinations of the ruling class. "You don't commit to an attack on an operational objective unless it supports the timing for a strategic move. They've done this to discredit you, but what's going on right now that involves your office?"

There was a short pause. "There's been talk," Hadrian Nathaniel replied cryptically. "The imperial court might need to appoint a new regent soon."

Paul shivered. Nobody really expected the *Childe* Roland to reach the age of majority but he was only nine years old; there was no rush to bump him off. The position of regent was far more dangerous because, for all intents and purposes, it was the same as being the emperor. Many moths had died from flying too close to that particular flame.

Was Hadrian Nathaniel in the running?

"Is there anything else, Senator?"

"There's been talk of sending the 488 to Irricana to pacify some secessionist activity," Hadrian told him, "but it's hardly a coveted assignment. Few senators want to be shoved back into uniform for a low-intensity operation out on the Rim."

"I'm going to follow the evidence," Paul informed him, "and see where it leads us." He could hear a soft chime over the link.

"I need to go." Hadrian sighed. "I have a Defense Committee meeting, but keep me informed."

Paul killed the link and brought up the copy he'd made of the evidence. Few ICI inspectors had the kind of military hardware that resided in Paul's sinuses but most of them had never served, either.

If you have a senator obtaining your early release from the Marines, you can easily leave the service with your implants intact.

When Julius' five-year term came to an end, Hadrian had arranged for Paul to be released from his own ten-year contract. The lower orders tended to serve for longer terms, but Paul had made himself useful to Julius on several occasions and the Nathaniels' sense of reciprocal duty had compelled them to patronize his career.

It wasn't entirely altruistic, of course. By engineering a knighthood for Paul and getting him into the ICI, they'd created a potent asset within the law enforcement community.

And his implants gave him a distinct edge. He'd managed to download the entire case-file and now he closed his eyes to take a look at the holo of Julius and the courtesans.

The decor was licensed to an hourly-rate hotel chain and the artwork scrolling across the side wall was from a video-pool contractor. The particular imagery was tailored by planet and this mix seemed to indicate the hotel was local.

He looked back at Julius. Not even a flutter of an eyelash. If he needed any further indication his friend was out like a light, he needed look no farther than the window.

Even if Julius was the type to engage courtesans, he would have closed the blinds. Paul frowned at a soft glow outside. "Frame advance," he subvocalized. The next image in the holo recording came up, and the soft glow was gone.

"Play holo," he commanded and the shadow of one of the courtesans began moving up and down against the wall by the window. "Stop."

Paul grinned. There, outside the window, was the bright neon glow of 'Raised Eire'. He did a quick title search for address proximity, pairing the hotel and bar names. Not only were they on this world, but he was only twenty minutes away.

He resisted the urge to go there. His presence would only serve as a warning to their enemies that he was still pursuing the matter. He connected to the hotel's financial portal but, instead of invoking ICI protocol to access their records, he used his quantum processor to hack their security by brute force.

He didn't want to alarm his prey.

The room had been paid for by one of the courtesans in the video. It made sense. Whoever had arranged the scene wouldn't want to pay for it from their own account — they'd simply turn themselves into a loose end in the process.

Paul used her identity to locate an address and tasked his vehicle to go there at best possible speed. The two women would be worth talking to.

Of course, that also meant they'd be worth eliminating and he forced himself to consider his next step in the event they were already dead.

He tried to open the courtesan's financial records, hoping to find the money trail, but he was unsurprised to find they'd been burned down using a warrant from a local city cop. He brought up the cop's dossier — unremarkable, under the radar. He was the cleanup-man.

Paul opened the tasking menu and saw the cop was on his way to a public disturbance call. He very much doubted the officer would survive the assignment.

He opened his contacts and selected the 488 MEF folder. "Major Anthony Nathaniel," he ordered, opening the connection.

"Paul, tell me you have something," Julius' younger brother demanded eagerly.

## A.G. Claymore

"Following some leads, Tony, but they have a habit of going cold. One of them is a city cop, badge alpha-245-golf-566-echo-4567. He's probably on his way to catch a bullet right now so I need him collected in the next ten minutes."

A disembodied voice intruded, announcing the launch of a tactical aircraft.

"I've a team on the way," Anthony advised him. "I'll meet you at the echo site."

## Dead End

**P**aul's vehicle slowed to a halt and slid sideways into an opening on his right. He stepped out of the ground car and crossed the small platform to a bank of transit shafts. Each shaft had a magnetic monorail at the back for the ubiquitous transit-capsules that sped throughout the city. The capsules tended to travel individually in remote areas but when entering a dense neighborhood like this one, they joined into long trains.

Just like the boarding platforms for horizontal tracks, this vertical station had no doors or guard rails. The only difference here was the three-kilometer drop for those who failed to exercise caution.

A short train arrived, the capsules separating to slide into the adjacent boarding shafts. Eighteen capsule doors slid open and Paul stepped into the nearest one, ignoring the curious glances of the three young women and two men inside. The conversation between two of the women had died as he stepped inside and announced his destination to the vehicle.

He didn't belong down here, so far from fresh air. His clothing, his bearing, both proclaimed him as someone who possessed wealth and influence. He wasn't the kind of person who entered the *rezzas* without a good reason and, whatever that reason was, it probably didn't bode well for the locals.

The rezzas were large, high-density neighborhoods, usually located near the labor-intensive industries. They typically occupied a cubic kilometer and had little or no access for independently controlled vehicles.

Not that the denizens of a rezza could afford to use one anyway. Transit capsules like this one were the only way in without climbing the stairs and nobody with any sense used the stairs.

# A.G. Claymore

There were no security cameras in the stairs.

The car slid to a halt and Paul walked out through the gate, turning right to head down an endless hallway. Every five steps brought another door, another argument or blast of music, another smell of rotting garbage or a backed-up toilet.

He came to the address and, seeing the open door, drew his sidearm. The scanner on the outside was missing three screws, looking like it had been hacked and quickly put back in place.

He took a deep, calming breath and glided quietly through the open portal. The small apartment had no windows — few did down here — and there was no place to hide.

Not that the occupants were concerned about hiding. Both of the young courtesans had been decapitated, posed on the sleeping platform with their heads cradled in their hands.

He knew the business with the heads was just an attempt to cover tracks, to obscure the true motive behind their deaths. The local cops would write it off as just another cult or lone maniac, if they even heard of this. He started heading back toward the transit gate.

He was halfway there when he noticed the two people headed his way. A man and a woman. Both had been on the transit capsule with him but they'd stayed on when he exited.

The only way they could've gotten back down here so quickly was if they'd exited on the next level and run down the stairs.

He'd been a cop his entire adult life and he'd already noticed the bulges under their light jackets. They each had a small-caliber weapon dangling under their left shoulders. Paul could clearly see the rhythmic movement of their clothing as the weapons collided with the fabric.

When he was still five doors away, the young woman pulled the man around and shoved him up against the wall, planting a deep kiss on him.

25

# Rebels and Patriots

It was one of the oldest tricks in the book. There's a natural urge to look away and that's the moment you catch a bullet in the head.

This would come down to resolve. Paul was certain they'd been planted on the transit system to watch for anyone coming to look for the courtesans. There would be others, seeing as there was more than one transit line leading to this neighborhood.

Considering how thoroughly they were cleaning up the loose threads, Paul had to assume they'd be inclined to kill anyone looking into it. What other reason for them to come into this hallway?

He also didn't want it known that he was investigating. If the conspirators got spooked, they might decide to liquidate Julius.

They'd want to wait until he was past them, looking the other way.

Now came the struggle. Instinct is like a half-tamed animal, caged in the cellar. You hear it screaming, warning you of danger, but the standard reaction is to turn up the stereo and ignore it. That's why people venture out of their bedchamber, armed with a lamp to investigate a noise in the middle of the night.

If you were sure there was danger, you would have stayed put and called the police.

Paul fought the urge to downplay the risks. He *was* going to be shot in the next five seconds unless he listened to his instinct.

He watched their faces, sure he could see the tiniest sliver of eyeball. The man was watching him, so he was unlikely to draw his pistol until Paul was past, but *her* right hand was obscured by their bodies.

Paul faked a cough, bringing his right hand up toward his mouth but he diverted it at the last second, reaching under his jacket to draw a compact 5mm pistol. He swung the weapon up as his left foot hit the floor behind them and fired a three-round burst into the back of her head.

## A.G. Claymore

The rounds passed through both heads and buried themselves in the aluminum-foam panel of the wall behind them. Both bodies slumped to the floor and he noticed a small handgun in her right hand.

Despite his certainty, he was still relieved to see proof that he hadn't just murdered a young couple whose only crime had been bad timing.

He kept walking, sliding his pistol into his right hand jacket pocket and keeping his finger alongside the trigger guard.

A shadow began to bounce its way down the wall across from a stairwell twenty meters beyond the transit gate. Paul broke into a run, slapping his palm on the car-call button as he reached the first gate.

A man emerged from the stairs at a trot, one hand inside his jacket and, seeing Paul, pulled out a pistol. Paul snapped off a three-round burst, horribly inaccurate at twenty meters, and jumped across the vertical transit shaft, barely managing to get a grip on the framework at the back of the confined space.

He scrabbled with his feet until he managed to wedge them above a cross-brace and swung his weapon back to cover the opening. The approaching footfalls slowed and he held his sights to the left side of the boarding portal.

The growing hum told him a new capsule-train was approaching from beneath, but he didn't dare risk looking down. A face popped around the corner and darted back. Paul held his fire, wanting his newest opponent to get cocky.

The man shoved his pistol around the corner and Paul fired a burst at the arm before he could aim. There was a grunt of pain and the arm withdrew.

The capsule was getting very near now and Paul was anxious to finish the engagement before he left. He took a quick glance around, seeing the usual collection of junk thrown in here by the locals. He saw a broken holo-camera sitting atop a transverse beam, only inches from his left hand and he reached across his body to shove it loose using the pistol in his right hand.

"Shit!" he exclaimed in mock anger as the camera tumbled down the shaft, doing its best to imitate a falling pistol.

The grinning assailant stepped around the corner, limp right arm hanging at his side and a pistol in his left hand. His grin turned to shock as he realized his opponent was still armed.

Three rounds took him in the center of mass and he went down. The small rounds were designed to tumble inside their target and his internal organs would be irreparable.

Within hours, the three bodies would be scavenged by the locals and dumped down a biomass chute. He finally looked down to see the capsule slowing in response to the button he'd pressed earlier. He fervently hoped he was at the right end of the platform. If he got it wrong, he'd find himself crushed between two capsules as they left the station.

He breathed a sigh of relief as he saw cars appear from beneath the top capsule, shifting to the left as they headed for their assigned gate. The top car kept coming straight for him, slowing as it approached the gate. He hopped onto the roof of the car, hearing the startled shouts of surprise from its occupants at the dead body on the hallway floor.

He leaned down to knock his pistol against the capsule roof. "Six twenty three, please."

## A Fireside Chat

Paul stood on the sidewalk for a few seconds, knowing he was being watched. He wanted to give the operators from Tony's grab-team enough time to recognize him before he began walking toward the door of the abandoned production facility.

He pretended to be looking up at the open space. Industrial areas were typically located deep within the cities of the Empire but they usually had several civic layers of open space above them. It allowed the high-density aerial traffic needed to keep raw materials and finished goods flowing at peak efficiency.

There was always some churn as businesses came and went, and this particular factory had been producing servo motors until the Nathaniels had bought it and shut it down.

Now it served as one of several safe locations, ready on a moment's notice for use by those who counted the Nathaniels as their patrons.

Paul moved across to the door and entered the code. He stepped inside, and his pupils dilated as he struggled to adjust to the lower light levels. He noticed a black-clad Marine on his right and nodded a greeting, accepting the offered respirator.

He pulled it on, adjusting the seals out of long habit. Years of hull-breach drills flooded into his mind as the Marine nodded in approval.

He moved down the hallway and stepped out onto the ordinarily quiet production floor. The equipment stood silent, except for a single arc-furnace, used to melt large quantities of metal. A red-orange glow emanated from inside, slashed by brilliant white light every time an arc of electricity crashed through its interior.

Three more Marines, faces obscured by respirators, stood over a kneeling man.

Paul approached, moving to stand in front of the kneeling policeman. The man looked up at him, registering the civilian clothes and probably assuming, correctly, that Paul was the man he'd been brought here for.

"Look," he pleaded, "whoever you think I am, you're mistaken. I don't know anything, I don't have anything. Why don't you just let me go? I haven't seen your fa…"

Paul pulled off the respirator. He'd caught a break, finding this cop before he could be eliminated, but who knew what other breaks were out there being eliminated while he talked to this man?

He had to move this along quickly — give the prisoner hope, take it away — rinse and repeat as needed…

The cop sighed, shoulders sagging as he looked at his captor's face. He shook his head morosely. "Why'd you have to go and do that?"

"Because I think we can be of use to each other," Paul replied, crouching in front of the man to reinforce the offer of mutual benefit. The polymer tarp beneath their feet made small crinkling sounds in counterpoint to the louder arcs.

"You're taking money from people that I don't like and that's fine, as long as you keep me in the loop."

"Are you bent?" The cop shook his head. "If they ever found out, they'd…"

"Kill you?" Paul cut him off, grinning. "You're already dead."

He watched the man's eyes widen, saw the rapid flaring of his nostrils as his gaze darted to the arc-furnace. "We sent a team to that 'domestic dispute'," he told the cop. "When our marines walked in, the squabble ended very abruptly and they both turned out to be armed, unrelated and registered as living at two completely different addresses."

## A.G. Claymore

They'd done nothing of the sort. For all Paul knew, there was a *real* domestic dispute at that address, but it was a safe bet the cop had been on his way to his death, so why stand on ceremony?

The cop looked away, staring off into a dark corner. "No," he whispered. "They wouldn't dare. Seneca would never tolerate..." His eyes darted to Paul as he shut up.

Jumping to conclusions was one of Paul's favorite investigative techniques. It was surprising what you could shake out of a suspect through the occasional leap of insight. "Seneca would tolerate them 'borrowing' you but he can't let them get away with killing one of his assets," Paul agreed, hoping he'd read the partial sentence correctly.

He leaned in, putting his left hand on the cop's shoulder. "That tells me they're prepared to escalate the matter beyond the original plan."

The plan was still a bit of a black box for Paul but he wanted the cop to think he was being questioned by someone who already knew most of the story.

"All I know," the cop pleaded, "is they gave me a pile of credits in return for having the courtesan's financial records burned down." He winced as another arc flared behind Paul.

"The agent may have gone rogue," Paul mused for the man's benefit. He focused on the cop's eyes. "Who contacted you?"

"He didn't exactly exchange *meishi* with me, did he?" he retorted, one eyebrow raised. "His info was shielded, but I managed to get his facial rec off a street cam."

"And?" Paul prompted.

"And he's Ruffus Hancock, a nobody, but a nobody who works for Romanus Kinsey."

Paul nodded impatiently, giving the impression he already knew who the agent belonged to. "But what exactly did he say to you?"

# Rebels and Patriots

A shrug. "Burn the records out of the system, keep my mouth shut, don't start spending the money for at least a full cycle and I'd be fine."

Paul sighed. "You ever tell a citizen to cooperate and they'd be 'fine'?"

Another furtive glance at the arc-furnace.

Paul took a moment to choose his words. "Look, you're already a dead man. You'd have died an hour ago, if not for us." He waved a hand at the Marines standing behind the cop. They moved around to stand behind Paul.

"Think of us as 'life support'," he urged. "We could just *pull the plug*, as they say, or we could help you out." He grinned suddenly. "Funny old saying, isn't it?"

"What?" A tone of exasperated fear.

"*Pull the plug*," Paul replied. "What plug? Did life support patients float in some sort of fluid in the pre-imperial days?"

"Do I look like a damned medico?" Exasperation was clearly winning out.

Paul shrugged. "Frankly, you've been of use to us, so I'm inclined to offer help."

"What sort of help?" the man asked, brows lowering.

"We'll get you off-world, take you out to the frontier somewhere." He held the cop's gaze. "Man can make a name for himself out there — a new name, of course — but it's worlds better than waiting for death here."

A sigh. He looked down at the floor for a moment, face twitching as a flash of arc-light washed over him. The arc screamed a tortured warning.

He looked up at Paul. "No, thanks," he said. "I'll take my chances."

A.G. Claymore

Paul brought his hand out of his pocket, the small pistol fired three shots and the cop fell back onto the polymer sheeting. "You already have," he said quietly.

He stood, backing off the sheet and tossing the pistol down next to the body.

Kinsey was an aristocrat of moderate means. In all probability, his holdings were less extensive than Paul's.

The Nathaniel family's concept of patronage included stock tips. From their perspective, it was a zero-cost proposition to pass along tips to trusted assets like Paul.

Inspectors from the 'Eye' were free to take cases as they saw fit, but they were only paid by the case. In making Paul financially independent, the Nathaniels were able to access his services more freely.

Paul, knowing the tips were the result of Hadrian manipulating the market, frequently bet heavily and rarely failed to come out ahead. He was now a major shareholder in several companies.

Kinsey's relatively average wealth meant he couldn't be the primary mover behind this particular conspiracy. That would be someone with far more wealth. Not just impressive resources, like Paul had, but startlingly obscene amounts of credits. Kinsey had been known to fall in with the schemes of several leading families and Seneca had made use of him before.

He looked over as the Marine on his left pulled off his respirator. His face was covered in sweat and his eyes were glued to the corpse on the floor.

Paul stepped over to him. "Are you OK, Tony?" He grabbed the man's shoulder, turning him away from the body. He lowered his voice. "You've seen bodies, even killed more than your fair share of people yourself."

"Yeah, but that was combat…"

"So is this," Paul hissed. "The Empire is always in a state of civil war. It's secret, it's dirty and it never goes away. If your father hasn't told you that, I'll eat that arc-furnace, piece by piece."

The light in the room increased dramatically as one of the Marines deactivated the shielding on the furnace. The unmitigated glow of the melted steel bathed the grisly scene.

"But his hands were tied," Tony growled.

"Don't lose track of what kind of war we're fighting here," Paul said quietly, watching the Marines roll up the body and weapon in the polymer sheet. "Just because a man's hands are tied doesn't mean he's no longer a combatant. He was in the fight right up to the instant I shot him.

"I even gave him the chance to surrender," Paul reminded the Marine officer. "We could have relocated him and we'd have even found a use for him, eventually. If we'd let him walk out of here, he'd have told the enemy everything he knew about us in exchange for a few more seconds of life, and then your brother would die in prison."

"Yeah," Tony grunted. "Yeah, right. So what's next?"

Paul was watching the Marines throw the body into the arc-furnace. "Kinsey's a small fish. Too small to be running a play against your family on his own. He's out in the Gliesan systems, supposedly 'stiffening' the sector defense forces against rebels."

"*We* don't have anyone out there, do we?" Tony finally tore his eyes away from the fading color variations in the crucible.

Paul tilted his head to the side a few degrees as he came to a decision. "Not until I get there." He looked over at Tony. "I need a couple of operator pairs."

Tony waved a hand at the two men standing by the furnace. "Ed and Mike, here, Sandy and Al at the door... best operators in the 488."

Paul noticed the lack of reaction at this praise from one of their officers. They *were* that good and they knew Tony was aware of it. He nodded at Ed. "Do you boys have civvies close to hand?"

"Yes sir." Ed pulled his collar back to reveal a blue shirt underneath. "Never can tell what sort of camouflage you might need on a city op."

"Good." Paul angled his head toward Tony. "Leave your uniforms with the major. We're heading straight up to Wayfarer Station. First ship taking wormholes for Gliese 667 will have us on it."

"Mmmm," Mike chimed in, grinning. "Ration paste — how I've missed it!"

Paul chuckled. "Sorry to disappoint, but the four of you wandering around in steerage practically screams 'covert military operation'. We'll have to put you in better accommodations. First class is the last place anyone would think to look for grunts."

Rebels and Patriots

A.G. Claymore

# RECONNAISSANCE

## *Boarding*

The clerk at the boarding gate looked up at Paul, assessed his clothing, hairstyle and general demeanor and flashed him her best welcoming smile. "Good afternoon, sir. How can Pulsar Lines help you today?"

Paul returned an easy smile. "I believe this vessel is bound for Gliese 667?" He waved a hand toward the window behind her.

She beamed. "Yes indeed, sir. The *Pulsar Intrepid* is leaving in three standard hours but I'm afraid we're down to second class and lower staterooms. First class is booked solid."

Paul placed his hand on the ident-square on her shield. Unlike the police windows, the systems here were far more discrete. His social rank and profession were only visible from *her* side and her eyebrows raised a fraction, followed by the corners of her professional smile.

It wasn't his equestrian status that raised her politeness a notch. Paul was a three-percent owner of the Pulsar line.

The Nathaniels had managed to float a rumor about the passenger line several years ago. One of the family's assets at Carbon Heavy Industries had 'confided' to a reporter that CHI was about to issue a category-one maintenance bulletin on their entire line.

The reporter had promised to keep it quiet and then put it on every feed an hour later. News that Pulsar's entire fleet was about to be grounded by CHI for weeks caused the stock to plummet.

Having been the one who arranged the 'chance' meeting between the CHI employee and the reporter, Paul had already borrowed several hundred thousand shares of Pulsar from his broker and sold them before the news broke.

Two days later, he repurchased those shares at a fraction of their original price, along with a three-percent stake. The original shares went back to the brokers and he found himself sitting on a large pile of stock and credits.

He grinned. "Are we still sold out for first class?"

She tilted her head to the side. "I'm afraid we still are, sir, but there *is* the owner's suite."

"How big is it?"

"Four bedrooms, a living room and a dining area!" she replied.

Paul nodded. "We'll take it. Please have our bags sent up."

He turned away from the counter, waving his four Marine companions toward the boarding tunnel. "Two of you will have to share a bunk." He started moving for the walkway himself when a man bumped him.

"Watch where you're going!" the man admonished Paul, his voice clearly indicating his high opinion of himself.

Paul simply continued toward the tunnel opening, hearing the man address the boarding clerk — ahead of the rest of the people in the line.

"My employer requires your best accommodations. I think you know what suite we're expecting…"

Paul grinned. The best accommodations on the *Pulsar Intrepid* now meant second class. He looked back to see his Marines closing on his position and, behind them, a man followed by a mostly alien entourage , also heading straight for the boarding tunnel.

Paul knew the type. A noble, but just barely. He was fairly certain most prosperous non-voters were happier than this man. In a highly stratified society like the Empire, few things were more galling than to be at the bottom of your particular social ladder.

Even when it was *still* the top ladder.

A man like Hadrian Nathaniel preferred to travel quietly, eschewing ostentation. He was one of the most powerful men in the Empire but he felt no need to impress that on everyone who saw him.

This low-level aristocrat, however, had a retinue of useless followers and most of them were inexpensive aliens from the various subjugated worlds. The few Humans on his payroll were the face men. It was as if he was constantly proclaiming that he *really* was an important man. Paul knew the man was trying to convince *himself* at least as much as he was others.

The boarding tunnel ended and he stepped out into the ship proper. A helpful steward greeted him and offered to lead him to his cabin.

As Paul and his four companions followed the young man, he questioned his own behavior. Here he was, being followed by a small retinue of his own and taking the best accommodations on the ship.

He hadn't asked Tony for these men so he could look important, though. He knew he might need a friendly military presence and, on a world where Kinsey held sway, he couldn't turn to local forces for help.

As for the owner's suite — screw it, he liked his comfort.

Was he deluding himself?

Was anyone ever *not* deluding themselves?

The steward reached the end of a hallway and pressed a button on the wall, opening a wide portal. He waved the five men through. "Your bags will be along shortly, gentlemen." He sketched an elaborate bow, his right hand held forward, ostensibly for balance but really for a tip.

"Thanks," Paul replied, waving his own hand over the steward's, automatically transferring his usual, generous tip.

Paul closed the door as the last Marine walked in. He looked around the room. Not bad at all. It was more or less equal to his own apartment as far as the interior went, but the view from the lounge was amazing.

It boasted a broad, curving balcony looking out onto the ship's atrium, providing a magnificent view of the gardens on the central column.

The column ran the entire length of the vessels atrium and its outer surface, roughly a half kilometer in circumference, was home, not only to the ornamental gardens, but also to the bustling shops, pubs and restaurants of the *Pulsar Intrepid*.

The Marines obviously approved. Ed pulled a bottle of wine from a wall rack. "Holy shit!" He carefully put it back, looking at the other members of his fire-team in wonder. "Real glass bottle! Must be worth a year's pay at least!"

"Well, don't put it back, Ed." Paul waved at the cabinet to the left of the wine rack. "Grab five glasses and we'll see if it's worth the money."

The Marines' grins were interrupted by a chime from the portal. Paul walked over and activated the monitor.

He chuckled. "This is rich!" He looked back at the four men and grinned. "Try to act serious."

He opened the portal to reveal the minor noble. His entourage waited behind him, encumbered with baggage. The man who'd bumped Paul was rushing down the corridor, too late to intercept his employer with the bad news about the accommodations.

## A.G. Claymore

Paul made a show of looking past the noble to see the baggage. "I'm sorry," he said, turning his gaze back to the bemused noble. "There's been a mistake."

The man obviously couldn't read Paul, who simply refused to give any definitive social signals as to his actual status.

As a class, Paul generally regarded aristocrats as a waste of Imperial resources, including oxygen. It was difficult to reconcile that attitude with his close association to the Nathaniel family, but he'd managed to rationalize that through his respect for their ideals.

"A mistake?" the noble repeated the statement as a question.

"Yes," Paul confirmed, leaning to point at the small group behind the man. "Those aren't our bags."

For a minor noble, being mistaken for a wealthy equestrian would be bad enough, but being mistaken for a baggage steward was intolerable. His face purpled.

"Do you know who I am?" he asked Paul, his voice a dark warning.

Paul leaned in, squinting slightly. "Can't say as I do," he mused. He suddenly brightened. "Didn't you work at the Continent Club?"

The noble was horrified. He sputtered indignantly and might have worked his way up to actual words if his employee hadn't caught up with him, whispering in his ear.

Hearing he was now destined for a second-class cabin probably didn't improve his day by much, but he at least managed to bring his response under control. He grabbed his servant's arm and turned him back down the hall.

He followed, turning one last baleful glare at Paul before waving his entourage to follow.

Paul held out his hand, and the man's glare slid immediately to the obsolete but highly fashionable timepiece on the extended wrist.

"Something for your trouble?" Paul offered in the standard gesture of a tip.

Without a further word, the man stormed off and Paul slid the portal closed. He was surprised to realize he felt a little bad about the encounter. Offering a tip might have been just a bit too much.

He looked over at Ed, holding five glasses and staring at the bottle, now on the sideboard. He was about to tell him to get on with opening the bottle but realized, just in time, that a Marine lance-corporal would have no experience in extracting a cork.

He walked over to the sideboard, grabbed the corkscrew and opened the bottle. "Suppose I should have gone easier on the poor fool," he muttered as he poured.

"Are you kidding me?" Sandy chuckled. "Even considering the room and the expensive booze, that was the highlight of the mission so far." He nodded at the door. "I've had to serve under fools like that. It's good to see one of 'em put in their place for a change."

Paul shrugged, raising the glass to take a drink. He looked up to see the four men, holding their glasses and staring at him. He shrugged a second time. "It's ok," he said. "One thing you learn if you drink enough of this stuff is that there's no such thing as a bottle of wine that's really worth more than a few hundred credits.

"The price difference is all in the marketing," he insisted. He finally got a grip. He was probably ruining the moment for them, but then these were practical men, not given to gullibility. He could see from their expressions that they appreciated his honest explanation.

"So our plan for tonight," he went on as they tried their drinks, "is to split up. I'll do dinner in the Atrium, you lads split into pairs and pick a couple of first-class restaurants. Keep your ears open and spend some time at the bar. We probably won't learn anything, but it never hurts to conduct a recon."

"The four of us in first-class joints?" Ed looked dubious.

"Camouflage, Ed," Paul replied. "It's just another op, so put on an attitude the same way you'd put on a ghillie suit." He waved his glass around, indicating the lavish suite. "I camouflage myself with foolishness like this on a daily basis."

"Hell," Sandy muttered. "I'd take this over a ghillie suit any day."

"Speaking of camo…" Paul looked at the civilian clothing the four men had worn beneath their uniforms. "Purser's office," he ordered.

"*Nin hao*," a cheery voice filled the room. "Purser's office, Kyle speaking."

"*Nin hao*, Kyle. This is Paul in the owner's suite. I'd like four tailors sent up right away. I'm going to need my companions ready for dinner tonight."

"Certainly, sir. Is there anything else you need?"

"No, that should be all, *xiexie*." Paul broke the connection.

"What's wrong with what we're wearing?" Sandy demanded.

"Nothing at all if you think 'first class' means the falafel hut down on the promenade." Paul drawled. "I need you to fit in on the upper decks. That means suits and it means some watches – nothing flashy, I think, something understated, discerning…"

"I understand the need for this… camouflage…" Ed assured him. "But what are we supposed to do with all this stuff when we get back to the 488? We don't move in the kinds of circles where this stuff fits in."

"Get your heads in the game, boys," Paul advised. "Get comfortable in your camo and tell yourselves you're officers. It'll help if you can assume a persona you're familiar with."

He paused in thought for a few seconds then nodded to himself. "Help me pull Julius' ass out of the fire and Hadrian himself will

Rebels and Patriots

know your names. I wouldn't be surprised if your next deployment sees you berthed up in officer country."

By the time the *Pulsar Intrepid* broke umbilicals and slid away from the station, Paul had effected a surprising transformation in the four soldiers.

To their credit, they were highly intelligent and motivated individuals and they already possessed the confident swagger of men who'd learned to manage their fears.

It had really only required a few tweaks. Imperial Marines are among the most cosmopolitan citizens of the Imperium. Their deployments immerse them in an incredible variety of cultures. When they'd seen the fashionably exotic menus of the various ship-board restaurants, they realized they were probably more familiar with the food than most of the upper-class patrons.

An hour out from the first jump gate, the four Marines were good to go, perfectly comfortable in the outfits they jokingly referred to as 'urban ghillie suits'.

"Eyes and ears open, boys," Paul told them as he opened the portal. He grinned. "And try to have some fun."

## Meet and Greet

**P**aul approached the elevator to Carbon. It was listed in the ship's systems as the premiere restaurant so it was no surprise to see a reception desk in front of the elevator door.

A slightly harassed clerk looked up, forcing a smile. "Good evening, sir." He gestured to his screen. "Do you have a reservation?"

Paul detected the slightest emphasis on 'you' and assumed he'd just missed a scene. "No," he replied, giving the clerk time to take a deep breath and then stifle the exasperated sigh that threatened to escape. "But I'm in the owner's suite."

The clerk brightened. "Ah, well that puts you at the captain's table." He glanced down at the screen. "Will your companions be joining you?"

"No, they're exploring other venues tonight."

"Very good, sir." The clerk pressed a button and the elevator door slid open. "Enjoy your meal… you might find four troublesome guests up there, so I apologize in advance for any disturbance."

When the door opened again, Paul was only slightly surprised to find the same noble he'd insulted talking to the maître d'hôtel. It looked like he was being stonewalled.

He must have bulled his way past the clerk downstairs but getting on the elevator and getting a seat in a hot restaurant were two very different things.

Paul caught a whiff of expensive cologne. His cranial processor identified several designer pheromones in the scent - illegal on most core worlds due to their aphrodisiac properties. Somebody was taking full advantage of the lax statutes of the Gliesan system. He looked to his right, following the source of the scent.

Three Marine officers, a major and two lieutenants, were waiting near the elevator door, looking like they'd like nothing better than to leave. Their Identification, Friend or Foe transponders identified them as serving in 538 MEF – Kinsey's unit.

It was a double opportunity. Paul *did* feel slightly bad for the earlier insult, but he also wanted a chance to talk to the three officers. If they were on their way to the Gliese system, he might learn something useful.

Paul briskly walked past the distracted maître d', not looking around at the restaurant, but simply picking a spot and heading straight for it. If you looked lost, some employee would inevitably intercept you. Once he was in the middle of the seating area, he took a quick look around.

The captain's table was easy enough to spot. It was more or less centrally located and it had a man in a brilliant white uniform, heavy with gold brocade and a sash of rank that bore decorations from previous service in the Imperial Navy.

Paul walked over and slid into the introduction chair on the captain's left side. The chair was a common fixture on passenger liners, saving the captain from the need to stand and greet passengers. It was bad enough he had to eat with his 'cargo' but nobody expected his meal to get cold while he socialized.

"Good evening, Captain. My name is Paul Grimm…"

"Captain Harold Williams." the captain nodded politely. "I've been expecting your party for dinner. Always a pleasure to have one of our owners aboard."

"A pleasure for the owner, perhaps," Paul grinned, "but less so for the crew, I'm sure."

The captain laughed. "You've behaved yourself so far, and you've been tipping the crew — which seems a foreign concept to most of our owners." He waved to a seat on his right. "I believe I can tolerate your company for an hour or two."

"Speaking of company, Captain," Paul spoke in a slightly more confidential tone, "there's a gentleman I gave inadvertent offense to — I mistook him for a baggage steward when he showed up outside my door — and he's over at the 'front of house' talking to your maître d' right now…"

"And you'd like to use my table to make amends?" The captain glared at him. "How many?"

"One noble *gentleman*," he explained, the inflection on 'gentleman' making it clear he was a man of relatively limited means for his class, "and three companions."

"The *gentleman* is welcome," the captain offered grudgingly, "but his sycophants will have to dine elsewhere. I'll not have them licking his bum at my table; it ain't sanitary."

"Oh, they're not sycophants, Captain. They're Marines."

"*Teufelhunden*, huh?" The captain grunted. "Well, that's different. Might even be interesting." He waved to the entrance. "Why don't you convey my respects to the four gentlemen and ask them to join us for dinner?"

The noble had a slight sheen of perspiration on his forehead as Paul approached. Obviously, the negotiation for a table was not going well and he was starting to lose face in front of the three Marines.

Paul put a hand on the man's shoulder and the noble turned to look at him. Before he could react to the man who'd taken him for a servant, Paul launched into an apology. "Terribly sorry for the mistake earlier, old boy," he whispered. "Imagine my mortification when I discovered who you *really* were."

Rebels and Patriots

He raised his voice just enough for the maître d' to also hear. "I've told the captain you're out here and he asked me to convey his respects and offer an invitation to his table."

He caught the look of surprise on the man's face as he started turning his head toward the three officers by the door.

"Your three companions as well, of course," Paul added.

The noble looked back at Paul, still somewhat flustered. "Well, sir," he managed, gruffly, "damned decent of you!"

Though the maître d' hadn't even noticed Paul until now, he didn't think to question the confident interloper. He simply nodded his assent and stepped out of the way, glad to be rid of the drama.

Paul waved the men toward the captain's table before leaning close to the maître d'. "What the hell *is* his name?" he whispered.

A chuckle. "Paronius Thatcher," he whispered back.

Paul grimaced. "Sounds like something you catch from untreated water..." He caught up with the party as they arrived in front of the captain.

He gestured toward the noble. "Captain, allow me to present Paronius Thatcher and his party."

They were all waved to their seats by the captain, just in time for the first course.

A well-dressed couple was seated next to the major and the wife turned to him as the first course was being cleared. "Major, why are you called Marines? I mean, it's not as though you have anything to do with water, right?"

The major smiled politely but, before he could reply, the captain jumped in.

"It's an acronym, my dear," he exclaimed with glee.

The major rolled his eyes, ever so slightly.

"An acronym?" she asked.

48

A.G. Claymore

"Indeed." The captain set down his fork and a steward immediately whisked the small plate away. "It stands for 'My Ass Rides In Navy Equipment'."

The Marines smiled politely at the chuckles. The major turned to the young woman. "Actually, ma'am, it traces back to a time before the Empire, when naval battles were still fought on water. We've always been needed on ships. If they get boarded, you don't want those poor, delicate little sailors getting a chipped nail…"

"Very true," the captain conceded amid the laughter. "Fifteen years in the service and I've never had a ruined manicure!"

As the laughter increased, the major nodded to the captain, raising his wine glass in an informal salute.

"So what takes you to Irricana?" Paul asked Paronius.

The noble set down an empty glass and it was filled almost instantly by an attentive steward. "We're actually on our way home," he explained. "We were trying to convince the empty heads at CentCom to authorize a planetary blockade."

"Against who?" the captain asked, his eyes wide with surprise.

"Not *against*, captain," he corrected earnestly, "*for*. We need to cordon off the Gliese-667 worlds." He leaned forward to look over at the captain. "You see, the only way we can starve the insurgents of new recruits is to stop them getting off-world in the first place."

"Starve may be the only accurate word in that sentence," the captain growled. "You *do* realize that a blockade means absolutely no ships are allowed to cross the gravity threshold? Those worlds are primarily minerals exporters. Without the off-world customers, they won't have the money to buy food, not that it would matter much, with none coming in…"

One of the lieutenants accompanying Paronius waved a dismissive hand. "Economic shipping would have to continue, of course, but…"

"Blockades don't work that way," the captain cut him off forcefully. "There are three inhabited worlds in the system, meaning we'd have close to five Billion square kilometers of orbital space to watch. D'you really expect the Navy to board and search every vessel trying to pass through that much space?"

Paronius' party was silent. Paul noticed that Paronius himself looked slightly surprised, as though nobody had bothered to explain the simple facts to him. How could the major traveling with him not grasp the logistical impracticality of a blockade? He certainly didn't seem like an idiot.

"Simple mathematics," Paul observed. "That much space takes thousands of ships to police, and that's just for a complete shutdown. Anything tries to leave atmo... they destroy it."

He leaned back, lifting his wine glass and gazing into the red liquid. "If you intend to board and search every single vessel..." He shook his head. "I'm afraid we'd have to strip every squadron on the Rim to get enough ships." He looked back at Paronius.

"The Grand Senate would doubtless deem it too costly, assuming CentCom bothered to pass the suggestion along. Wage cost alone would cripple the plan. I doubt the Gliese-667 system could afford to pay a single squadron, let alone several entire *fleets*."

He could see, out of the corner of his eye, a furtive glance from the major.

His implants let him read others like a book. Paronius' heart-rate was fifteen percent above baseline and his face was growing darker by the minute but, though he usually found a confused noble unremarkable, this seemed a bit much.

Then the elements fell into place.

Paul resisted the urge to look over at the major. Whatever his official mission, the Marine officer was the *real* purpose for

A.G. Claymore

Paronius Thatcher's voyage to home-world. Thatcher was simply too clueless to have been sent for any serious reason.

He was just window dressing.

Governor Balthazar must have been politely ignoring Paronius' insistence on a blockade, writing it off as his idiot-brother's typical nonsense.

But if Balthazar needed to coordinate something delicate, something he didn't want picked up by Imperial monitors, he'd have to communicate via the old-fashioned Mark I data-storage-unit.

In this case, the major's head.

Suddenly, a barely aristocratic dimwit with a half-baked idea would be just the ticket. His ill-advised plan provided the perfect cover. The major could spend a few hours watching the blockade plan being laughed out of CentCom and then he'd be free to meet with co-conspirators on home-world.

Paul was still no closer to identifying *what* they were up to, but he was at least starting to build the order-of-battle – military parlance for a chart identifying the enemy's structure.

Paronius wouldn't be sent off to home-world without the governor's blessing, so Balthazar was involved. The major was almost certainly a go-between – he doubted the two junior officers would be trusted with information that could get senior officials executed.

He stored the facial patterns of the major and his two lieutenants in his cranial implant. When the ship crossed threshold at the Sumpter wormhole station, he'd be able to pull a real-time data query on them before the event horizon normalized.

"A bad business," Captain Williams insisted, "starving your civilians. Especially when it has no effect on the secessionists. Creates resentment…"

51

"It would only be until we stopped them," Paronius countered weakly.

Williams shook his head. "When you outlaw travel, only the *outlaws* will travel and you'll have a damn sight more folks turning to the cause if you interfere with their livelihoods."

"But we have to make an example," the young lieutenant insisted, gamely coming to Paronius' defense.

"Hardly the example you want to make." The captain shook his head before leaning far forward to point at the hapless aristocrat. "It's folk like your young Miss Urbica who're making the *right* kind of example."

Thatcher recoiled, both from the pointing hand and from the name invoked. "Her father needs to reel her in," he declared. "It's unseemly, staying in uniform so long after her demobilization option, and in a *combat* role? Ridiculous — she's just a wisp of a girl with a Zhan-Dark complex!"

It was a common enough insult in the Imperium. Women who showed too much independence were labeled with it, even though nobody had any idea of its origins.

Any man who felt he was being upstaged by a woman was almost sure to use it, and Paul couldn't help but feel the comment meant Thatcher felt inadequate where young Miss Urbica was concerned.

The aristocratic young woman leaned toward the major. "She's a Marine, isn't she?" She clearly didn't care for Paronius Thatcher's views and wanted to keep him squirming.

A nod. "Yes, ma'am," he confirmed. "A colonel. Daughter of a middling noble family out of the Ganges system."

"Came out with that adviser team under the late Rear-Admiral Crispin," Williams explained.

## A.G. Claymore

"Pardon me, Captain," the young woman interjected, "Did you say 'late'?"

Williams touched a finger to the side of his nose. "Crispin had an *accident* with his sidearm shortly after they arrived in-system. Apparently, the poor fellow managed to shoot himself in the back three times, so now it's a bit unclear as to who's in charge. "They're supposed to *stiffen* the sector defense forces, but *she's* the only one doing any stiffening…

"Pardon my carelessness, ma'am." He hastened to mollify the shocked young noblewoman. "I mean no double entendre. She's just a damned good officer. Instead of endless lecturing on how to fight insurgents, she took them off to the edge of the Rim and beat seven kinds of Hell out of the raiders – even tipped into a skirmish or two with the Greys."

"When she could have been back at 667, stopping secessionist terrorist attacks," Paronius groused.

The captain turned on him with barely concealed disgust and Paul suddenly felt less guilty about tweaking Thatcher earlier. The fool really did have his own blood in the water and here he was, splashing it around like a maniac.

"How exactly would the SDF stop a stadium bombing? Fire on the bomb from orbit? They'd crack open the dome in the process and let that nasty weather in. I suppose you could at least claim the thousands of dead citizens weren't casualties of the secessionists."

Paronius developed a sudden interest in the restaurant's ornate decor.

The captain turned back to the young aristocratic couple "She kept giving the SDF units victory after victory, y'see," he resumed his explanation to the young woman who was now giving him her undivided attention.

"When they came back from the Battle of the Carbon Well, she gave them a present, the best kind of present a beloved leader could ever give her troops."

"What?" the noblewoman demanded breathlessly, eyes shining.

"An *identity*. She declared they would no longer be miscellaneous, numbered SDF units. From that moment on, they would all be known as the 1st Gliesan Dragoons."

"And that pleased them?"

"Ma'am, after that, they'd follow her straight into a black hole. She welded them together into a single unit, gave them something to hang their pride on. They don't have to explain that they were with 724 Regional Defense Squadron which was one of the units that fought at Carbon Well. They just wear the *1GD* on their shoulders and everyone knows what they did."

"Random citizens buy them drinks," the major drawled, rolling his eyes.

"Not to mention commercial captains," Williams added emphatically. "We used to have six or seven piracy incidents a year — per ship — but since young Colonel Urbica and her dragoons started patrolling the Gliesan Main..."

He leaned back, spreading his hands. "Not a single attack in two years."

"They're that effective?" the young woman asked.

"It does strain credulity, just a bit," her husband added. "The raiders were quite bold the last time we came out this way. We were overtaken and boarded in full view of the Iridium colony just four years ago." He looked at his wife and shuddered.

"We were completely in their power."

"Your lovely wife would have been quite safe, I'm sure," the captain offered gently. "Most of those raiders are nothing more than businessmen, when you get right down to it."

# A.G. Claymore

"Businessmen?" Paronius exploded. "They're criminals, plain and simple."

The captain arched an eyebrow. "What businessman *isn't* a criminal? Perhaps their only fault is their lack of circumspection? I've known aristocrats who commit atrocities on a planetary scale and get Imperial commendations for it."

He turned back to the young couple. "My point was that they usually have the sense to keep their hands off their high-born captives. Stirring up moral outrage is bad for cash flow." He shrugged. "Last thing they'd want is a Marine Expeditionary Force sent to slap them down.

"That, in essence," he explained, "is what Colonel Urbica is using against them. She knows she just has to make it too expensive for them to continue operations on the Gliesan Main. They've gone elsewhere."

"Chasing off pirates doesn't stop the secessionists," the major observed.

"No," the captain agreed, "it doesn't, but it does slow them down, or do you think they get their supplies from legal sources?"

The major tilted his head, acknowledging the captain's point.

Paul drained the last of his wine and set the glass on the table. "If you'll excuse me," he said, rising to his feet, "I believe I'll explore the rest of our excellent ship. Sir." He returned the captain's nod and headed for the elevator.

## *Major Trouble*

**P**aul wandered down the *Grande Allee,* a seven-story atrium in the ship's main cylindrical hull, noticing the incredibly expensive merchandise with more than a little disgust.

The aristocracy was obsessed with their *things*. He gazed at a pair of shoes in a shop front. They cost enough to feed a family on a Rim world for an entire year.

What made a couple pounds of silicone and leather worth so much?

The value of things — such an artificial concept.

He shook his head and moved on. He was no paragon himself. The anachronistic mechanical timepiece on his own wrist would *house* a family for an entire year.

And he'd just given four of them to his Marine companions.

He'd bought them as camouflage, or at least that was what he'd told himself at the time. Even if it *was* camouflage, was it justifiable to spend so many credits simply to confuse aristocrats?

He knew it helped to move investigations along. When nobles couldn't figure out what social order he belonged to, it kept them on their heels, made them slip up.

But he still enjoyed the effects of his camouflage and that always left a taste of guilt. If he'd had the money for just one of those watches as a child, his father wouldn't have died as an impoverished miner on Hardisty.

He turned right and followed a corridor toward the center of the ship. The ornate hallway turned into a bridge as he stepped into the massive, cylindrical central atrium.

Roughly a kilometer across, the atrium was dominated by the central column. The sounds of music, shouting hawkers and passengers grew in volume as he reached the sliding joint between

A.G. Claymore

the bridge and the rotating central cylinder. He stepped onto the column and, preferring a little quiet to order his thoughts, angled toward the garden side.

That major would be his best bet. If he could find out who the Marine was reporting to on Irricana, he'd be able to move on to the bigger players. He knew there was no guarantee that the major's plot was connected with Julius' predicament, but it was definitely probable.

He suddenly caught a hint of cologne.

Those damned pheromones…

Faint footsteps approached, accelerating. He detected ozone.

A stun ball. He grinned, continuing to walk through the park as though he didn't have a care in the world.

The major would be counting on his augmented abilities — implants that gave Imperial Marines incredible strength, speed and agility. He probably didn't know he was approaching a target that represented a very rare convergence of factors.

Paul was ex-military and he'd won the patronage of a powerful aristocratic family. The Nathaniels had arranged for him to keep the basic military augment-suite on his discharge.

Then they sent him for testing.

He wasn't part of that fractional percentage of citizens compatible with full augmentation, but he was eligible for a hell of a lot.

The Nathaniels had him tweaked within an inch of his life. There were times when he hated them for it, but it did come in handy at moments like this.

He felt a tingle at his lower back as the stun ball made contact. He turned to find his assailant twitching on the stone pathway. He crouched, offering his erstwhile attacker a friendly smile as though they were bumping into one another at a coffee shop or bar.

Rebels and Patriots

"Part of the electronic warfare package," he explained casually, tapping his own chest. He brushed off the man's feeble attempt to grab his arm. "Not to worry, the effects will wear off over the next twenty minutes."

The Marine was purple with rage. His attack had been turned against him with alarming ease. He glared at Paul, who affected not to notice the hostility.

"Directed ionization, or something like that," he mused. "I wasn't really listening at the time — the pain was absolutely excruciating."

He tilted his head. "But here I am, telling you what you already know. You've got the standard Marine package, I'm sure."

There was no answer from the stunned officer, but he did hear approaching footsteps. Someone was moving through the trees to the left of the path.

Paul stood as Ed and Mike emerged, pistols in hand. "Gentlemen," he greeted them warmly. "Your timing is impeccable." He gestured to the helpless form. "We need to help the major back to our quarters. Seems he's had a little too much."

"Too much electricity, you mean." Ed grinned. "We saw you come into the central atrium and figured we'd keep an eye on you." He gestured down at the incapacitated Marine. "When this one pulled a stun ball, we almost dropped him, but I had a feeling you knew he was there."

"Perceptive." Paul raised an eyebrow. "And if I'd failed to detect his attack?"

Mike shrugged. "Well it *was* just a stun ball. We would've been able to get you both back to the room."

"Well, we need to camouflage him before we start back to the room." Paul nodded at Mike. "Dump some whiskey on him, get a bit of it down his throat as well."

A.G. Claymore

"What makes you think I have…"

"Flexi-flask, right front pocket of that new dinner jacket," Paul cut him off. "I was in the suite when you put it in there, remember?"

Mike pulled out the small rectangular bladder and popped the spigot open, pausing to take a sniff. "Y'know, this stuff ain't cheap."

Paul bit down on the impatient response that leapt to the tip of his tongue. For a Marine non-com, whiskey, any whiskey, was an expensive luxury. Even the cheap rotgut currently leaking its aromatic compounds from the flask.

"Up in our suite," Paul began in a salesman-like tone, "there's a bottle of single malt, distilled on Iona. It spent fifty years in oak before they bottled it, five hundred years ago." He tilted his head. "Some don't care for the woody hints, but you," he emphasized, pointing at Mike, "you, my friend, strike me as the kind of man who might just appreciate such a brilliantly composed whiskey."

Mike was spellbound.

Paul knew he'd closed the bargain, but he just couldn't stop himself. He might be a cynic where wine was concerned, but he had a real love for good whiskey and the anticipation was half the fun, something he wanted to share with Mike to the fullest.

"Fifty years in a sherry barrel," he continued. "It was one of only eight hundred that survived the bitter trade-war between the Campbells and the MacGregors. It was bottled during the conflict, but then it sat, forgotten, for three hundred years while the Ionans rebuilt their war-shattered planetary economy.

"And then one day, they found the caverns where the last production run of Campbell's distillery had been stored, and the bottles have been circulating throughout the Imperium ever since. Every now and then, someone dares to open one."

Mike was nodding, his grin threatening to split his head in half. He stepped over to the major. "Ed, get his mouth open."

Ed held the major's nose and, when the man finally opened his mouth for a breath, Mike was ready, pouring almost half down the officer's throat. Ignoring the strangled coughing, he poured the rest on the man's tunic and pants.

"Right, let's get him back to the rooms." Paul gestured at the coughing form. "Gentlemen, perhaps you could give our inebriated friend a hand? I don't think he's quite ready to walk."

A.G. Claymore

# *Interrogation*

**S**andy and Al walked into the suite, just back from dinner, and stopped, staring at the scene before them as the doors slid shut.

Paul, Ed and Mike were sitting on the couches in the main lounge, laughing their heads off at the antics of a holographic cat and mouse.

A major of the Imperial Marine Corps sat in one of the club chairs, his hands tied and a lamp shade over his head.

"Pre-Imperial stuff," Paul explained, waving at the cartoon animals. "It's a wonder it isn't banned. The cat's constant failure to catch the mouse despite his huge advantage in strength could easily be seen as a sinister commentary on the Imperium."

He looked back as Ed and Mike broke out laughing again. "That thing on the cat's tail is evidently a trap and, from its size, designed for killing mice but it's been turned on the cat instead."

He shook his head as he chuckled. "How the Imperial censors never saw the allegorical reference to revolution is completely beyond me." He looked at the newcomers and followed their gaze. "Oh, the major?" He smiled. "A real party animal, that one, but he didn't care for the show, so…"

He stood, waving a hand to bring up a holo-menu and pausing the program. He walked over to the prisoner, removing the shade from his head.

"Let's get started, shall we?"

He sat on the coffee table in front of the major. "Are you *sure* you wouldn't like some whiskey? One sip and you're transported back five centuries to the trade-war on Iona."

The major gave him a look of pure loathing. "Might as well start slicing into me," he growled, "cause I'm not going to play along with any of this, you psychotic freak."

"Well, of course you aren't," Paul said in mild surprise, as if he'd always taken the point for granted. "You're a Marine, after all – incorruptible, after a fashion."

He looked up at his companion's frowns and waved a placatory hand. "It's practically unheard of for a Marine to be bribed or compromised," he allowed, "but what if you serve a leader who's so morally compromised that you're faced with a decision between obeying illegal orders or engaging in mutiny?"

"Like I said: start cutting."

Paul shook his head. "I have no intention of torturing you, but I *will* destroy your reputation as well as that of the 538."

The major frowned but kept his mouth shut.

"I can easily access a burner account," Paul said as he opened a new holo-menu. "Easiest thing in the worlds to move several hundred thousand credits from that account into yours." He closed the window.

"There! Payment received; now we just need to make it look like you carried out your little freelance assignment." He leaned forward. "You've just been paid for the demise of one Paronius Thatcher, an aristocrat of some mild comedic value, but the Imperium's better off without him, don't you think?"

The captive's eyes widened. "You murdering bastard…"

"And what was your plan for *me*?" Paul countered. "After you'd stunned me and done God-knows-what, were you just going to let me go, knowing who you were?"

"You wouldn't have seen my face," the major insisted. "I was behind…"

"Behind me, yes," Paul admitted, "but wearing so much of that cologne you smelled like all the brothels on Narbonne combined. You're so inept at this." He shook his head. "You leave a trail like a

A.G. Claymore

quick-slug. It will be no surprise to anyone who knows you that you received a fatal defensive wound while murdering your target.

"Or you can tell us who you report to and I'll remove the offending funds from your account."

"Go to Hell!"

Paul sighed. "Are you so sure we aren't already there?" He stood, looking at Ed. "Well, if he isn't going to comply, we only have one use for him. Let's get him down to Paronius' cabin and…"

He tumbled back onto the coffee table as the officer lurched out of his chair and raced across the room. The major leapt, getting his right foot onto the low railing overlooking the central atrium, and pushed off, easily escaping the artificial gravity field of the suite.

As the five men stared in surprise, their escaped prisoner writhed in agony as he floated toward the central column. His skin slowly turned blue and ice crystals formed around his eyes and mouth.

Paul chewed the inside of his lip for a few seconds. "Well, that was certainly unexpected." He looked at his companions. "Do you think he was aware of the extreme cold and lack of oxygen out there, or did it come as a surprise?"

"Came as a surprise to me," Ed admitted.

Paul nodded. The atmosphere in the central atrium was held close to the central column through a process that involved an artificially created energy gradient. It drew oxygen and energy away from most of the vast, open space.

"Oh, shit," Mike exclaimed. "His wrists are still tied. It's going to raise questions."

Paul gave it a moment's thought, then shook his head. "No, it's just as though he'd been dropped in a vat of liquid nitrogen. He'll shatter when he hits the garden. Shipboard security will have a hell of a time figuring it out — probably write it off as a drunken leap."

He opened a holo screen and located the ship's outgoing message queue. He hacked into the secure folder easily and found one message from a major in the Imperial Marines. Just to be sure, Paul deleted it.

No sense in letting a message get out that might identify Paul as a threat.

"What exactly were you hoping to get from him?" Ed asked.

"I'd originally planned to keep a discrete eye on him to see who he's dealing with on Irricana," Paul explained as he watched the major impact the garden, too far away to see the grisly details. No sound reached them across the airless space.

"Unfortunately, he developed suspicions about me and tried to… Well, we'll never know what he had in mind, but he forced a change in the plan. I was hoping he might trade a little information in return for my abandoning a plan I never would have carried out in the first place."

"You were bluffing about the contract killing?" Mike was surprised.

"Nothing to gain in actually carrying it through." Paul shrugged. "I was just going to toss him off the balcony."

"Well, I suppose it's nice he did it on his own," Ed mused. "Death before dishonor…"

"Well, he *was* a Marine, after all," Paul agreed. He looked at Sandy. "Did you guys learn anything of interest?"

A grin. "We had a first rate jaeger-schnitzel at a place on the *Grande Allee*, drank a bit too much lager and talked to a hell of a lot of idiots."

Al picked up the story. "Then we went looking for that falafel hut you mentioned." He held up a hand. "Don't give us that look," he insisted. "We didn't learn a damn thing in the first-class areas,

## A.G. Claymore

but it's the vendors on the promenade that have to pay attention to what's going on if they want to earn out their franchises.

"They need to read the crowds and identify the potential customers if they want to stay in business. Some of those guys would ace the deep recon course — they're perceptive."

"All right," Paul held up his hands. "I withdraw my earlier remark. What did you learn at the falafel hut?"

"First off, this guy's had the franchise on the Gliese run for more than twenty years, so he's got a good feel for what's normal and what isn't," Sandy explained. "He took one look at us and pegged us as officers in the 538."

"The 538 specifically, huh?"

"That's right," Sandy nodded. His eyes suddenly lit up when he saw the open whiskey bottle on the sideboard. He nodded inquiringly in its general direction.

"Help yourself." Paul dropped onto a couch as Sandy and Al made a beeline for the bottle. "Grab flasks from the drawer and fill 'em up while you're at it. That stuff's too pricey to leave any behind for the crew to guzzle."

Sandy rooted through the drawer while Al poured two tumblers. "So he knew the 538's been shifting troops to the Gliese system for a couple of years now." Sandy said. "Used to be a couple hundred per trip, at first, but now it's just a dozen or so. That many grunts — some of them are bound to spill a few beans."

"And they're always in civvies," Al added. "He made us for Marines in a heartbeat and the way we're dressed had him thinking we're officers. He asked us if we're planning to move the entire unit to Irricana.

"We acted as though we had no idea what he was talking about, with a nudge and a wink thrown in so we wouldn't scare him, and he took great delight in showing us what he knew."

The four Marines were all at pay-band twenty or above. That meant they all had the advanced Prisoner of Conflict course. A big part of POC training was resisting interrogation which, of necessity, involved an understanding of interrogation methods.

Paul was pleased with the results of their efforts, but he wasn't terribly surprised.

He held up a hand to pause the conversation. Accessing his cranial processor, he opened the queue with the facial recognition queries from dinner and added in a request for logistical records from the 538th Marine Expeditionary Force.

He'd seen more than a few sneaky deployments over the years and the troops themselves were usually hidden with great care, but a unit with fifty thousand personnel was a complex beast. Somewhere, there were details that the conspirators might miss.

The new request would synch with home-world as they traversed the event horizon at Sumpter station.

"OK," Paul said, picking up his tumbler. "We should be able to find corroborating evidence if the 538 is really involved, but what *is* it they're involved in?"

He looked into the amber liquid. "That's a question we'll have to answer when we reach Irricana."

## ENEMY CONTACT
### Landing

he view from orbit was more interesting than usual. Most planets were a more-or-less homogeneous spread of wildlife and habitation, but Irricana was very different.

The station was situated above the capital, Vermillion, and it offered one of the strangest views in the Imperium. Because the northern pole was constantly aimed at the system's three suns, a broad, doughnut-shaped band of vegetation circled the day-side.

On the edge bordering the central dead-zone, the foliage tended more toward the green shades and faded to reds, oranges and yellows toward the equator, where the light was fainter.

There were cities down there, Paul knew, but they were all too small and compact to be seen from orbit. Though many colony worlds had been built with quaint, separate buildings, the vicious climate on Irricana ruled out any arrangement that required walking around outside.

With proper planning and a constant eye to the weather, one could go outside, but it was far better to simply employ the standard Imperial arco-designs. The arcologies were massive structures containing entire cities within one shell.

On Irricana, the arcos were built mostly underground. Storms coming from the eye of the day-side were incredibly corrosive, carrying sand at hundreds of kilometers per hour. They could eat away the outer shell of a concrete arco in less than a decade.

And speaking of storms, he could see a circling, reddish-brown mass closing in on the section of the band where Vermillion lay.

That was why they were all standing in the departure lounge, staring out the window rather than sitting in a descending shuttle.

Ed took a quick look around the lounge to see if anyone was standing too close to them, but most of the waiting passengers were in a nearby bar. He stepped a little closer to Paul. "You told us, back at Sumpter, that the 'ghost grunts' were coming from 538 MEF, but you never told us what the proof was."

Paul chuckled. "For future reference, Ed?"

A shrug. "Never know when a fella might get caught up in a scheme," he replied cheerfully. "The 488 *is* closely tied to the Nathaniel family, after all."

The Nathaniels always had someone serving in the 488, usually at the rank of major or higher. Julius had commanded the units aviation group for five years and his younger brother, Tony, would be promoted into that role within two years.

Though there were rules preventing the noble families from suborning the Imperial Marines, there were always means of building a relationship with particular units.

The connection between the Nathaniels and 488 Marine Expeditionary Force went back to a time when the leading families were *expected* to provide troops for Imperial service.

Constantine Nathaniel had founded the unit as a naval infantry brigade five hundred years earlier, equipping the force at his own considerable expense. Eighty years later, the unit had been integrated during a reorganization of the Imperial Marine Corps, but the Nathaniels never forgot the unit's origin.

Nor did the unit.

Not only did the 488 always have a Nathaniel serving in their officer cadre, they also got some of the best equipment and augmentation available, thanks largely to Nathaniel patronage.

Imperial apathy over military readiness had led to some surprising loopholes in the laws designed to keep the nobles' hands off military units. The scarcity of official funding had led to a semi-official support system through various 'associations'. The Marine Association and others like it, allowed public support, usually manifested in the form of better housing for military families.

Hadrian Nathaniel had caused one hell of a blip in the news cycle when he'd used the Marine Association to present the 488 with a brand new, Light-Hull, Voler-class planetary assault ship.

It may only have been half the cost of a super-dreadnaught, but there weren't any companies left that could even build one of those monsters anymore. The LHV's were now among the most expensive pieces of equipment the Imperium could produce and a private citizen had bought one for the 488.

It made them one of the few units that could deploy without relying on cooperation from the Navy.

Paul knew his patron was playing a dangerous game. Hadrian was now positioned as a go-to guy in the Grand Senate. If disaster loomed out on the fringes, the Grand Senate would see in Hadrian a man who could return to active duty and take the 488 to the trouble zone in a matter of hours.

It also made his colleagues nervous of his ultimate intentions. A senator who actively cultivated the loyalty of Imperial troops was a man to fear and that meant he had to live with a target on his back.

Paul broke out of his reverie as he noticed the shuttle's flight crew running toward the boarding gate from the meteorological office.

"Flight IV-2332 to Vermillion will be departing in five minutes," the dispatch system announced. "Passengers wishing to board this flight must pass the scanner within the next four minutes."

# Rebels and Patriots

Paul looked back out the window. What had been a dense storm now looked like a faint haze. The weather here could turn in an instant.

But the remnants of the storm were still there and he hated flying in abrasive conditions. He sighed, waving his comrades toward the gate.

Hopefully, they'd make it down in one piece.

The shuttle was half empty, most of the first-class passengers electing to finish their drinks while waiting for the next one. Paul and his group were able to have a ten-passenger compartment to themselves.

The passenger shuttles plying the orbits of Dangerous Weather Planets were always compartmented. In the event of an engine failure or a catastrophic weather incident, the compartments would be ejected, relying on their own emergency lifters and, as a last resort, parachutes.

Irricana was near the top of the scale, as DWP's went, and more than a few shuttles had been lost to a sudden blow of hot, abrasive sand.

Ed sealed the hatch and strapped himself in. "So," he began, resuming the conversation, "the proof? What did you find in the data?"

There was a distant clunk as the shuttle broke umbilicals, and Paul was suddenly glad of the chance to think of anything but flying through a hostile ecosystem in a three-hundred-year-old shuttle.

"There were a few things," he began. "They were clever about it, but there are just too many details when you try to hide three quarters of an expeditionary force."

Sandy had been looking out the portal at their destination, but he turned wide eyes on Paul. "Three quarters?" he blurted. "That's tens of thousands…" He trailed off in shock.

## A.G. Claymore

"I figure they have a couple of battalions in barracks at most," Paul replied. "Keeping the lights on and making it look like they're all still there."

"But how do you know that?" Ed demanded.

"For one thing, there's the maintenance records." Paul gave his restraint harness a quick tug as they hit the edge of the atmosphere. "There's a constant flow of new parts for any unit — you guys know that — and the broken parts from equipment usage in a force that large always conforms to a statistical pattern.

"The inflow of new parts has continued to fit that pattern," he continued, "but the outflow of broken parts to refurbishing contractors has dropped to a level indicating activity at a battalion level, two battalions tops.

"I found that by tracing an increased income in their parts flow. They're still shipping out the expected number of parts, but they're not going for refurb; they're being sold back to the original supplier for nearly the full price."

"So, the parts aren't being used because the equipment's not there to break down?" Sandy asked.

"That's what I thought at first," Paul agreed, "but their circuit usage is right where it should be."

The Marines nodded. Most of their equipment had multiple redundancies built in because the electronics had a high failure rate. Everything from personal weapons to assault craft had organic circuitry that had to stand up to heavy abuse, and those circuits had a limited lifespan once taken out of an incubator and installed in an operational system.

An assault craft would go through twenty circuits a month, just sitting in the hold of an LHV-class carrier.

Rebels and Patriots

"So it's just the personnel that came out here, not even sidearms," Paul emphasized. "What the hell are they doing out here?"

"How do we find out?" Ed asked.

Paul risked a look out the window, regretting it immediately as the reddish haze proved the storm was still out there. He shuddered. "I know the local police commissioner." He looked at Ed, mostly to get his eyes off the homicidal weather. "He used to be my boss."

A.G. Claymore

# *Catching Up*

**P**aul led his small team off the shuttle the instant the hull doors were unlocked. He wiped perspiration from the back of his neck as he moved toward the exits. The air was cool and, surprisingly, moister than he expected, having just flown through a sand storm.

The upper surface port was located at the border between the commercial and residential levels, centered in the middle of the huge core space. A network of bridges connected the terminal to the city proper.

Vermillion was shaped like a giant cone sunk point-first into the ground. The top two hundred meters were residential, a huge ring, two-kilometers in diameter, where three levels of parkland provided citizens a taste of the varied plant-life of the Imperium.

The commercial and business districts sat beneath and they took up the next five hundred meters, the cone narrowing to roughly one kilometer in diameter at the top edge of the industrial sector.

It was the industrial region, at the bottom of the cone,that provided the city with its life-blood. It recycled the air and water, but it also opened onto hundreds of tunnels leading to the region's countless mines.

There were only two reasons for a colony in the Gliesan system — a bulwark against aggression from the technically advanced Grays, and erbium. The erbium mines on Irricana were keeping the computer and data transmission industries alive.

Without erbium doping, the power required to push information through glass and crystal would increase dramatically. The resulting heat would melt the fragile systems.

There were other sources of erbium, but this world was the biggest producer. More than three quarters of the current market came from this planet.

The occasional mining franchise was awarded from time to time for a competitor to develop a new world's resources, but they were almost always bought out by the consortium running Irricana.

The few who had the clout to evade their clutches usually found supplies artificially expensive and the markets rather dry. Circuit producers preferred the lower-priced Irricanan erbium, even if it put them at the consortium's mercy.

Paul stepped over to the railing that ringed the station and looked down into the misty depths. From this height it was impossible to see the industrial sectors.

He took a look around at the bridge network, hanging like a spider web between the residential and commercial zones. It was a hotbed of enterprise. Small shops, cafes and open-air restaurants covered every possible space. Even the mag-lev tracks used by the passenger trains were put to use.

He'd been watching a train as it approached the shuttle terminal and he couldn't figure out how it would actually reach the structure. As he watched, a spice vendor concluded a transaction, rolled up his samples and dodged out of the way only seconds before the train roared past.

All along the route, shop keepers were vacating their spots, just moments before disaster. As the train passed, they flowed back into place like tidal birds chasing the waves.

Paul grinned. "This is the best place to start looking for my old boss."

"Yeah," Ed grunted noncommittally, "or you could just call his office — he *is* the top cop down here, right? He shouldn't be all that hard to find…"

"Shouldn't," Paul admitted, "but, for me, he would be. It's best if we just surprise him."

A.G. Claymore

He started at the center, near the station, and began checking out the spice vendors. They seemed to concentrate near the center of the bridge networks and Paul had a hunch that the type of spices gave an indication of the kind of restaurants one might find farther out.

He found what he was looking for and started working his way out toward the city proper. After a hundred meters he approached a local, a young woman with a small child. "Pardon me, ma'am," he began politely. "Could you tell me where the best green curry might be found?"

She shrugged and he moved on, selecting a young couple. "Pardon me, folks, but could you tell me which shop makes the best green curry?"

"Slumming it, are you?" the young man asked with a grin. "Not many folks of 'means' bother to eat out here at a walk-shop. He leaned in a little, lowering his voice to a mock-conspiratorial whisper. "They have no idea what they're missing!"

He straightened, returning to a normal tone. "Seriously, though, if I tell you, you'll keep it to yourself?"

Paul squinted at him. "Why the big secret?"

"I'll tell you why," the young woman declared. "If word gets out, the place will get trendy and overrun with rich folk. The prices will go up and we won't be able to eat there anymore."

Paul nodded. "Fair enough. We don't know many people here anyway, so it's not like we'll ruin it for you."

The man regarded him for a few seconds, then sighed. "OK, it's over that way." He pointed past Paul. "Take that diagonal bridge over there and then double back for fifty meters or so. It's a place called Aunty's."

Paul thanked them and moved off to look for the restaurant.

Ed was walking alongside him. "Green curry?"

Paul chuckled. "The man we're looking for makes a virtue of predictability. There are a limited number of dishes he likes to eat, and he tends to return to the same place for each one.

"If Aunty's really is the best, then it'll be the place he goes when he's craving..." He stopped walking and almost fell over as Al bumped into him.

They'd found Aunty's and he was pretty sure the man sitting with his back to him was Morgan Alexander. Two men sat at an adjacent table, but they weren't eating. They'd be the security detail.

Paul shivered, his thoughts reaching back across the years to his time on TC-465. Morgan had been a junior officer back then, in charge of ten men, including specialist Paul Grimm.

Then things had started changing, and a mentor became an opponent.

Paul took a deep breath and walked over to the table. The man looked up and frowned for a second. His eyes grew wide and his security detail came to their feet, hands reaching inside their jackets. It was Morgan, all right.

Morgan made a subtle gesture and the two men returned to their seats.

Paul gestured to the empty chair across from Morgan, raising an eyebrow. Morgan nodded his assent and Paul settled into the chair with a sigh. "You're looking good, Morgan. Done well for yourself, I see." He cast a glance at the residential levels that surrounded them.

"Surprised you aren't back on home-world helping your little friend weasel out of the jam he's gotten himself into," Morgan drawled. "Or are you selling *him* down the river as well?"

"You're still angry I called you up in front of the Provost Marshal?" Paul gave him a tired look. "I didn't ask to be promoted over your head..."

## A.G. Claymore

"And you used to bitch about patronage even more than I did," Morgan cut him off. "At least you *did* until young Julius showed up with all his wealthy connections."

"And I suppose *you* would have refused a chance at promotion?" Paul arched an eyebrow. "I can see it all now: 'No, thanks. I'm happy having no prospects. I'll just keep on shoveling shit like I've always done...'"

"Six months in rank as a lieutenant," Morgan stated flatly, "and then you're my captain?" He looked away, into the crowd. "I always said the system's broken."

"Well, of course it's broken," Paul retorted irritably. "It's been broken for centuries now, so we have to find ways around it or settle for what we have." He looked at Morgan for a moment, then shook his head, ever so slightly.

"Matter of fact, I suppose you *did* turn down a promotion, back on TC-465."

"Running the homicide cell out in the alien quarter?" Morgan snorted. "You call that a promotion? I'd still have been a lieutenant, *and* I'd have had to put up with all the crazy shit those little goolies get up to..."

"It *was* a promotion, you halfwit," Paul insisted. "Captain Thule had Flinter's Disease. He hadn't been informed yet, but he would have been taken off active status within the month. You would've been the senior man in rank out there if you hadn't been a massive jackass, sticking around to sabotage me."

He caught the waiter's eye, pointing at Morgan's drink and holding up five fingers. "It was the perfect way to get you promoted. Nobody with the money to *purchase* a captaincy would be willing to serve in the alien quarter."

Morgan stared. "You might have said something..."

A shrug. "Didn't know he was sick at the time. They just told me you'd be running the shop within five weeks. You and I weren't exactly on speaking terms. I figured you'd be happy to get out from under me. After, when you were stuck with me, I didn't figure it would do any good for you to know you'd pissed away a captaincy."

"Yeah, well..." Morgan groused, "you're still an ass."

Paul nodded judiciously. "It seems to be the consensus."

"So, what brings the *Eye* all the way out to Irricana?"

Paul wasn't entirely sure he could trust Morgan but he figured the man would've been more friendly if he were playing some devious game. He decided to take a plunge, since he had no other potential allies on this world. "There's something going on out here, right under your nose."

Morgan chuckled. "Oh no! 'Something going on' on Irricana?" He shook his head. "Listen, sonny, I have two million Humans in this hole-in-the-ground, another eight million spread around the other habitable-zone cities and then there's at least sixty million alien laborers living in homes they dig off the sides of the mine tunnels.

"There's always 'something going on' under my nose, so you'll have to give me a little more to go on."

"538 MEF has been sneaking troops out here for the last couple of years."

Morgan stopped in the middle of raising a mouthful of curry rolled in a piece of flatbread. He gestured at Paul with the morsel. "How many, why are they coming here and how do you know?"

"Looks like they left behind a battalion or two to keep up appearances; the rest are here."

"That's got to be at least thirty thousand, closer to..." Morgan trailed off, staring off into the hazy distance above the awning that covered the kitchen.

"*Jiàn ta de gui,*" he muttered quietly. "Would you say it's close to thirty-seven thousand five hundred personnel?"

Paul had waved his four comrades to sit. He'd just indicated an order for a round of green curry by catching the owner's eye and pointing at Morgan's food when the oddly specific question was asked. "Yes. Pretty much exactly. Where did you get that particular number?"

Morgan sat back, his food forgotten. "Couple of years ago, folks started going missing. Thousands at first and then it trailed off to a trickle."

He looked absently at Paul as he talked. "Round about that time is when we started having incidents."

"Incidents?" The food arrived but Paul didn't notice.

Morgan nodded. "Bombings, mostly. Transmission arrays, infrastructure disruptions, shuttles in transit…"

"Terrorists?" Paul suggested. "Secessionists?"

Morgan released a short, sharp sigh. "That's what our idiot governor seems to think. Balthazar Thatcher," he spat out the name. "Sharp as a bag of rocks and half as pretty."

"I met his relative on the way out here," Paul advised, "Paronius."

"His brother," Morgan confirmed. "He does come in handy. Makes Balthazar look smarter by comparison. The two of them are so plug-stupid, they'd be living in the mines if they didn't have Irricana's economy to embezzle from."

"So, not terrorism?" Paul nudged him back to the topic.

"I'd be surprised." Morgan took a drink of his ale. "None of it is ever serious. Very few civilian casualties, and the damage to infrastructure is always easily fixed within hours."

It did seem odd. When a terrorist attacked your infrastructure, it was an attempt at reducing public confidence in the administration.

# Rebels and Patriots

A short interruption in service was more likely to draw attention to how well the government was responding to the unrest.

"Just had an attack on the HSVL a couple of days ago," Morgan went on. "They used a small shaped charge to blow a hole in a maintenance hatch, but they only blew the inner hatch. Maintenance sealed the outer hatch and replaced the damaged one from the inside. Total down time was twenty-six minutes.

"One guy got killed because he hit the air before the safeties could stop his vehicle, but he was the only casualty, aside from the 'bomber' himself."

Paul caught the inflection. "You don't think he was the bomber?"

Morgan shook his head. "Real scumbag," he growled. "I'd have killed him myself and slept easy the next night. He wasn't the sort of guy who falls in with idealists and he didn't have the brains to be trusted with explosives."

"Just a scapegoat," Paul mused, "to throw you off the scent?"

Morgan waved off the owner, who was gesturing at his drink. "It's exactly what happened," he insisted, grinning. "I'd bet your life on it."

"Not your own?"

"If I had to, but I'd rather bet yours," Morgan replied cheerfully. "I think this is the key to all our missing citizens. The Thatchers insist they're running off to join the secessionists, but we didn't even have a hint of secession until two years ago. It's just too sudden. It built up way too fast."

"They're not *joining* the secessionists." Paul had worked with Morgan for years and he could still follow his train of thought easily. "They're *covering* them. Thousands of scapegoats…"

"Except there *are* no secessionists," Morgan insisted. "Why hide where they're really coming from unless they're up to something?"

A.G. Claymore

"But what?" Paul still hadn't noticed his food. "It can't be an attempt to break the Gliese system out of the Imperium."

Morgan raised his eyebrows as he nodded. "Even the Thatchers aren't that foolish. Sure you can take a system, with enough force, but the Imperial Navy would show up sooner or later... or the Marines."

"The Marines are already here," Paul pointed out. "At least, the personnel are."

Morgan nodded absently. "They just need a reason to come here officially. They can smuggle the troops out here, but ships and weapon systems are a little harder to hide."

"So they're providing their own justification by posing as secessionists." Paul finally looked down at his food. He pulled loose a piece of flatbread and scooped up some of the aromatic mixture. "Kick up enough fuss and whoever's behind this can have Kinsey request a full deployment."

Morgan grunted. "And with your pal in prison for mass murder, the Nathaniels will be out of the running as the saviors of the Imperium. Kinsey will ask for the 538, since he officially has half the senior staff here as advisers anyway."

Paul finished chewing. "This is so much better than that garbage you used to eat on TC-465."

Morgan replied with a less than helpful suggestion of an auto-reproductive nature.

"So that gets 538 MEF out here, with their equipment." Paul took a drink. "But what the hell are they going to do, once they're here?"

"You're talking to the wrong guy," Morgan managed to say before belching. "My jurisdiction ends at the edge of the atmosphere. If you want to know what's going on out in the black,

Rebels and Patriots

you'll need to talk to Kinsey, for form's sake, then go have a quiet chat with Colonel Urbica."

He stood, his guards following his lead. "I'm going to make a few new inquiries, now that I have a better idea of what's going on."

Paul nodded. "We'll go visit the local forces."

Morgan walked around to Paul's side of the table and stopped, facing away into the crowds on the bridge. "Arresting an Imperial inspector would be problematic," he said quietly, "so keep your nose clean, or your organs will end up in the under-market."

Paul looked over his shoulder just enough to see his old co-worker in his peripheral vision. "So, I'm still an ass, huh?"

Morgan simply chuckled as he walked away.

"And here I thought we'd get a chance to see the sights," Ed muttered.

"You will," Paul returned to his food. "Same as on the ship, pair up and be tourists. Talk to people, go everywhere. I'll put enough money in your accounts to cover food and lodging.

"We need to figure out what's going on down here. They could be pulling these shenanigans anywhere, but they chose this planet, so I need you to keep your eyes and ears open. If thirty-seven thousand people have gone missing, it's bound to be a popular topic."

"And you'll be visiting the local forces?" Sandy had finished his own plate and pulled Morgan's half-finished lunch over.

"I will, and it'll go easier if I don't have to explain four Marines from the 488 to everybody." He found the owner, paid the bill – including Morgan's meal beacause the man had stiffed him with his own check – and started making his way back toward the surface station.

He fought down the growing unease. The Nathaniels were counting on him to solve this riddle but there was never a guarantee

# A.G. Claymore

of solving any particular case. Julius' life was hanging in the balance and Paul had no idea how much time he had left.

He knew conspiracies became harder to conduct as you added more players. This one had thousands. He took a calming breath as he moved through the crowd.

The answers were here.

He'd better find them.

## In the Enemy Camp

**P**aul looked out the side portal of the naval, ship-to-ship shuttle. Officially, traffic was kept out of a naval vessel's exclusion zone for security reasons, but it quickly became evident, as you approached, that there was a secondary reason.

With vessels like the INV *Dauntless*, the Imperium was showing its age. The closer you got, the worse a super-dreadnaught began to look.

The newest in the class was several centuries old. They had been through a few refits over the decades but their exteriors bore the scars of a hundred fights and a thousand small accidents.

An almost uniform patina of damage and discoloration testified to the long service of the massive ship.

At a distance, she was awe-inspiring but, up close, she showed a critical weakness in Imperial politics. Not that anyone dared to speak such a thought out loud.

They passed the nav shields and settled on the deck of the main receiving hangar. Paul joined the back of the debarkation line, ignoring the curious glances of the crewmen returning from shore leave. He knew the rumor of an inspector from the *Eye* being aboard would spread quickly enough, but he could at least slow that spread by waiting till the rest had passed the officer-of-the-deck before explaining himself.

He waited while the last crewman saluted the emperor's crest at the aft end of the hangar and received permission to come aboard. Paul stepped forward and, since he no longer wore a uniform, turned to face aft and stood at attention for a few seconds.

He executed a smart left turn and came to attention once more, facing the OOD. "I request permission to come aboard, ma'am. Inspector Paul Grimm, ICI."

A.G. Claymore

The ICI had broad jurisdictional powers and an inspector from the *Eye* could assume control over a military case for almost any reason. As a rule, naval officers had the good sense to cooperate with the ICI, but it never hurt to show respect.

Paul always observed the proper procedures when dealing with the military.

The lieutenant commander nodded. "Permission granted." She waved him through.

Paul was instantly transported back to his years as a military policeman, even more so than during his meeting with Morgan.

In some ways, the military was almost like an alternate universe. It had its own internal economy, its own rules and punishment, and its own smells.

The scents of hydraulic fluid, lubricants, and sweat mingled with the metallic tint of untreated deck plating. Paul felt the unease of commanding his former boss, almost as fresh as the day he'd brought Morgan up on charges of dereliction. He even noticed a sneaking dread of the usual queue of data-work documenting the various crimes of TC-465.

He shivered, trying to shake off the past, and headed for the main starboard passageway. He followed the passageway aft for a few hundred feet until he came to the central monorail line.

Several crewmen waited on the platform and, from the sound of their banter, they were commuting home after completing their duty shift. He followed them onto a three-car rapid-transit unit, grabbing a strap as they lurched into motion.

Three stops later, only one crewman remained, and he showed no interest as the civilian exited the train in Marine country.

Paul placed his hand on a screen by the transit exit and a Marine guard waved him in. "Sir, you're now in a class two zone. Your safety is your own responsibility. Are we clear on that?"

85

Paul nodded. "No problem, Lance-Corporal. I know the drill." He nodded toward the Marine hangar. "Must be pretty quiet when you're just doing an advisory mission."

The Marine grinned. "Quiet as a temperance meeting on Donnegal Six, sir!"

Chuckling, Paul headed straight for the hangar entrance. Marine hangars on a monster like the INV *Dauntless* were designed to carry an entire expeditionary force, but this ship only held a small detachment.

There was a pretty good cross-section of the ships used by a Marine force. Five dropships sat in a row near the barracks entrances. The squat, large-engined ships were so ugly they actually looked good in a twisted sort of way. They each carried eighty grunts in EVA suits and full packs.

Next to the dropships were two gunboats. The gunboats consisted of a twelve-man hull wrapped around an antimatter cannon. The antimatter weapon fired 30mm rounds designed to contain a minute amount of antimatter.

The explosive yield of the tiny payload was the equivalent of a thousand tons of TNT. The source of the antimatter itself was something of a mystery. Naval logistics ships left through the Solitude wormhole under heavy escort, returning several weeks later to offload their deadly cargo at TC-122-b.

TC-122-a had been inadvertently converted to an asteroid field in the early years of the antimatter program. The official response from the Navy at the time had been along the lines of 'Mistakes were made — let's move on.'

Eight ship destroyers were sitting in a neat row, closest to the launch doors. The ship destroyers were lightly armored and, like the gunships, consisted of a twelve-man hull. The main difference from the gunships lay in the ship destroyer's primary weapon.

## A.G. Claymore

The 155mm launcher in the central axis of the small ship fired a much more devastating round than the main armament on the gunships. At an equivalency of twenty-six kilotons of TNT, the ship destroyers could wipe entire cities out of existence with a single shot.

A row of smaller, sleek craft were suspended from the ceiling. The Salamanders were used for amphibious operations and their main armament consisted of torpedoes. They used conventional warheads because the short ranges of underwater weaponry combined with water's ability to transmit force made anything more powerful into a suicide weapon.

Of course, being Marine ships, they all bristled with an array of automated close-in weapon systems. 'You never know when you might find yourself alone and surrounded.' Paul remembered Julius' response when hearing the vessels compared to a cactus.

He shuddered again. Julius *was* alone and surrounded. Paul needed to figure this out as quickly as possible and see if he could find the leverage to save his old friend.

He walked around to the boarding ramp of the first dropship. It had seen better days but, compared to the INV *Dauntless,* it was practically brand new.

He heard someone moving around inside and he climbed the ramp, surprising a Marine who was looking around the floor.

"Hello there," the man said, moving out of the forest of stalactite-like suit clamps to get a better look at Paul. He was wearing standard battle dress uniform but his BDU's had creases consistent with recent storage. His hair was slightly too long and he had at least two days' growth on his face.

Drop-ships didn't carry seats because they took up too much space. Instead, the Marines stood in EVA suits. The suit clamps, hanging down from the ceiling, attached to the front of the EVA suits, leaving room for packs on their backs.

If the landing was being done without packs, the clamps could be moved closer together and more installed to carry extra troops.

"Hello," Paul stepped toward him. "Lose something?"

A nod. "My ration counter. I had it when I boarded so I figured this would be the best place to start looking."

As good as Marine augments were, Paul's implants were the best that money and lucky genes would allow. He opened a discrete, short-range RFID query. It was at a low enough setting to avoid being detected by the ship's internal systems so he figured it was minimal risk.

He found the counter's signature under the co-pilot's seat. Now he just had to camouflage how he'd found it. "If your pilots are anything like the ones I remember, it would have slid forward on shield approach."

The man chuckled. "Marine?"

Paul nodded. "At the end of the day..." It was a common phrase in the Imperial Marine Corps. Those who had a non-combat trade, such as military police, were still able to fight, if it came down to it.

And, unless you were drummed out of the service, you never stopped being a Marine if you'd earned the title.

A raised eyebrow. "What was your MOS?"

Paul moved toward the cockpit. "Military police. I did most of my hitch out on the Rim."

"God," the man exclaimed quietly. "Those were still the good old days, when we saw regular action." He shook his head. "Now we just keep getting redeployed a little closer to the core every few years."

"It didn't feel so great at the time," Paul muttered. "Do you have any idea how many domestic disputes you have to deal with on a

Rim colony? The isolation, the stunted social networks, the incredible lack of resources..." He shook his head. "Families move out there expecting to find opportunities on a growing colony only to find they've been duped."

"Just warm bodies to bolster a territorial claim, huh?" The Marine leaned over to look under the pilot's foot pedals.

"Pretty much." Paul leaned over and picked up the counter from behind the co-pilot's seat. "They end up blaming each other and it escalates until folks like me get called in. Here's your counter." He stood up, holding it out.

"Thanks! Last thing I want is to get docked a day's food for a re-issue." He took the chip. "So what brings you to the *Dauntless*?"

"Senate wants a review of the current situation with the secessionists," Paul explained in an offhand manner. Just another boring assignment. "They want to know if they need to go to the effort of putting a response force together."

"So what's your feeling?" The man's mannerisms had changed slightly. His arms crossed.

"Just got here," Paul admitted. "Thought I'd come down here first and get the straight goods from the *real* Marines before going up to the combat information center."

The man nodded. He was a real Marine, after all, not some rich youngster who'd bought a commission. "It's pretty bad," he said, uncrossing his arms. His right hand came up to scratch at the light stubble on his neck. "We've just heard of an attack on the high-speed vac line down on the surface and the signal repeaters between here and the neighboring gates have been going down on a regular basis."

"Would you say the incidents are becoming more frequent?"

A nod. "Oh yeah. Those guys are turning into a real pain in the ass." He leaned against a suit brace, effectively putting an intervening brace between himself and Paul. His voice dropped in tone. "We need to deal with them."

Paul nodded. "Well, thanks for the honest assessment. I'll keep it in mind as I talk to the empty shirts in the CIC."

He headed for the hangar exit. The man was almost certainly one of the 'Secessionists'. His modified personal grooming indicated covert work and he didn't strike Paul as an undercover operator assigned to infiltrate a secessionist cell.

The man had no training for that kind of work. He seemed to have no idea how strongly he was signaling his lies. His uniform, recently out of storage, indicated the man had been rotated to the ship from his 'insurgent' duties.

That meant the Navy or, at least, the crews of the *Dauntless* and her escorts might be involved as well. It would be hard to hide a steady flow of personnel on and off the ship.

Of course, it might just be a coincidence, or the young Marine might have been brought back for medical reasons, but his attitude had been unmistakable. He didn't really believe there was a secessionist problem out here, but he was trying to convince Paul that there *was*.

Paul felt a growing sense of alarm as he headed for the transit platform. Whatever was going on out here, it was big enough to involve not just one expeditionary force but the Navy as well. Someone senior enough to assign a capital ship and her escorting vessels was involved in this.

The danger to Julius was even greater than he'd first thought. The risk might even extend to Hadrian himself. A man who makes himself indispensable to the Imperium also makes enemies in equal measure.

He needed to get a coded message out as soon as possible. Hadrian had to be warned. He frowned as he stepped onto the train.

A.G. Claymore

That Marine had claimed the signal repeaters were being hit. He might not be able to send a signal all the way to one of the wormholes.

Paul was headed for the forward station, ignoring the chattering crewmen grasping straps in front of him. The bridge was mounted near the bow and he had to at least check in with the captain. It would be taken as an insult if an inspector from ICI came aboard without saying 'hello'.

And it would look very suspicious.

When he reached the station where he'd originally boarded, seven officers stepped into his car. The chatter in the car ended instantly as the bare-headed seven found hanger straps.

Paul looked them over. Two women and five men, all wearing full CIC implant suites but they weren't command and control staff. They were command-grade officers — decision-makers.

That was a rare thing in the Imperial military. Most command officers, especially the aristocratic majority of the officer corps, preferred to rely on NCO's for coordination. The CIC staff would advise the officer of enemy activity and the officer would reply with orders.

The seven officers in front of Paul obviously took their jobs far more seriously. They weren't willing to wait the precious seconds it took to pass data orally. For them, it was far more important to trim wasted time from the decision cycle than it was to look good at cocktail parties.

Paul suspected these officers didn't have the luxury of capital ships to buffer any inefficiencies in their methods. They either took immediate decisions or their ships and crews would suffer the consequences.

He'd found the command staff of the 1st Gliesan Dragoons. One woman, the shorter of the two by a couple of inches, was clearly

# Rebels and Patriots

their leader. She wore the insignia of a full Marine Corps colonel and she had an air of unmistakable authority about her. A patch on her right shoulder depicted a pair of crossed, carbine-length accelerator rifles behind the Emperor's personal sigil — the crest adopted by the new unit. They'd taken the nickname 'Roland's Own' to show the nine-year-old Emperor where their loyalty lay.

Her head was shaved, like the rest of her officers, exposing the tattooed helmet-positioning glyphs on her scalp, and she had several external implants running from her chin, along the jawline, to her ears. The glyphs spoke of the kind of work they must be doing. They weren't really necessary unless the wearer needed an absolute perfect fit.

It was usually only needed if you engaged in hand to hand combat while wearing the suit.

They all had electrochromatic tattoos around their eyes, allowing the skin to be darkened at will. The tattoos allowed better visibility in bright starlight conditions and most personnel turned them off while not in combat. The seven dragoon officers seemed to prefer leaving them on full time. It gave them a dangerous, brooding look.

Paul had to admit he was impressed, even a little awed. Most aristocrats were a waste of valuable resources, as far as he was concerned, and the women of that class were mostly simpering fools.

Julia Urbica was hardly that. Though he knew she wasn't from one of the leading families, she'd still left a life of almost unimaginable luxury to serve in the Marines.

The train slid to a halt at the bridge terminal and he followed the seven out onto the platform, hearing the excited chatter grow behind him as Urbica's imposing presence no longer affected the crewmen so strongly.

## A.G. Claymore

They passed through the security checkpoint at the bridge/CIC and Paul simply fell in behind the seven officers, scanning his wrist for the guards and lowering his hand to allow a polite sniff from the guard's German Shepherd. He was rewarded with a friendly lick.

The dragoons were standing in the middle of the space, looking over at a small knot of officers. Paul recognized Romanus Kinsey from the files he had in his CPU implant. The superior sneer in his file image was, presumably, his everyday face.

Kinsey glanced at the newcomers for half a second, then turned his attention back to the junior officer in front of him.

Paul recognized the game. Kinsey wanted to make Urbica wait. Both were full colonels in the Imperial Marines but he was trying to send a subtle signal about who was more important.

Colonel Urbica already knew the answer to that and she was accustomed to making quick decisions. She nodded toward a situation room, walled in ballistic glass, on the port side of the bridge and led her officers across the deck.

Paul fell in with them, waving down a mess steward who was just on his way toward Kinsey with a carafe. "In the situation room," he ordered peremptorily. He caught the lad's nervous glance toward Kinsey and deduced he was stealing the colonel's coffee. "I'm pulling rank," Paul warned him casually.

He caught up with the dragoons as the last man stepped through the door. Paul stood in the opening, keeping the door from sliding shut while he waved the hapless steward in. "Just on the sideboard is fine," he told him. "We can serve ourselves."

When the young man left, Paul stepped all the way in and the door slid quietly into place. He locked it and turned to grin at the staring officers. "Paul Grimm," he announced. "ICI."

If Urbica's expression changed, Paul hadn't seen it. She continued to stare at him in silence. It was hardly surprising she

# Rebels and Patriots

might be suspicious. She'd taken what might be described as excessive liberties with the local Sector Defense Units, welding them into a new unit without authorization.

Paul might have been sent to take her into custody.

Paul looked out the window. "Nicely done, by the way," he nodded toward Kinsey, who started and turned back to the junior officer he'd been talking to. "Now he needs to come to *you*, after he's done with his fake conversation. You've turned his little tactic on him.

"But now he's probably reluctant to barge in here while you're talking to the *Eye*, especially an inspector you seem to have brought in with you." Paul chuckled darkly. "He looks nervous." He turned back to Urbica, seeing the other six dragoons resting their hands on the butts of their personal weapons.

"Don't you think he looks nervous?" he asked her.

She made a subtle gesture and her comrades relaxed slightly. She walked over to the sideboard and poured herself a cup. "You stole this from Kinsey?" She turned to lean against the low cabinet, keeping her eyes on him while she took a sip.

Paul nodded.

She sighed in appreciation of the dark liquid. "Well, that's a point in your favor, so I suppose I can unbend enough to answer you." She glanced through the glass wall at her rival. "Yes, he does look rattled."

"And *you* don't look the least bit nervous," Paul mused. "Even though you have to be wondering if I've been sent out here to bring you in for trial."

"Trial for what?" a major to her left blurted indignantly.

"Reorganizing Imperial forces without prior authorization," Paul began, "engaging in combat against dangerous species like the Grays or," he nodded at Urbica, "most damaging of all, being a

A.G. Claymore

competent officer. The military can hardly afford having officers who know what they're doing."

He jerked a thumb over his shoulder. "Makes idiots like that look bad."

He was sure he detected the faintest hint of a smile from Colonel Urbica but, if it was real, she'd quickly covered it by taking another sip.

He started moving around the large central table, suddenly craving coffee. "I'm not here for you, Colonel. I'm here because I think there's a very good reason why Kinsey looks so nervous."

He filled a cup, suddenly aware of how long it had been since he'd had any sleep. He poured half the steaming liquid down his throat in one gulp, his throat accustomed to such punishment from his years as a cop.

"And do you have any ideas that might explain his nervousness?" Urbica took another sip, then gave one of her dragoons a meaningful glance, raising the cup. The man grinned and left the room.

"You're thinking of stealing Kinsey's personal stash of coffee!" Paul exclaimed in surprise.

"Inspector," she replied in mock reproof, "my dragoons are punished severely for getting caught stealing."

Paul laughed. "For getting *caught*, not for actually *stealing*, yes?"

She tilted her head to the side, giving him a polite nod of approval. "A soldier who gets caught is a careless soldier. A careless soldier gets himself and his comrades killed. I would be careless indeed if I didn't press you to explain why you think Kinsey should be nervous of you."

Paul took another look out at Kinsey before he answered. "You didn't serve with the 538, did you?"

95

She shook her head. "No. I was with the 'trip eight'."

"Well, Kinsey has a lot of the 538 with him out here."

Urbica looked out at the colonel. "A few hundred, maybe, but..."

"Try thirty-seven thousand," Paul cut her off. "He's been sneaking them out here for two years, and he's been snatching a matching number of citizens from Irricana to make it look like the Marines are actually locals. Their equipment's still back on home-world, but the troops are mostly out here."

He had everyone's undivided attention now. "They're the 'secessionists'."

"But what the hell for?" Urbica demanded.

"If they can engineer a big enough incident, they can justify the dispatch of an intervention force, get their gear shipped out."

"But it wouldn't be the 538," Urbica pointed out. "The 488 has that shiny new LHV; they'd call Senator Nathaniel back into uniform and send *them* out here."

Paul shook his head. "A few days ago, his son Julian was drugged, infected with the 'happy ending' virus and turned loose on a diplomatic shuttle."

"Oh, hell," the major exclaimed softly. "Are you saying he's susceptible?"

Paul nodded. "I was the one who told him to get tested when we were serving together on TC-465. He knew what would happen if he ever engaged one of those courtesans."

"How bad was it?" Urbica set down her mug.

"Killed everyone aboard. They found him wearing the skin from one of his victims. Hadrian's been severely damaged, needless to say."

"So no 488," she said quietly.

A.G. Claymore

"Clever scheme," the major said, grudgingly. "Sneak the troops out here to create the pretext, then have orders cut to send them officially to put down the trouble they caused in the first place."

"So why are you telling us all this?" Urbica's dark brows knit together. "We could be a part of this incomprehensible scheme."

"You *are* part of it, unfortunately." Paul finished his cup and set the mug on the table. "I think the low-level stuff they've been doing is just background noise meant to create a believable backdrop for the *really* big incident that'll light a fire under the Grand Senate."

"Hold on, you son of an indent," one of the two lieutenants nearly shouted, "if you think we're a party to what's…"

"Stow it, Lars." Urbica put a calming hand on his shoulder. "I don't think that's where he's headed."

Paul nodded. "I think Kinsey will try to set you up as sacrificial lambs. The loss of the brave Gliesan Dragoons would be enough to dispatch a full intervention."

He looked over as Kinsey started moving toward the door to the situation room. "I'm afraid my presence here will likely accelerate that scheme. He's definitely nervous so he'll be anxious to see the lot of us dead."

Kinsey reached the door, but it was still locked. He looked around the bridge to see who was watching him.

Urbica glanced at him then looked at Paul. "What I don't understand," she said, "is what they hope to accomplish out here. They can certainly seize a world or even an entire sector, depending on how much force they can get their hands on, but they can't *hold* any of it for very long.

"Sooner or later, CentCom will scrape together enough force to come out here and crush them."

97

*Rebels and Patriots*

Paul spread his hands "It's the one thing that makes no sense in all this. We can see how they plan to put their pieces in place, but we have no idea what they plan to do with them."

"So maybe we aren't seeing all the pieces yet," Urbica suggested.

"I agree," Paul got up to unlock the door so Kinsey could stop pretending to examine a nearby terminal. He stopped halfway there and turned to Urbica. "Colonel, are you planning to be anywhere that I could get a signal to home-world? I need to pass on what we've learned so far."

"No problem. There should still be enough repeaters around Trochu. They can amplify your signal and get it to a gate."

Paul opened the door and dropped into a seat.

They had to wait at least a minute before Kinsey decided it would look like he was entering the room on his own timetable. The man walked in without a word and headed for the carafe.

"Romanus," Urbica greeted him casually. "I see the orbitals are secure. I'm sure the rebels will think twice before taking on a super-dreadnaught."

If Kinsey realized he was being called a coward, he showed no sign. "Colonel Urbica, I called you in for orders, not to steal my coffee."

"I'm busy, Romanus," she chided. "Surely you could arrange affairs here without having to seek my orders for every little thing."

Kinsey made an obvious effort to control his anger. "Don't push your luck," he warned. "I called you here because we need to put an end to these secessionists, once and for all."

She looked at him as though regarding a mildly amusing child. "You have a plan, do you?"

## A.G. Claymore

"I do," he insisted in clipped tones. "You will draw your forces in, concentrate them here around Irricana and, when the rebels come, we'll crush them."

Urbica stared at him for a few seconds, then frowned over at Paul. Her look was clear enough to Paul. Kinsey was initiating the incident.

She managed to cover it by pointing out the obvious flaw in the plan. "I doubt the secessionists would be so obligingly stupid, Romanus. They specialize in asymmetrical warfare; why would they develop a sudden interest in high-intensity combat against superior forces?"

"Because this is their only source of supplies now that..." Kinsey trailed off when he realized where he was headed.

Urbica smiled. "I conceed the point, Romanus. Driving off the raiders has limited the rebel's options, but I doubt they'd be desperate enough to commit suicide in front of our guns."

She started toward the door. "I'm taking the dragoons out to the Trochu system," she told him. "There are a lot of repeaters out that way that they haven't hit yet. We should be able to bag a few secessionists, if we're patient."

"I'll be making a note of this insubordination." Kinsey threw the warning at her back.

Urbica stopped, turning to face him. She kept staring, black rimmed eyes boring into him until he looked away. "Have the master-at-arms write it up, Romanus. It's a conflict of interest to report your own disobedience."

She gave him a wolfish grin. "Or are you planning to officially claim that poor old Crispin wanted you to take charge if he should ever happen to shoot himself in the back? That might raise questions, might even cause the 'Eye' to drop out for a visit."

She turned and led her officers out of the room.

Rebels and Patriots

"Well, they're giving me a ride so…" Paul heaved himself out of the seat and walked out past the enraged colonel. Seconds later, he slipped back in and grabbed the carafe. "For the road," he told the incredulous Kinsey. And then he left without another word.

A.G. Claymore

# *Dragooning*

**P**aul opened his eyes. The ceiling seemed wrong somehow. It looked like the same modular panels used on passenger liners but several of the filthy panels were either broken or entirely missing. On a commercial liner, they would have been replaced immediately. The passengers were more at ease when they weren't constantly looking at conduits and cable trays. They liked to forget they were on a fragile ship in the void of space.

He swung his legs over the edge of the slightly dusty bed and sat up, looking around at the grimy, dated decor of the stateroom. It was the smell that helped his brain to catch up with his senses. He remembered the faint musty odor from several hours ago. The ship's atmospheric scrubbers were being cleaned rather than replaced and they were being shoved back into their ducts while still wet. It was the kind of jury-rigged solution you tended to see out on the Rim where parts were hard to come by. The sort of thing you'd expect from dragoons trying to keep an old passenger liner running.

He was aboard Urbica's ship.

The *Rope a Dope* was a former passenger liner, dilapidated by civilian standards, but luxurious to military personnel. It's new name was a backhanded comment on her role, or at least that had been the gist of Urbica's cryptic explanation.

He glanced at the door to the washroom but decided on food and caffeine before hygiene. He opened the door to the passageway and started in mild surprise to find an armed guard facing him from across the hall. The man was wearing the lighter-weight combat EVA suit common to the sector defense forces and he had 1GD stenciled on the shoulders.

"The colonel wanted me to bring you up to the bridge," he said with a grin, "after you'd had your 'beauty sleep'."

# Rebels and Patriots

"Mind if we swing by a mess deck and pick up something along the way?"

"No need, sir." The man gestured to his left. "There's usually something laid on in the ready room so the bridge staff can rotate through a meal more quickly. We're operating this beast with less than two full shifts."

Paul fell in beside the guard as they headed aft. At the first big intersection they turned inboard and the narrow passageway gradually widened onto a large open area. They descended a grand, curving staircase and made their way through the lounge that sat at the bottom of a twelve-story atrium.

Close to two hundred members of 1GD were in the lounge, talking, playing dice or simply listening to the music provided by a trio of amateur musicians.

Paul amended that assessment as they approached a bank of elevators. The three sounded good. It was a bouncy little folk tune; the guitar, drum and harp-cordion playing off each other with practiced ease.

He wondered if they had been a group that volunteered for the SDF together. A chime sounded from the address system as he passed the bar, and everybody dropped what they were doing and headed up the stairs.

Paul and his guard walked into an elevator and rode up to the command deck. Immediately outside the elevator door was a guard station. The modular scanner was an obvious addition and it looked out of place amid the lurid pastel carpet and wall coverings.

As they rounded the corner to the bridge, Paul noticed Urbica through the glazed wall of a boardroom. He assumed, from the mug in her hand that it must be the ready room where food was, hopefully, located.

A.G. Claymore

He caught a hint of a smile from her again and he thought he had a good idea why. This class of ship had recently been retired from service in the Pulsar Line but Paul had seen one during an owners' tour.

There were a few peculiarities in the White Dwarf class and one of them was the difficulty in locating doors. Anywhere the ship had a glass wall with a built-in door, the door simply looked like another pane of glass.

Urbica and the two other officers in the room with her were waiting for him to start pawing at the glass like an idiot. Paul smiled to himself as he stepped up to the door panel and reached out to touch the panels on either side. It was an unpopular design among stewards, who rarely had two hands free.

The door slid up into the ceiling and he walked in. "Good morning, Colonel," he greeted her with a polite smile and headed for the food at the back end of the boardroom table. He tried not to look smug as he caught the other two officers exchange looks of surprise.

"Your quarters are to your liking?" she inquired.

"I've had worsh," Paul mumbled around a mouthful of an unidentifiable purple fruit. He nodded his thanks to a lieutenant who handed him a mug of coffee, and forced himself to wait until he'd finished chewing this time. "What was that alarm I just heard?"

Another smile, but this time it was just a crinkling of amusement around the eyes. "The *Rope a Dope* is about to live up to her name. We picked up some suspicious activity near a repeater junction."

Paul swallowed. "We're going after them?"

"That would spoil the illusion," she told him. "We're just a helpless private charter, carrying passengers to Trochu. They'll want to board us and slap us around a bit so we'll scream to home-world about how dangerous it's getting out here."

103

## Rebels and Patriots

"And we want to be boarded?"

"Oh, we do," she replied emphatically. "We could sure do with a good boarding, couldn't we fellas?"

The two dragoons chuckled. "I haven't been boarded in *months*," a dragoon captain declared. "Those three little Khlen-class ships will make us heave to, and then they'll sweep us into a close embrace in order to swamp us with boarders."

"And *they'll* get what someone in a close embrace typically gets..." Urbica's lips curled up at the corners in a wolfish smile. She set her mug down. "Grab something that won't leave crumbs all over the bridge and let's go put on a show."

Paul selected an egg-filled roll and followed the officers out to the bridge. It was surreal, seeing the lightly armored dragoons with their shaved heads sitting at civilian terminals. The carpeted floor and enclosed ceiling further enhanced the contrast. In the large, open central space a portable CIC suite had been erected. The holo screens showed three approaching raiders.

"I'd say it's just about the point where some half-drunk, has-been bridge officer might actually notice them," Julia announced. "Helm, give us a couple of course changes, then go to all-ahead-full."

"Aye, ma'am," the helmsman replied. "One 'Panicky-Pete' coming up."

The stars began to shift back and forth for a few seconds.

"They've gone to full speed," Urbica announced. "They should be..."

"Unidentified vessel," a harsh voice emitted from the overhead speakers, "heave-to and prepare to be boarded or you *will* be fired upon."

"Reduce thrust," Urbica ordered. "Give us a couple more course changes."

A.G. Claymore

A streak flashed past the windows.

"That was pretty close," Urbica said cheerfully. "We don't want to look *too* brave or they'll get suspicious. Full stop. Secure the reactor."

"Full stop, aye."

"Operations," she called across the bridge, "get ready to move the starboard teams, it looks like both incursions will come in on the port side."

"Both?" Paul had finished his breakfast and he came to stand near Urbica. He took a sip of coffee. "I thought we had three inbounds."

"You've never done a boarding operation?" She spared him a quick glance. "They'll want to keep one ship ready to fire on us while the other two carry out the boarding. That way they can give us a face-full of depleted-uranium if things start to go sideways."

"We have a cunning plan to deal with that, right?" Paul looked out the window as a hull appeared above them.

She nodded. "All this plan is missing is a tail and you could call it a weasel. To begin with, they're assuming the show-bridge is where we'll be. It's the most prominent from the outside, so they can fire all day and have no effect on our ability to fight."

The show-bridge was where passengers were allowed to sit behind dummy consoles and believe they were on the *real* bridge. They could push buttons and distract the crew all they wanted without driving the company's insurance through the roof.

The main display holo showed two streams of red heat signatures entering the ship on the port side. They began leapfrogging their way in toward the center of the *Rope a Dope*.

She nodded, her hand reaching halfway to her ear. "Acknowledged. All units, this is Colonel Urbica. Execute. Execute. Execute."

105

Paul watched the holo as the invading red heat signatures converged in the main lounge and green signatures moved forward, lining the railings above them.

A distant rattle of automatic weapons fire signaled the beginning of the uneven fight. On the screen, white lines lanced out from each dragoon as they cut down the invaders. It looked as though the boarders' vessels might be completely empty. The boarding parties numbered close to fifty men in total.

The Khlen class ships, built for the export market by the Grays, could carry thirty troops if they weren't in armor, twenty if armored. If the crews joined the boarding parties, they might be able to put twenty-five armored fighters aboard the ship from each of the two Khlens.

Urbica had thousands of dragoons aboard the *Rope a Dope* and they'd known the most likely place for an armed band to effectively subdue a ship filled with civilians would be the central lounge. It was where they would be most visible with their intimidating armor and weapons.

Some of the dragoons had doubtless lived through just such an attack in their civilian past.

Life on the Rim was hard.

"All units, this is Colonel Urbica. Phase two. Phase two. Phase two."

Two knots of green signatures poured out of side passageways and up the main corridors to the two open airlocks. They flowed aboard the two vessels in single file.

It was accomplished in seconds. Both docked ships were empty, their crews caught in an ambush at the lounge Paul had walked through moments earlier.

"All units, Urbica. Phase three. Phase three. Phase three."

A.G. Claymore

Seven small ships swarmed out from behind the bulk of the *Rope a Dope*. It was the standard dragoon formation. Three mutually supporting patrol units of two ships each and one troop leader.

They came at the third Khlen from the side, taking full advantage of Gray tactical thinking. The Grays were firm believers in the concept of specialization. The Khlen's were their version of a dropship.

They each had a large, forward-facing cannon with a twenty-degree traverse limit. The gun was only there to soften up ground targets on approach. If a Khlen needed support against other ships… well, that was what the Hichef fast-attack ships were for.

If the attackers were really Marines, they'd be accustomed to operating vessels that could defend themselves. The Gray ships were never meant to operate alone.

It was easy shooting for the dragoons as they tore open the third Khlen from its undefended flank, their conventional rounds making short work of the lightly armored hull.

"We salvaged a few loading doors from a derelict ore freighter," Urbica explained as the dragoon troop reformed and disappeared aft. "Converted the aft atrium into a hangar. We've got two squadrons in there and another in ready-launch slots.

"We just pull an entire cabin module out and mount an airlock in the neighboring cabin. Gives us the ability to put three, seven-ship troops out in a matter of seconds if we need to get frisky."

She gestured toward the exit. "Let's go see what we managed to capture." She led the way to the elevators. "We'll start with the prisoners."

The lounge they stepped out into was very different from the congenial gathering place Paul had passed through only minutes earlier. The chlorine-like stink of linearly accelerated rifles mingled with the stench of torn bodies.

107

*Rebels and Patriots*

Eight prisoners had been taken alive. They kneeled in a row, hands tied behind their backs.

She turned to Paul, leaning close. "Bet I can get one of them to reveal who they really are in less than sixty seconds," she whispered.

"Colonel," he hissed in her ear, "are you trying to show me up at my own profession? What magical method of interrogation are you planning to use?"

She leaned in closer. "Maybe I'll just bat my eyelashes at them?" Chuckling, she strolled over to the youngest-looking prisoner.

Paul put a hand to his ear. He could still feel the heat of her breath. He was surprised to realize that, even with the shaved head and the tattoos and implants...

...batting her eyelashes would probably work on *him.*

"You," she said loudly, nodding at the young prisoner. "How many people do you have out here attacking the repeaters?"

He threw her a defiant look. "Hendricks, lance-corporal, Mike four twenty-three, seven two eight, six six one."

"So your serial number starts with 'Mike', does it?" She grinned down at the dawning realization on the young man's face. "So you're an ex-Marine."

He'd been given the usual training for a new inductee and it had been his undoing.

The basic resistance-to-interrogation course was nowhere near as comprehensive as the training received by Paul's four Marine companions on Irricana. It concentrated on capture during high-intensity conflict.

They were run through endless scenarios where any deviation from name, rank and serial number would result in severe punishment. It was the best way to avoid talking to an interrogator. The minute you start talking, the game is up.

# A.G. Claymore

Urbica had used that conditioned reflex to slip past his guard. If she'd asked his name, rank and serial number, she probably would've gotten some bullshit about striking a blow for freedom.

"Separate them," she told the officer in charge. "Start with Hendricks, here. He's chatty. If he doesn't talk, give some thought to the fact he's connected with the disappearance of your little brother."

The dragoon had been heading for prisoner Hendricks but he snapped his head around to look at her. "Are you serious?"

She nodded. "We're pretty sure the missing person cases on Irricana all trace back to these assholes. They want to make it look like folks are sneaking off-world to join the secessionists so they 'disappeared' enough people to account for their fake rebellion."

The dragoon officer took a deep breath. He turned back to Hendricks, pulling a wicked-looking knife from his hip sheath. He nodded to two of his men and they grabbed the prisoner.

"You'd better start talking the second we get you in that room over there," he told him, "or I'm gonna start carving you up like a Rundlemass goose."

'You can't!" Hendricks' eyes darted around the room. "The Ceres Convention prohibits torture. We're Marines taken in…"

"You *were* Marines," Urbica shouted. "There are only *two* Marines in this room." She gestured toward Paul. *"You* were taken, out of uniform, while committing an act of piracy. I'm not going to bring disgrace to the Corps by processing you as Marines or even as ex-Marines."

One of the older prisoners spoke up. "You'll never get away with this. We're not as alone as you think."

She walked over to the man and kicked him in the chest. "You have no idea what I think," she said as the man landed on his back.

"You were from the 538. You left a couple of battalions in barracks but the rest are out here.

"I very much doubt any of you have enough information to buy your lives. Most of you won't even die as males, considering how many of my dragoons have lost family members over the last two years.

"Every one of you is a pirate. Forget about personal honor, forget about the honor of the 538. Standing orders dictate that all pirates be executed upon capture. Spacing is specifically recommended but it has no prohibitions against the employment of extreme prisoner conditioning.

"We're going to interrogate each one of you, put you in a hell of a lot of pain and, if we don't get any answers, carry out your mandated punishment in accordance with the Emperor's Regulations and Orders, chapter one hundred twenty-eight, paragraph sixteen."

She looked back to her officer. "I'm going to have a look at their ships. Let me know when you're done turning young Mister Hendricks into young *Miss* Hendricks."

Paul followed her up the grand staircase. They turned left and headed toward the open airlock at the port end of the passageway. They walked through, into the captured ship, and looked around at the forest of poles in the cargo area.

"The export versions of Gray ships tend to be pretty low tech," she told him. "No suit clamps and the avionics are actually reverse-engineered Human electronics. They never let their *real* gear fall into alien hands." She shivered.

Of all the alien races, none elicited such a deep visceral feeling of revulsion as the Grays. Legends went back through the veil of recorded time about abduction and experimentation. Even now, the few Grays within the Imperium gave the impression that they viewed their Human neighbors as little more than speaking animals.

It was an impression that had led to more than a few murdered Grays, but the investigations were always half-hearted.

She looked over at Paul. "No opinion on my handling of the prisoners, inspector?"

"Not really." Paul gave her a tired smile. "You're absolutely correct in your assessment. They aren't in uniform and they forced their way onto this ship. They're pirates. You're not just splicing the regulations here — this was a real-life act of piracy. I know the section of the ER & O you quoted and there's no room for mitigation.

"They might claim they were just following orders, but they have a responsibility to recognize an illegal command. Attacking Imperial citizens is about as illegal as it gets. They forfeited the right to call themselves Marines and I'll shove them into an airlock myself if nobody else wants to."

Her smile was grim. "You'd have to get in line for that particular honor. By now, half the regiment knows they're behind the missing Irricanans. I dropped that bomb so they'd be less conflicted when we get around to taking on the rest of the bastards."

Her eyes widened suddenly and she looked toward the cockpit. "We might just have a way to get the drop on them…"

They both turned as an ordnance tech walked in with a case of antimatter grenades. "What are you planning to do with those," she asked him, nodding at the case.

"Orders to blow the ship, ma'am." He raised an eyebrow. "Or perhaps, orders to return these grenades to the armory?"

"Good man." She gestured him toward the door, but called out to him as he reached the airlock. "Were you told to blow *both* ships or is someone placing demo charges on the second ship right now?"

"Uh, just me for both, ma'am."

With a quick nod of acknowledgment, she gestured him on his way and opened a channel. "Majors Harris and Flokison."

After a brief pause she began issuing orders. "Tim, I've rescinded the destruct order for the captured ships; we might have a use for them. Ivar, do you have any pilots checked out on export Gray ships? Good, get them up here. I want both brought into the hangar. Run a full maintenance cycle on both."

She killed the channel and cast a sidelong glance at Paul. "I doubt we'll be able to waltz onto the *Dauntless* once things heat up, but we can use these ships to sneak our people aboard."

"You think you can take a super-dreadnaught?"

"Yes," she said simply. "It may come to that. I don't want to find myself caught between fake rebels and treasonous Navy gunners.

A.G. Claymore

## *Turning the Ambush*

**P**aul had just stepped into the shower when enemy contact was announced over the PA system. Cursing, he killed the water and stepped into the drying cubicle. Instead of getting clean, he was just baking the stink to a new level of offensiveness.

He ran out to his cabin and backed into the SDF armor they'd provided him with. It closed around him at full deployment. He manually retracted the helmet and gloves and headed for the bridge.

In the hallway, three cabins aft, a ground crew chief was shouting at his pilot to get his ass in gear. The running pilot ducked into the cabin and the chief followed, shouting obscenities at his ordnance tech.

Paul raced down the stairs, through the lounge and started mashing the call panel for the elevator. It seemed stuck on deck seven, so he turned and raced back up the stairs, continuing across the passageway and up the next flight of stairs behind.

He was surprised at how easy the steps were in the light SDF armor. He'd had the basic courses in the heavy Marine suits, and he'd expected the SDF versions to be even more difficult to operate.

This armor may not offer much in the way of ballistic protection, but it seemed to enhance the user's capabilities. Even Paul, augmented in every way money could buy, found he was able to move faster in the suit.

He bounded out onto the command deck, waved at the guard and raced into the bridge.

Colonel Urbica was already there, looking at the holo screens with one of her majors. She nodded at Paul as he approached. "Looks like Kinsey has decided to throw us a party after all."

Paul stood next to her and followed her gaze to the main screen. Four Khlens and one Hichef were swarming around a medium-range passenger carrier. The carrier had its back to an asteroid field so it had nowhere to run.

Urbica grabbed the projected screen and stretched it out to provide a three-dimensional view. "They're sure as hell taking their time about it, aren't they?" she muttered.

Paul nodded. "When that patrol thought we were harmless, they were on us in seconds, but these guys seem to be more interested in creating a sense of urgency."

"Hmmm…" Urbica responded absently. She stood near the projected passenger ship and peered into the asteroids behind it. "Inspector, give me a hand."

Somewhat bemused, Paul simply stood there, so she took his hand and led him into the asteroid field. She held it up, palm toward the beleaguered passenger ship and returned to her original position, once again, peering past the holographic ships.

"Up a bit," she told him. "Now move straight back. More… More… Wait! Come back a bit… There! Hold still." She walked back over, putting her right fist against his palm. "Target," she ordered.

A target sphere appeared around her fist and she touched its edges, dragging her hands apart to enlarge it. She moved to starboard, holding up a fist. "Right here," she told him.

It had become clear to Paul that she was identifying lanes of fire through the asteroid field. At least, it had become clear once she'd let go of his hand and started giving directions.

They identified seven probable lanes that overlooked the area around the apparent pirate incident. The incident still hadn't reached the boarding stage, which indicated the dragoons might have a slight advantage in sensor range.

A.G. Claymore

They might have been flying around the ship for hours, waiting until the dragoon ship was spotted before pressing home their 'attack'.

She stood back, looking satisfied with her work. A movement outside the bridge caught her eye and she closed the targeting overlay before the three squadron leaders walked in.

"Gentlemen," she greeted them, gesturing toward the holographic projection. "It looks like we haven't been spotted yet, so we have time to sort out our dispositions."

They gathered around the projection.

"What's it been, five minutes since contact was called and they're still sniffing around their victim?" a dark haired-squadron leader asked. "Colonel, I smell rotten fish…"

"You have a good nose, Liang," she replied. "So what would you say we're looking at?"

He spent a few seconds taking in the overall picture, then, just like his boss had done, leaned in to peer past the passenger ship. He moved his head back and forth, nodding thanks to one of his fellow squadron leaders who moved into the field to help mark positions.

The pair spent less than a minute at it and they conferred with the third squadron commander, who'd been looking at more extreme angles. They added two more targets to incorporate his findings.

"Excellent," Urbica declared. She re-opened her own overlay and they matched almost perfectly. "You managed to find one that I missed. She closed hers again.

"We'll work off your version. We have eight probable locations for ship destroyers. Liang and Dimitry, get your squadrons out of the hanger and infiltrate through the asteroid field. I want you to start with the SD's," she ordered, waving at the targets, "then start working your way out toward us.

# Rebels and Patriots

"They'll probably be operating in accordance with standard Marine doctrine, so we can expect four or five fast-attack ships for every SD we find. There's a good chance the FA's will be concentrated here." She indicated the outer edge of the field.

"They'll be planning to swarm out and overwhelm us when we charge in to save the passenger ship." She looked at the three majors. "You might find easy pickings with those SD's. They're used to ship destroyers that can defend themselves, so they probably don't deploy the same way Grays would. Chances are, they'll be all alone back there.

"Kill what you find, then spread out and sweep the field. This many SD's would indicate they've committed two thirds of their aviation assets to this ambush. If we're wrong, we might have three or four more lurking out there, meaning you might not have a ship to come home to."

"We'll find the bastards," Liang assured her.

"Good." She turned to the third major. "Eddie, we're going to give the flanking attack twenty minutes to get in place, then we'll charge in. As soon as the engines go to full ahead, you'll launch all three ready-troops and move ahead of us.

"The ship destroyers won't waste fire on you unless they can destroy us first, so you can help build the illusion that we're falling for their trick. Kill the ships we can see. By the time you finish with them, the SD's should be handled and you can cordon off the field from the outside."

Liang grinned. "And we'll drive the FA's out toward you!" He gave Dimitry a thump on the shoulder. "Sounds good — let's do it!"

She smiled at them. "All right, get going, but leave some for Eddie's boys." She turned to the back of the bridge. "Beat to quarters."

"Beat to quarters, aye, ma'am."

# A.G. Claymore

As the alarm klaxon for General Quarters sounded throughout the ship, the three raced off like excited schoolboys heading for mischief.

Urbica chuckled. "I had to shake the hell out of this regiment to find those three," she told Paul. "The local SDF units were a mess. Some absolutely horrible officers with enough money to keep them in place and a few hidden stars like those guys.

"I ended up fabricating evidence to get rid of some of the better-connected deadwood, but I'd do it all again in a heartbeat. You should have seen them fight at the Carbon Well. They sent the Grays home with green faces."

It was a common saying among the Grays. Their blood used copper to carry oxygen instead of iron. It tended to turn green after a few moments of exposure to oxygen.

It took roughly fifteen minutes to get the two flanking squadrons out of the converted hangar. One squadron was already sitting in the massive airlock and it was a simple matter of opening the outer door to launch them.

The second squadron had to wait while the crew sealed the door, pumped the air back in, moved their ships into the lock and pumped the air out before opening the outer door again. An energy shield would have been far more efficient, but there simply wasn't room. Military hangar-shields required a string of redundant reactors to keep the power-hungry emitters running.

Paul watched the holo as the hazy green ships began working their way toward the rear of the suspected ship destroyer positions. It was hard to believe the moving icons represented a battle in the making.

It had all seemed plausible when they were formulating their plans but he suddenly felt the whole thing was a huge gamble based on very little data.

"Well, of course it is," Urbica told him when he confessed his thoughts. "Welcome to combat. The next fight I get into where I know all the angles will be the first."

She waved a hand at the five ships. "They still haven't done anything but fly around in circles. When they came after us, we had their ships in our hangar by this point. I'm about as certain as I've ever been.

"I suppose Kinsey thinks he's being clever, using our own tactics against us." She looked away at the sound of a chime. "Time to go. Helm — all ahead full. Unmask the batteries."

"All ahead full, aye,

ma'am."

"Weapons unmasking, ma'am."

The ships of the ready-squadron came streaking out from the flanks of the *Rope a Dope* as the old liner accelerated. They angled in toward the mock battle, forming into troops as they spread out.

The five 'attackers' milled about for a few seconds, then ducked into the asteroid field. It was what you would expect from raiders. They wouldn't dare fire on a superior force for fear it would ensure a pursuit into the dubious refuge of the asteroids.

A red flash caught Paul's eye and he turned to see a holographic image of a ship destroyer at the back of the nearest estimated position. Almost as quickly as he'd noticed the ship's icon, it went gray.

"Splash one Sierra Delta," an officer called out.

Three more blinked into view and were gray within thirty seconds. Before Paul could even form an opinion on the speed of the dragoon's advance, two more SD's were found and dispatched.

The holo showed the blocking squadron had reached its assigned position and the *Rope a Dope* was coming into the firing envelope determined by the assessed SD positions. If Urbica was nervous

A.G. Claymore

about the undiscovered SD's, Paul certainly couldn't tell from looking at her.

The two flanking squadrons were now moving toward the blocking units but they had already passed through the last of the likely positions for a ship destroyer.

"At least the Grays don't mount antimatter weapons on their export versions," Urbica muttered.

So she *was* worried, Paul realized; she's just very good at concealing it.

The deck plating shuddered beneath them and a shrieking noise battered at their eardrums as a two-hundred-kilo slug sliced down the starboard flank. It vaporized against the hull, much of its force dissipating into space.

"Still not showing up on anyone's sensors," an officer yelled.

Julia stepped into the holo and marked a point. "It came from this neighborhood. Open fire on the asteroids in between. Maybe we can put enough rubble in the way to stop their rounds from getting to us."

The chatter of the ship's guns was intensely satisfying for Paul, who was trying very hard not to shake. It felt good to be shooting, even if it was just at rocks.

"Any second now," she announced.

As if on cue, there was a brilliant flash as the next round impacted a rock and sent a maelstrom of rock and plasma in their direction.

A red icon showed up near Urbica's target and the two ships that had found it put it down before it could recharge its launch rails.

A haze of red icons began to appear near the edge of the asteroid field. Paul counted close to thirty but it was hard to be sure. They were moving out of the field and into the fire of Eddie's troopers.

Even though his squadron only had twenty-two ships, he still held the advantage. The enemy were tumbling out of the asteroid field in no particular order. They were desperate to evade the overwhelming enemy contacts coming from an area where they expected nothing but supporting fire.

As they left the asteroid field in piecemeal fashion, the blocking squadron was able to concentrate a devastating hail of fire on the individual ships. Some tried to break out at the edge of the battle, but they were easily dealt with by the widely spread ships of the two flanking squadrons.

The order-of-battle table on one of the holo screens showed seven ship destroyers engaged and eliminated, twenty-eight fast-attack ships engaged and twenty-six destroyed as well as four command and control ships, three destroyed and one disabled.

Urbica was looking down at the deck, reviewing the results through her own retinal projections. The implant had a much better resolution than the modular system Paul was looking at.

She nodded at something only she could hear. "Roger that, Liang. Bring it in. We'll see if we can fix it. Might come in very handy. Good work every one." She let out a deep breath as she killed the channel.

"Any casualties on our side?" Paul asked her.

She sighed. "Two ships, nineteen troopers." She was still looking down at the floor. "Sounds like they just happened to fly past the guns of enemy ships who snapped off a shot at the right moment. Just dumb luck."

She looked up at him. "Speaking of dumb luck, we got seriously lucky. If the enemy were using their own ships instead of that Gray garbage, their dispositions would have been a lot harder for us to pick apart."

## A.G. Claymore

"I was looking at a Marine ship destroyer the day we met," Paul told her. "The defensive weapons are probably equal to the *offensive* weapons on your ships."

"We still would have killed them," she said, "but it would have taken a hell of a toll on the flankers. And the fast-attack ships would have been firing AM rounds."

"The slug that hit *us* would've been antimatter as well." Paul shuddered, thinking about the massive cloud of energy that would have replaced the *Rope a Dope* and all her crew.

"I should be thanking that idiot Kinsey," she said, her skin flushed. She looked away from Paul, taking a deep breath. "He handed us two thirds of his flight personnel on a platter. The 538 is little more than a basic Naval-Infantry unit now."

Every time she looked away from him, Paul was surprised to find himself staring. The lines of her profile, the curve of her neck… He forced himself to look away. He'd served as a Marine but never in combat.

He wasn't familiar with this particular side effect of near-death experiences. For some, it increased the urge to reproduce, no doubt an evolved mechanism to preserve the species' numbers in the face of a hostile environment.

He'd already noticed a few urges where Colonel Urbica was concerned but he was a big boy and he'd managed to put that aside. She'd come out here to fight the Emperor's enemies, not to flirt with fools. Now, however, still dealing with the after-effects of the adrenaline rush, he found it much harder to ignore.

He forced himself to look at the holographic battleground. Two enemy ships had managed to escape. Probably not a huge loss. Kinsey would find out, sooner or later, that he'd lost the majority of his flight crews.

## Rebels and Patriots

"Secure from General Quarters," Urbica ordered. She ran a hand over her stubbled scalp as she looked over at Paul. "As soon as we get squared away, we'll resume course for Trochu," she told him. "I'm assuming you still need to send…"

"Distortion alert!" a sensor officer shouted. "Multiple inbounds."

"Beat to quarters," Urbica snapped. She titled her head to the side for a moment and then the three squadron commanders were projected in front of her.

"Inbound ships," she told them curtly. "Re-form to face the coordinator's marker."

Before anything else could be said, the blackness of space was filled with blinding, bluish light.

Ships traveling any distance outside of the wormhole network relied on their phase drives. The drives created a compression of space-time in front of the vessel and a corresponding dilation behind its stern.

It essentially shifted space past the ship, giving the passengers and crew no sensation of movement despite traveling many times the speed of light.

One aspect of phase travel was that the 'bow-wave' of compressed space picked up any cosmic debris along the way. That debris was then released on 'dropout' with almost unimaginable energy.

The massive plume of high-energy particles and gamma rays meant phase-traveling ships had to arrive in civilized systems on strict schedules and only in approved approach corridors.

Here in the middle of nowhere, however, rules didn't exist. Fortunately, the inbound ships weren't on an intersecting course and the dragoons survived unscathed.

At least for the moment.

A.G. Claymore

"No IFF transponder, but that's a Marine force," Urbica declared. She turned to her three squadron leaders. "I'm all out of clever, fellas. They caught us flat-footed."

Liang shrugged. "Nobody said we'd live forever. If we use a couple of squadrons to hold them here, you could pull out..."

"Wait a minute," Paul cut him off. "That's an LHV. I know more than a few units have them, but what are the chances of a Marine unit showing up where we are *and* having a brand new LHV?"

He could feel the hair on the back of his neck rising. "Colonel, hail them; it could be the 488."

"Whatever we do," Dmitry advised, "do it fast. They're launching their aviation assets."

Urbica looked straight through Paul as she accessed menus to hail the newcomers. "Inbound vessel, this is Colonel Julia Urbica of the Imperial Marines, commanding officer of the 1st Gliesan Dragoons. Please identify yourselves."

There was no response for a moment and the attack craft continued to form up around the LHV. "If we're going to fight," Liang warned, "we need to fire first. Once they start sending AM rounds our way, the balance will shift fast. We need to keep as many of them from firing as possible."

Urbica was staring intently at the holo-projection of the new ship. She drew a breath and, before she could speak, the answer came.

"Colonel, this is Major Anthony Nathaniel of the 488. Ma'am, we were told you'd been killed near these coordinates by raiders. Frankly, we thought your ships *were* the pirates."

"Yeah, you did seem a little aggressive," Urbica replied dryly. "No doubt that was the reason for the lies they told you. Major, what are you doing out here?"

# Rebels and Patriots

"Ma'am, it's complicated," Tony replied. "Would you be able to join me over here? It really would be best if we talk in a secure room."

"Very well, Major. I'll be there in a few minutes."

"I'll clear you for landing in the main hangar." Tony paused and the inflection at the end of his previous sentence indicated he might have more to say. "Do you happen to have Inspector Grimm with you?"

"I'm here, Tony." Paul's implants allowed him to join the conversation. "What the hell's going on?"

"It's best if we wait till you're aboard." Tony sounded exhausted.

A.G. Claymore

## *Bad News Travels Fast*

The *Xipe Totec* was vastly different from the *Dauntless*. She was half the size but, more importantly, she didn't seem to age as you came closer. She had glided out of the graving dock at Michigan Junction only eight years ago and her hull was flawless.

The shuttle slipped through the nav shield and followed an orange-vested ground guide to their assigned docking zone. The landing points hit the deck with a muted clunk.

When Paul stepped out, he found a Marine captain waiting for them. He accessed the unit files and noticed he'd met the man before. His CPU implant came in very handy at times like this.

"Harrison," Paul greeted him. "How's Emma?"

A pleased smile. "Full recovery," he replied, "thanks to the senator."

Paul thought he detected a falter in the man's smile and it added to his concern. "Major Nathaniel's up in the bridge with General Pullman?"

"It's best he talk to you," Harrison gestured toward the central lift.

With a glance to Urbica, he followed the young officer to the lift and rode up through the cavernous space. He cringed slightly as they passed through a small hole. They continued through seven more decks before coming to a stop.

They waited while an armored Marine walked past with a German Shepherd. He shared a glance with Urbica. Both knew that ship security only wore armor if they were on a wartime footing.

They were ushered onto the bridge. Unlike the super-dreadnaughts, Marine ships tended to put their bridges deep inside the vessel, behind layers of heavy armor.

125

## Rebels and Patriots

There were no windows with pretty views. Holo-displays filled the space and the flame-proof metal decks and exposed ceilings were somehow reassuring to Paul after the plush bridge of the *Rope a Dope.*

Tony stepped through a hologram of the local region and held out a hand toward a door at the back of the bridge. "We can talk in here," he said.

"Tony," Paul began as soon as the door started to slide shut, "what the hell is going on? Why are you out here? We need to get a signal out to your father..."

"My father is dead," Tony cut him off, his voice flat. "Julius is presumed dead as well. General Pullman ordered my detention as soon as word got out."

Paul stood rooted to the floor, staring at Tony. *Detention...* He was a cop, he knew the difference between arrest and detention. There were no official records for detention.

If you put someone into detention, it would be very easy to kill him and claim you hadn't seen him. Pullman was hoping to sit on the fence, holding Tony as a pawn. Paul knew he was seeking refuge in the relatively mundane, trying to ignore the constricting feeling in his chest.

His friends were gone and his quest to redeem Julius' name had been a failure. He had no intention of stopping, however. He would find the people who did this and make sure they paid.

"What happened to Hadrian?"

"Assassination," Tony spat the word. "Someone walked up to him in the grand rotunda and detonated an internal charge. Vaporized them both and killed another three senators and two aides."

Paul's entire body tingled with the urge to run, to fight, to seek revenge. He wanted to punch the walls, trash the room and scream,

# A.G. Claymore

but he knew it would accomplish nothing. He waited until he could master his voice before speaking again.

"I'm sorry, Tony." Paul's fists were clenched so tightly his fingers were growing numb. He flexed them. "If I'd been there instead of poking around on the Rim…"

"You couldn't have known this was coming." Tony insisted wearily. "We knew there was a play against us, but we had no idea they were going to escalate so heavily and so quickly."

"What about Pullman? I can't help but notice you don't seem very detained…"

A wry smile. "Pullman ordered the officer of the deck to lock me up, but the general ended up in detention *himself* along with most of the senior staff in our wing. I was lucky Chris had the duty watch that afternoon; we came up through the academy together."

"So they're hunting your family down," Paul said. "Probably to keep you out of the way of whatever their play is at Irricana, but we still don't have any theories that hold water. What the hell are they hoping to gain out here?"

"That's one of the reasons I came out here," Tony said. "My father found out Seneca had managed to sneak the 726 out to Santa Clara. We thought it had something to do with all this, since Kinsey is in Seneca's pocket."

"Santa Clara?" Paul put his hands on the back of one of the chairs. "So, what's the connection between Santa Clara and Irricana?"

"*Wŏ de ma!*" Urbica had been quiet while Tony talked about the death of his father but now she couldn't hold back.

"Erbium," she said. "Irricana is really only known for erbium. The planet represents more than seventy percent of Imperial production and at least ninety percent of known reserves."

# Rebels and Patriots

"You're right." Paul looked over at her. "Without erbium, the factories on Santa Clara will shut down. They can't produce circuitry without it."

He turned to Tony. "And you know how quickly your pretty new ship will die without a steady flow of replacement circuits."

"*Aiya, bù hǎo!*" Tony's face went white. "We carry incubators with a six-month supply, but that's only because this is a mark seventy-three. The older models only have a month at the most."

"So, they take those worlds," Urbica said, "then they put a stranglehold on the military. The only thing that still doesn't fit is the probability that CentCom will throw every ship in the Imperium into the effort to recapture both worlds quickly."

Paul's eyes widened. "Unless they're willing to cripple both worlds as a last resort. Would CentCom still send in a strike force if they thougt the rebels would destroy production at both worlds?"

Tony had regained his color, but now he was turning a dark shade as shock gave way to anger. "Those bastards have thought this through, alright. It's just enough of a threat to tie the Grand Senate in knots and CentCom certainly won't care for the risk ratio involved in a direct assault.

"The Senate will dither and pose for the cameras while the idiots at CentCom will war-game a thousand covert options."

"And the whole time," Urbica added, "the Imperium's warships will grind to a halt from lack of replacement chips."

"How the hell did two worlds manage to develop a stranglehold on something so critical?" Tony demanded. "Military logistics is never supposed to rely on single-source supply. It's the law, dammit!"

"Yeah, well, we've been staring at this for a while and never saw it," Paul told him. "It's not surprising nobody's done anything about this; the Imperium's got its fair share of weaknesses. Which ones

## A.G. Claymore

are we supposed to prioritize? And the law doesn't talk about percentages. It just states there has to be more than one potential supplier."

"Ganges makes circuits," Urbica told them. "Just nowhere near enough to keep the military in operation. There are other sites as well but, even if you put all of us at full production, we'd never be able to replace the output from Santa Clara."

"Even if you could ramp up production," Paul added, "you'd still need erbium and most of the Imperium's reserves are on Irricana."

"We need to put a stop to this," Tony insisted, "before they get settled in."

"I've been working on a plan for that." Urbica looked at Tony for a half minute, a slightly amused expression on her face. "How much of the 488 did you manage to steal, Major?"

A sheepish grin. "All of the aviation assets, ma'am, and a battalion of ground troops. Our family has always had a good relationship with the unit."

"So I gathered from Inspector Grimm's conversation with Captain Harrison," she replied approvingly. "Do you have any issues with putting yourself and your men under my orders?"

"Not at all, Colonel." He looked relieved to find a competent superior with a plan. "What exactly do you have in mind?"

"We need to start with Irricana. We have to sneak some forces into Vermillion and find their 'plan B'. It's probably an antimatter device so it's going to be hard to find."

"Hell, I was thinking Kinsey would just eradicate the city from orbit," Paul exclaimed, "but, yeah, he'd want to make sure the threat could be carried out even if he lost his ships."

"So I'll take a team and sneak into the capital," she said. "My dragoons all have family down there, so I owe it to them. When we find it, Major, you'll take out the super-dreadnaught."

Rebels and Patriots

Tony tilted his head back slightly, regarding her with mild skepticism. "Something tells me you have a daring scheme in mind…"

She grinned.

## Hiring a Guide

"**Y**ou *think* we'll be in the right spot?" Paul asked the pilot.

"Give me a break, buddy," the dragoon officer shot back. "With this export Gray garbage? My son's flow-board has better avionics than this flying turd." He glanced at Paul. "Close up your armor, jackass. If Kinsey gets a look at your face, the whole plan falls apart."

Paul took a final look over his shoulder. Urbica was tied to one of the hand poles in the back of the captured Khlen-class assault carrier.

Her face bore several new bruises and her armor had been removed, leaving her in her skin-tight under-armor suit. He realized his eyes were wandering and forced them back to her face.

She gave him a wink. "Don't worry, it'll work as long as you keep your head."

He nodded, turning back to face the plaz windows just as they darkened to protect the crew from the plasma of drop-out. He deployed his full helmet.

"Not bad," the pilot muttered. "We're forty seconds out from the *Dauntless*." He opened a channel. "Ghost call-sign to INV *Dauntless*. Requesting passage of the nav shield. Also requesting a quarantined landing zone and immediate, personal direction from Sunray, over."

"Roger, Ghost call-sign, passage approved. Please advise as to request for Sunray, over."

The pilot hesitated for a few seconds so it wouldn't sound rehearsed. "Ahh... *Dauntless*, roger that. We have an unscheduled passenger who might turn his frown upside down, over."

There was a short pause. "Ghost, Sunray will be standing by."

# Rebels and Patriots

"Everybody stay cool," Urbica ordered. "This is going to work. We're going to show him exactly what he wants to see. Just play the roles you've been assigned."

Six of Tony's Marines were in the back with her, dressed in the modified suits captured by her dragoons. They should be able to pass for Kinsey's men as long as they avoided close contact with personnel in the Marine hangar.

They landed in the hangar without incident and Paul saw Kinsey approaching the side door of the Gray-built shuttle. He got up and moved back to stand behind Urbica.

The door slid out of the way and Kinsey remained outside, no doubt suspicious that this might be some trick.

Two of Tony's Marines moved outside and took up guarding positions at either side of the door. As soon as they went still, Paul activated full interior illumination. His blood ran cold as he watched Kinsey.

The man's eyes grew wide in shock as he realized he was looking at Urbica.

She made a show of trying to turn her back to him. Her under-armor suit left little to the imagination and she was using that to sneak past Kinsey's guard.

Not terribly pleased about his own role in this farce, Paul grabbed her arms roughly and turned her to face him. He pushed her forward, arching her back.

Romanus Kinsey was one of those average officers who didn't like being shown up by a woman and he was also someone who actively wanted her eliminated. Seeing her bound and vulnerable was an irresistible lure and her revealing pose was also affecting his decision-making abilities.

## A.G. Claymore

His legs carried him inside the shuttle as if they had a mind of their own. He was letting his eyes roam freely over her form and Paul forced himself to stick to the plan.

Kinsey would be of no use to them dead.

The colonel grabbed her chin and lifted her battered face, forcing her to look at him. "Playing at soldier," he whispered to her.

The two Marines came back inside and closed the hatch.

"Perhaps," Kinsey continued, "you'd like to play with a *real* soldier…"

He doubled over as Paul let go of Urbica's arms and drove an armored fist into the colonel's stomach. The man was still alive, surprisingly.

Marine armor was incredibly powerful. Piloting a suit like this could take months of training for an un-augmented candidate. Paul's implants made it much easier to control, but he barely had a handle on his own anger at the moment.

He could easily have punched his fist straight through the man's unarmored torso.

Urbica released herself and gave Paul a wry grin. "You didn't have to do that, you know." She tilted her head slightly as his helmet retracted. "I can handle myself."

"I know," Paul agreed. "I'm sure you could put *me* down if you had to. "I just couldn't help it."

A very slight smile. "It's alright." She looked down at their prisoner. "As long as you didn't kill him…"

"The person you're asking for…" The pilot's voice drifted back to them. "…can't very well confirm his intentions over official channels, now, can he?"

There was a pause. "Yeah, why don't you just do that. Listen, our mutual acquaintance is going to be pissed if he has to go all the way back to the bridge just to explain his plan to your replacement."

## Rebels and Patriots

Another pause. "Hey! What a super idea! Next time, show that kind of flexibility from the start, you moron." The pilot killed the channel and started firing up the engine.

"This is gonna be the death of me," he declared. "Strap in. They're giving us clearance to leave."

"You went kind of hard on him." Urbica had slid back into her armor and dropped into the co-pilot seat. "Good work. They'd expect attitude from a man who has their CO breathing his neck."

"Yeah, well, they're gonna see all kinds of attitude when our guys show up." He lifted them off the deck and headed for the hangar exit. "You sure this'll work?"

"If Kinsey values his own hide, it will," she replied. "Keep your fingers crossed because there's no plan B."

They passed out through the shields. The point defense batteries didn't so much as twitch when they started their descent toward Vermillion.

"Weather ain't so hot," the pilot called out. "At least it's a night-side storm, so mostly rain — almost no particulates."

The small craft began to buck and heave as they dropped into the swirling weather system. Water pounded against the hull and streamed past the side portals.

Paul was far less nervous this time. He knew the heavy weather was less than safe, but it was a walk in the park compared to the abrasive sand of a day-side storm.

The turbulence dropped off sharply as they entered the yawning mouth of an approach tunnel. They moved through the heavy gates at the inner end and descended to the same surface-station where Paul had landed when first arriving.

He sent a quick signal to Morgan's office and the four Marines that he'd left behind in the city.

# A.G. Claymore

Urbica walked into the back, finding Kinsey tied to the same post she'd been attached to a few minutes earlier. "We're going to hold you here," she told him, "until the attack is finished. I don't want you getting killed in the fighting. I'd hate to miss your execution."

"Attack?" he frowned "What the hell are you talking about? What attack?"

"We know you're trying to use Imperial forces to seize this planet," she explained. "Why you think you can continue to hold it is beyond me, but we aren't going to let you succeed."

Kinsey stared at her for a few seconds, then shook his head in amazement. "No imagination," he sneered. "I shouldn't be surprised at how limited your assessment is…"

"Save it for your trial," she snapped at him. "We'll wait down here while our forces attack the *Dauntless*. After the smoke clears, we'll drag you back to home-world in chains."

Kinsey was suddenly very focused. "We're in Vermillion?" His eyes darted toward the portals. "We can't stay here!"

"What's wrong, Colonel," Paul retracted his helmet. "Do you owe someone money down here?"

"No… just trust me. We can't stay here if an attack is about to take place against the *Dauntless*."

"Trust *you*?" Urbica laughed. "Based on what — your stellar track record?"

Paul saw the four Marines from 488 approaching and he slid the side hatch open and hopped down to the tarmac.

He walked over to talk to them before they could get close enough for Kinsey to overhear. "What did you boys find out?"

Ed spoke for them. "Nothing specific but there's a really strange pro-Gray bias in the local media."

# Rebels and Patriots

Sandy picked up the thread. "A lot of similar garbage on the micro-chat forums. We traced more than ninety percent of it to the same five hive-addresses."

"And your buddy, Morgan, said to tell you he found DNA evidence of the missing Vermillians." Ed added. "Seems they were taken out to the south ruins and shipped out to God knows where. Still alive when they left traces…"

"So we might be able to save them" Paul looked over his shoulder at the shuttle. "We'd better keep that to ourselves for the moment. Don't want to end up spreading false hope." He turned back and lowered his voice. "I have some bad news, guys," he warned them. "The senator's been killed by an assassin."

"*Aiya! Huàile!*" Ed exclaimed. "What about the colonel and the major?"

"The colonel's presumed dead," he told them, "but the major made a run for it with the *Xipe Totec*."

"Thank the Emperor for that, at least," Ed growled. "Proper officer, the major. Does what needs to be done and to hell with the consequences."

"Mount up." Paul turned for the shuttle. "We'll get you back to the 488 when we finish down here."

"Oh yeah," Ed called as they followed him to the Gray ship, "Morgan had one other message for you."

"Let me guess," Paul turned to walk backwards. He grinned at the Marine. "I'm an ass?"

"Close enough," Ed told him. "He was slightly more specific as to which exact part, but 'ass' will do."

They climbed aboard, not paying a great deal of attention to Kinsey. They gave surprised nods of recognition to the six Marines from the 488 but, realizing something important was going on, they kept quiet.

## A.G. Claymore

"You morons!" Kinsey seethed. "You want to know how we plan to hold this world? We'll blow it if the Navy comes anywhere close."

"I'd say you've already blown it, Romanus," Paul offered mildly. "You let yourself get captured like a scale-monkey in a water pit." He looked around the small craft. "Anyone else hungry? There's a place near here that serves the best green curry…"

"There's an antimatter warhead hidden down here!" Kinsey yelled, his face turning crimson. "If it looks like we're losing a fight in orbit, they'll blow the warhead. We can't stay down here."

"Right," Julia answered, nodding in a manner that clearly indicated she wasn't taking him seriously. "So we need to launch immediately and get caught by the combat fleet patrol." She chuckled. "You really do think we're a pack of idiots, don't you?"

She turned back to Paul. "You're thinking of going to Auntie's, aren't you?" It was more a statement than a question. You've only been here a few days; how the hell did you find the place so quickly?"

"I know a guy," Paul told her. "Used to work together on an outer Rim dust-ball called…"

"I can't believe you people," Kinsey blurted. "Even if you think I'm lying, just move us to the next city. We can wait out the battle in Westlock and you don't need to worry about…"

"Give it up, Romanus." Urbica adopted a warning tone. "I'm not leaving till we've had lunch. Inspector Grimm's awakened a craving and I mean to see it satisfied."

"OK!" He was nearly shouting now. "Forget about leaving Vermillion. I'll *show* you where the damn thing is so you can shut it down. Just forget about your damned stomachs for ten minutes!"

Urbica put a hand on Paul's shoulder. "What if Kinsey's telling the truth? It's bound to happen from time to time, right?"

Paul sighed. "Fine. It's your call, Colonel." He turned away as though disgusted with her gullibility, but he was actually afraid he might start smiling. He was worried he might start everyone laughing and so he had to turn away and master his expression.

"Where is this convenient bomb of yours?" she demanded.

"It's in the old river-city ruins. Near the reactor housing." His earnest expression was almost too comical. "I swear; it's really there. We don't have much time."

"Get us back in the air," she told the pilot. "We need to drop down into the industrial sector and follow the aqueduct into the ruins."

The old linear city had been the first Imperial attempt to colonize Irricana. The ambitious plan had resulted in a fifteen kilometer long metropolis following an underground river.

Eventually, the city would have been long enough to allow orbital flights from different weather systems, but the design was too susceptible to tectonic activity. Several bad quakes had wreaked havoc on the city, shutting down the power plants and flooding the city.

A previously unknown underground river had been released into the city and a general evacuation had left the world uninhabited for several decades.

The newer, cone-shaped design was far more resistant to earthquake damage and Vermillion had been built adjacent the site of the original city's surface station.

Paul followed Urbica to the cockpit, crouching to look out the front windows as the city slipped past them. They dropped below the commercial district and banked to follow a massive concrete-bound river that leapt across the open space. It flowed through the central generator on its way out the other side of the city.

## A.G. Claymore

The pilot brought them down within meters of the rushing water and followed it into a man-made tunnel. After a kilometer of flying on sensors only, they emerged from the darkened tunnel into the dim twilight of the ruins.

More than thirty stories high, the ruins only showed the top twenty levels. The lower ten had been submerged since the flood, hiding the park areas and docks. They slowed to a hover and stared out into the hazy distance.

The city stretched out of sight. Massive concrete pillars and cantilevered walkways, grimy with centuries of decay, marched off into the mist. Shafts of light lanced down from broken skylights. Wild avians circled above the flooded area, occasionally diving for fish.

It would have taken forever to find the antimatter warhead. Fortunately, they had a guide.

A large circular pipe was releasing a stream of water that was far too small for its diameter. Just below it, a ten-meter-wide cascade of water poured from a crack in the concrete. It fell for eight stories to where it had been wearing a depression in a walkway for centuries.

Julia pointed. "That outlet looks like a hydro-electric exhaust. Probably the backup power for the containment field. Take us over there."

As the small craft lurched into motion, she looked at Paul. "Let's get Kinsey up here."

Paul cut his bindings and dragged him into the cockpit.

She gestured out the windows. "The generator was over there," she indicated. "Where's your bomb?"

Kinsey aimed a finger. "Down there, through that waterfall."

Paul gave him a cuff to the side of the head. "You mean that deep recess with no way in?"

139

# Rebels and Patriots

"We can't even approach," Julia added, "with *our* ship." She jerked her thumb back toward the passenger area. "Tie this jackass up. I'm too hungry to waste any more time on this."

"No!" Kinsey shouted, grasping at Urbica's shoulder. She shoved him backwards into Paul.

"Watch it," he warned, shoving the colonel into a bulkhead.

"I'm telling you," Kinsey whined, reaching out for Paul but deciding at the last minute to keep his hands to himself, "it's in there."

"How did you even get it in there?" the pilot asked dubiously.

"They had a small sledge," said Kinsey, eager to provide corroborating details. "They rode it through the waterfall and came out after about twenty minutes."

"Then it wouldn't be very far past the water," Urbica mused, "given how long it would take to unload and activate the thing."

Paul went to the side portal and slid it open. Ten feet away, he could see a ledge that led along the side of the recess, passing through the waterfall. It appeared to be roughly a meter wide.

He backed into the craft and stepped out of his armor. He lined up and made a run for the door. His implant conditioned muscles allowed him to clear the distance with ease, but he slammed into the concrete wall at the back of the ledge and rebounded a step and a half, teetering wildly on the edge.

After a heart-stopping moment, he regained his balance and leaned against the wall to collect himself.

Urbica landed in front of him with the grace of a cat. Unlike Paul's clumsy impact, she'd allowed her limbs to flex and absorb the energy of the landing. She hadn't even touched the wall at the back of the ledge.

He stared at her. "What the hell are you doing?"

# A.G. Claymore

"Well, that depends, doesn't it?" she stood, dusting the grime from her under-armor suit.

He forced himself to keep his eyes on her face, but he was certain she knew where he wanted his eyes to go. "Depends on what?"

She leaned in a little, raising one eyebrow. "Ever diffuse an orbital-range remote detonator?"

"Well... no," he rubbed a hand on the back of his neck. He had access to the instructions, but doing it for real was a very different beast.

"Well then, what I'm doing here is saving your dumb ass." She slid past him and headed for the waterfall.

Paul had to admit, she had a point. He may have served in the Corps, but he'd been a cop, not a combat operator. He followed her through the water and into the gloomy space behind.

He looked back at the distorted image of the alien assault shuttle, hoping he'd get the chance to jump back aboard.

"In here," Urbica called.

He looked back in her direction. She nodded at a large opening where the ledge wall simply ended. Optic fibers were still bringing in light from the outside, casting an eerie glow around the foggy interior. Huge piles of debris and office furniture lay everywhere.

"You've got to be kidding me," she growled. "This room's got to be at least a thousand square meters. Where do we even start looking?"

Paul suddenly felt useful. "I may not know anything about diffusing orbital-range remote detonators," he said, "but finding hidden weapons is kind of my thing."

She gestured at the mess. "Alright, detective... let's see the Emperor's finest at work."

"A little sarcastic," Paul told her with a good natured grin, "but I suppose it will have to do." He waved a hand at the closest debris.

# Rebels and Patriots

"They'd prefer to keep the sledge above a level surface. No sense risking the cargo tumbling off while angling to get over a pile of junk. It also wouldn't do to snag something on their way over a pile."

He moved to the left. "Only one path from here so it's very likely they went this way." They followed the path until it split.

"You go left," he said. "I'll take the right."

"If you find it," she warned, "don't touch anything, *dong ma*?"

He nodded. "Got it." He turned and headed down his branch of the path. Fifteen meters in, he came to a dead end. He started to turn but something registered in his brain. He turned back to the dead end.

There was a desk in front of him, standing on end. The top was heavily rusted. He looked around at the other debris. Every other metal object was more heavily rusted at the bottom, where gravity pulled the water as quickly as it could condense from the air.

He grabbed the desk and pulled it out of the way. His skin felt as though he'd wandered into an electrical storm.

A one-gram antimatter warhead sat brooding in front of him. A box-shaped device with two lifting handles was attached to the side and he assumed it was the remote detonator.

"It's over here," he shouted.

Urbica came jogging around the corner. She knelt next to the weapon and took a close look at the assembly. "Well, the good news first — it's just a basic remote."

"There's bad news?" Paul asked, "aside from the presence of an antimatter warhead?"

"It'll take a few minutes to reset the safeties." She leaned in and touched the side of the remote detonator, activating a holo menu.

A.G. Claymore

Paul fidgeted as he watched her hands dance across the projected screen. Red windows turned green and slid down to the bottom as she worked.

She stopped suddenly and stared at a new window. "Oh, Hell!" she whispered.

"Hell?" Paul stepped closer. "What do you mean — Hell? That doesn't sound good at all."

She pointed at the screen. A counter was running down. "Looks like something is happening up there because this thing just went live. It's going to blow in less than fifty seconds."

"How long will it take to finish re-engaging the safeties?"

"Three minutes."

"So... plan B? We have one of those, right? Like a red wire, green wire moment?"

She stood and pulled out her sidearm. "Standard procedure in a case like this is to abandon all sense and try something desperate."

"You're gonna shoot the remote?" Paul stared at her. "What are the chances?"

She shrugged. "Fifty-fifty." She stepped over, grabbed the back of his head and kissed him.

Paul was stunned. "For good luck?"

"Nope." She aimed at the detonator. "Just wanted to do it and, considering the circumstances..." She squeezed the trigger.

They both stood there for a few seconds, cringing — as if that would help in the event of a detonation. Finally, she reached down and yanked the detonator free of the weapon and tossed it onto a pile of debris.

Paul shuddered. There it was again. That overpowering reaction following a near-death situation. He wondered if Urbica felt the same way and how she managed to master it. He realized she was staring at him, her breathing shallow and rapid.

143

## Rebels and Patriots

"Never did like leaving unfinished business," she said quietly. Before Paul could work out what she meant, he found himself shoved up against the back of the desk so hard it fell over behind him.

This kiss was far more passionate than the previous one and she dropped her pistol, freeing another hand for reconnaissance duty.

Paul found himself on his back without even remembering the fall onto the desk. He was a little rusty with the catches of under-armor suits and she moved his hand out of the way to do it herself.

Clearly, he'd been less effective than he'd thought at hiding his growing attraction for her.

A.G. Claymore

# *Things Can't Get Worse... Right?*

"**O**h, shit!" Urbica sat up and began tugging her under-armor suit back into place.

"That's not what a fella usually hears afterward," Paul mused, staring up at the grimy ceiling.

"No..." She stopped herself from saying something and turned to face him. "Not that. The detonator was activated for a reason. Something is happening up there and we're down here acting like a couple of horny teenagers."

"Dammit!" Paul sat up and shoved his arms back into his suit. "This was time we couldn't afford..."

She spared him a lopsided grin. "Yeah, well, don't flatter yourself, mister. It wasn't *that* much time..." She grabbed the 30mm warhead and raced back along the path to the ship.

"Ouch," he muttered as he stumbled after her.

Fortunately, the occupants of the ship were far too occupied with the threat of a rogue warhead to notice any peculiar behavior from the pair. "Warhead's been neutralized." She tossed it to a Marine and continued into the cockpit. "Get us back into orbit," she ordered. "The remote was activated on us so something alarming is going on out there."

They banked hard and raced into the tunnel at full velocity.

"Orbital control," the pilot began in a calm voice, "be advised, the export Gray vessel coming out of the aqueduct tunnel is an irregular Marine call-sign on emergency duty. Open the main egress doors or they *will* be blasted off their mountings."

He nodded with satisfaction. "Should buy us a few seconds," he muttered. He pulled back hard on the control yoke as they exited the tunnel. The industrial and commercial zones flashed by and Paul's

# Rebels and Patriots

feet lifted off the floor as the small ship angled down toward the gates at the edge of the upper ring.

Paul and Urbica both flinched as the gate frames flashed by. In less time than it took to say 'gate' they were through the egress tunnel and back into the buffeting atmosphere.

"Holy batter-fried forest gnomes!" the pilot exclaimed. "The orbitals are lousy with Gray ships!" He punched in a sequence on the main pad.

"If nobody has any objections..." He shot a quick glance at Urbica. "I'm gonna bend space back to the rendezvous."

"Do it," she ordered. "Do it from down here. We don't want to go out there and get splashed." She nodded out at the stars.

"I'll give us a little more angle at the other end, seeing as we'll be bringing a chunk of high-energy atmosphere with us." The pilot engaged the distortion drive and the hazy weather shimmered out of existence.

Urbica blew out a deep breath. Her gaze lost focus on the outside world and Paul realized she was reviewing data. "Mind if I link?" he asked her. "I'd like to get a look at what we're facing."

She nodded and his retinal display activated, showing a new connection option. He accessed the highlighted data pool and opened a visual room.

The visual room was a way of occluding external input while reviewing data. His brain only saw the ship and its passengers as a faint haze while the 'room' appeared solid and neutral in color.

He put the tactical data into the room and rotated the display to put the *Dauntless* closer to his position.

"About eighty Gray ships?" he asked out loud.

"Yeah," she replied. "Are they taking advantage of the rash of internal conflicts in this sector or are they in bed with the conspirators?

# A.G. Claymore

"Never mind that," she amended. "Their dispositions clearly indicate their intention to support the *Dauntless* rather than attack."

"Seneca," Paul declared.

"You think he's behind this?"

"I found one of his assets tied up with the courtesans back on home-world. He'll use any angle to get an advantage. I wouldn't put it past him to make an alliance with the Grays."

"If he's going to hand Irricana and Santa Clara over to the Grays, then the doomsday threat isn't going to stop CentCom from attacking. They'd rather destroy the planets than see aliens get them."

"I don't think he's planning to take those worlds out of the Imperium," Paul replied slowly, marshaling his thoughts as he talked. "I think he plans to become the power behind the throne. He can shut the military down in a matter of weeks if he holds the two planets.

"Hell, the entire data-net throughout the Imperium would be at his mercy. All commerce would cease if we don't keep him happy."

She sighed. "He wants the Grays as support. An added deterrence against a sneak assault by Force Recon."

"And the Grays would go for it, purely for the face gained," Paul added. "They already exert a lot of influence on their side of the Rim. If they could call the shots *inside* the Imperium…"

"*Tamade!*" she cursed softly. "*Zhentama yàomìng!*"

"To put it mildly," Paul agreed. "If they pull this off, they can finally stop paying reparations."

The windows in front of them went dark and they dropped out of their distorted bubble of space. "Comms are back up," the pilot advised.

"Take us to the *Xipe Totec*," she told him. "We'll drop the Marines and then head straight back to the '*Dope*'."

She focused on a random screen in the dash for a few seconds and then Paul saw a queued message in his on-board CPU, inviting him to join a conference. He opened another visual room and synchronized it with the conference address.

Tony was already there standing next to her, staring at the projected dispositions around Irricana. He gave Paul an absent nod. "Thanks for bringing my guys back in one piece. Were they any help?"

"It was your boys that found out the 538 had been smuggled out here," he told him, "and they just told me there's a big media push going on out here to make the Grays look like the second ascension of Montgomery."

"Told you they were my best."

"No argument here," Paul said. "They'd make good officers."

A grim smile. "The only thing the Nathaniels can offer them right now is an early grave." He shifted gears. "So if the Grays are here, it must be Seneca."

Paul nodded in agreement. "That cop we tossed in the arc furnace was one of Seneca's assets. He doesn't loan anything or anyone…"

"You killed a cop?" Urbica interrupted.

"He wasn't a very nice guy," Paul assured her. "And besides," he continued, aiming a thumb at Tony, "he's done worse."

"Ass," Tony growled.

"You know, I've been hearing that a lot lately." Paul shook his head mournfully.

"If we can get back to the matter at hand," Urbica said forcefully, pointing to a red icon. "What's this?"

"We think it's the 538, or their ships at least," Tony explained. "We've been picking up the synch beacons from the local gates and it looks like these ships are heading for Irricana."

A.G. Claymore

"ETA?"

"Three hours from now." He touched the icon and a second copy appeared next to Irricana. "We estimate the dropout point to be here, but it'll take time to get full crews into them."

"They don't have full crews, Tony," Paul told him. "They lost most of their guys just before you showed up."

Urbica bit her lower lip as she took in the situation. "This could work. We're five minutes out so we've got enough time to brief everybody." She looked up at Tony.

"This is going to get hairy."

## The Battle for Gliese

The two Khlen-class ships tumbled into the black just outside Irricanan orbit. The lead pilot hailed the *Dauntless* immediately after clearing the plasma burst, requesting a docking pattern and advising of a potential abduction threat against Colonel Kinsey.

The traffic control officer was suddenly very concerned that he may have already allowed an abduction team aboard. He realized, from the warning, that Colonel Kinsey may have been snatched off the *Dauntless* through his own incompetence.

In his distracted state, he allowed the two Khlens to land, each one packed with forty dragoons.

Though the Khlen could carry twenty-five Marines, the dragoons wore lighter armor and they didn't worry about having everyone stand in front of a hand pole. They were crammed in so tightly they might as well have been wearing five-point harnesses.

And then they'd shoved more men on top, like crowd surfers.

The landing struts of the cheaply made ships groaned as they set down inside the main hangar. It had been a gamble, but Tony had convinced Urbica that non-Marine ships would be received in the main hangar rather than the Marine bay.

It made the initial fight a lot easier. The Dragoons poured out of the two small vessels like the crew of a vaudeville ship. They quickly cut down all resistance and set the entry shielding to full power. Now a clever commander wouldn't be able to insert a team of Marines behind them by ferrying them outside the ship.

The assault commander led them over to the cargo sledges, chopping his hand along an imaginary line, bisecting the twelve vehicles into two groups of six.

"The team heading to engineering, take those," he shouted. "The CIC team comes with me in these ones."

The dragoons grabbed breaching blankets from the damage control lockers and draped them over the front of their sledges. They secured the upper edges to the control station at the front of each vehicle.

The breaching blankets were two meters square and filled with a fixatropic liquid metal compound. In the event of a hull breach, the blankets could be thrown over the hole and the filling would turn solid from the force of the air.

They also came in handy as impromptu armor. The flexible plates would turn temporarily solid when hit by small arms fire. A similar type of material was used to seal the gaps in combat armor.

The two convoys maneuvered out into the main passageway and went their separate ways, scattering unarmed crewmen as they accelerated toward their targets. They knew better than to trust the ship's own monorail. If it was shut down, they'd be trapped.

"Well, well," Tony muttered under his breath. "Aren't we all just a cozy little pack of traitors…"

The display that had populated on dropout showed the *Dauntless* and her escorts sitting close to the ships of the 538. None of them seemed the least bit concerned about the large fleet of Gray warships sitting in Imperial territory. Though the two fleets faced one another, their shields were down.

He opened a channel to the commander of his air-group. "Launch everything," he ordered. "You know the plan. Good hunting."

On the holo-display he could see his ships leaving the *Xipe Totec* and streaking through the formation of 538 ships.

The skeleton crews aboard the 538 vessels were in no position to take action, even if they could find the resolve to fire on Marine ships without direct orders.

Tony's ships headed straight for the Gray fleet. As they crossed the maximum range threshold, they opened up with their forward batteries.

Seconds later, the first antimatter rounds began impacting the Gray ships and the initial results were devastating. Even the smaller rounds were sufficient to destroy a medium-sized city and they were fired from multi-barrel guns.

The first few rounds of the salvo stripped away the navigation shielding and the very next round was all it took to vaporize the ship itself. Almost a third of the enemy fleet had been destroyed outright by the surprise assault.

Now, as their combat shielding came on-line, the Marine ships wheeled around and fled back toward the ships of the 538. Every Gray ship still able to answer to helm instructions began turning toward the undermanned Marine ships.

They began to concentrate fire on the rearmost ships of the fleeing 488 squadrons.

"Five of ours are down so far, sir," the sensor officer advised.

"Now would be a good time, Colonel," Tony said under his breath.

The screens returned to normal shading as the plasma burst faded. Urbica stepped forward though the reflex wouldn't improve her view of the maneuver's effects. Not that it was in doubt.

"Yes!" the sensor officer shouted. "We ripped them a new one!"

Tumbling sections of hull were spreading out from the drop wash of the *Rope a Dope*. As they watched, a Gray cruiser tried to shear away but she was too late to evade the impact of a large piece of wreckage. The large warship began drifting.

"We're away," Liang advised. His squadron had gone through the short distortion hop attached to the outside of the mother-ship's hull. Eddie had already launched his ready-squadron and the third, under Dimitry, was just waiting for the hangar door to finish opening.

Liang's ride had been risky, but there would be no need to wait fifteen minutes to get the third squadron out of the hangar.

"Good hunting," she told him, "and keep to your zones. The 488 are coming back in and I don't want you shooting each other." She muted the channel and set a new icon in the holo display. "Helm, bring us alongside that Gray cruiser. I want a backup flagship for the regiment."

The forward boarding team reached the bridge of the *Dauntless* with surprisingly little resistance. The majority of her Marines were away playing at rebels and most of the crew were unsure whom to follow. Most of them hadn't signed on for treason and they showed little interest in fighting Imperial troops, even if they *were* boarders.

The assault commander led his team onto the bridge. "This vessel has given aid and support to secessionists," he declared. "The command staff are under provisional charges of treason against his Imperial Majesty; long may he reign."

Silence and fear.

"Shut down the transit system, lock down all portals and set all weapon systems to safe mode." He waved his team forward and they moved to stand behind the operators.

"Failure to comply will result in summary conviction and a sentence of death will be carried out immediately as per the ICI investigator of record, Paul Grimm."

"In simple tones that even the Navy can understand," he explained, "if you don't shut down everything but life support, we're under orders to blow your heads off."

"This is *not* how my investigations usually go," Paul told Urbica through his suit's short-range communications system. He was standing on the outside of the *Rope a Dope's* hull, along with Urbica and more than a thousand of her dragoons. He tried not to think about the weak magnetic plates that held him in place.

It was so quiet out here.

He looked up as the enemy cruiser grew closer. "How many crew does that thing carry?"

"Less than you'd think," she replied. "Their real ships are heavily automated. They probably only have a couple hundred crew and they don't seem to think boarding is a possibility. We boarded three ships at the Carbon Well and resistance was minimal."

"You've taken real Gray ships?"

"For a little while," she answered obliquely' "They managed to activate self-destruct mechanisms."

"Are we sure we want to do this?" Paul was starting to wonder at her sanity. Her taste in men was dodgy enough, but boarding a ship that had a high likelihood of exploding seemed a little askew.

A.G. Claymore

"Well, you know the old saying," she breezed. "Fourth time's the charm."

"Actually, it's supposed to be the third time," he corrected.

"Is it? Ah, well that just means we're due for a break, doesn't it?"

Before he could think of an answer to that, she crouched, cut power to her mag plates and jumped for the cruiser. Paul scrambled to follow, heaving away from the *Rope a Dope* with all his strength.

He reflected, as the cruiser filled his field of vision with alarming speed, that it might have been a little too much strength. His own augmented strength, coupled with the ability-enhancing light armor worn by the dragoons had sent him on his way with far more speed than he'd expected.

He slammed into the alien ship with alarming force, rebounding past an antenna array which proved to be his salvation. He grabbed one of the long metal rods and arrested his momentum.

He saw a shape flit past in his peripheral vision and turned to see Urbica land feet first on the hull with a graceful bend of the knees.

She looked up at him. "Quit goofing around and come down from there before they try to transmit and fry your dumb ass."

Feeling like an idiot, he activated his mag plates and pushed against the antenna to rotate his body and achieve enough momentum to reach the hull. He managed to land feet first and, after a breath of relief, set off after Urbica.

They reached an airlock and she punched the big red button to open it. "Told you they don't give any thought to being boarded," she told him. "They don't even bother with a simple pass-code on the airlocks."

She looked around. "I see eight people heading for this door. We'll wait for them before going in."

Rebels and Patriots

As the last of the eight moved inside, Urbica and Paul followed. "Remember, it only takes one of the bastards to blow the ship, so kill them all. They'd kill themselves anyway, but our way is a hell of a lot better." With that, she punched the inner red button and the outer door slid shut.

The inner door slid open as the pressure equalized. Two startled Grays were standing in a passageway leading away from the hatch. Urbica brought her assault weapon up and put three rounds into each.

"Split up," she ordered. "Break into pairs and cover as much ground as you can. Move fast and cut them down. They don't seem to carry much in the way of shipboard defense but they *will* try to destroy the ship if they realize how much trouble they're in."

She thumped Paul's shoulder. "You're with me." She raced aft and he fell in behind her. They encountered a dozen more Grays on the way to the bridge and put them down with embarrassing ease.

They rounded a corner and cursed. Marines guarding the bridge of a Gray ship?

He accelerated to full speed and dropped to get under the fire of the Marines' weapons. He knew his assault rifle had no chance of penetrating the heavy armor but there were still options.

He'd been trained in the armor before heading off to the military police school. Any Marine, whether a store-man, a recruiter or a military cop, has to know how to fight and he knew the strengths of the armor.

And its weaknesses.

He slid up to the guard's feet and aimed up beneath the chest plate. His rounds hit the fixatropic armored panel protecting the gaps between the composite plates.

The rounds slid under the outer composite plate and broke the seam between hard and fixatropic plates, tumbling into the

A.G. Claymore

operator's torso. He rolled to look for an angle on the second man but pulled his weapon up as Urbica slammed into the target.

She wore the same light armor as her dragoons and it was two thirds the weight of a Marine suit. Though it may seem a disadvantage, in the right hands its agility could give an operator a distinct edge.

She'd taken advantage of the second man's distraction. He'd been turning to bring his weapon to bear on Paul when she launched herself into the air, slamming her feet into his chest plate as he desperately turned to meet the new threat.

She was lighter, but applying that weight to an impact point high above his center of gravity was enough to ruin his balance.

Arms flailing, the man fell on his back and she shoved her own rifle under his chest plate and pulled the trigger.

The heavy suit shuddered and went still.

They pushed on into the bridge. Eight crew were there and they fell at their posts, cut down by disciplined bursts. Urbica wanted this ship intact. Shooting wildly in a room filled with control panels was a recipe for disaster.

She touched a hand to the side of her helmet. "Excellent. Team leaders, keep your people moving. Continue to sweep the ship until I say otherwise. I don't want a Gray popping out of a storage locker and setting the self-destruct."

She retracted her helmet. "You did alright," she told him, "for a doughnut commando."

His helmet folded out of sight. "Is that it? I thought boarding actions were supposed to be a little more desperate."

She nodded to the two dead Humans outside the bridge entry. "This was tougher than the boardings at Carbon Well. They must have asked Kinsey to give them Marines after that. There were five more down in engineering."

157

"That *pì jǐng* Seneca has a lot to answer for," Paul fumed. "I'm going to walk into the rotunda and slap restraints on him in front of the media. We've got enough evidence to roast him alive."

"Can you prove he was pulling Kinsey's strings?"

A nod. "Check the intel we've pulled out of the *Dauntless* systems so far. He's been giving Kinsey some pretty specific directions. Even if he buys his way out of this, he's finished in the Grand Senate. His family is about to go into decline."

"Then he'll be desperate to salvage the situation." she warned.

Paul sighed. "He can still threaten Santa Clara. It's not as complete because there are still other, smaller producers who'll have access to all the erbium they want, but…"

"But he can still use it to suppress the Imperial economy," she finished for him. "We need another clever plan."

**D**imitry swung his small attack craft around and dove back into the melee. One of the few remaining Gray Hichef attack ships was lining up on Eddie's junior call sign. The man was watching his squadron leader's back but his own backside was about to get ripped apart by sunspots – the Gray ammunition of choice.

The sunspots were nuclear rounds. A miracle of miniaturization but far less impressive, gram for gram, than the antimatter rounds used by the Humans.

According to official record, only the Imperium had cracked the mystery of antimatter. How it was harvested was a closely guarded secret and only the Navy and Marines were authorized to use it.

Dimitry had been pragmatic about that when Urbica had robbed the *Dauntless* blind. The armories aboard the super-dreadnaught

# A.G. Claymore

were now largely stocked with conventional ammunition, though they still believed it was AM stock.

He'd rather survive to stand trial than die as a law-abiding citizen. Pragmatism was a way of life on Kamchatka, a forested world orbiting another Gliesan system.

He closed in on the Hichef. AM rounds were not to be used lightly. One didn't simply spray and pray because their destructive power was too dangerous to friendly forces. You had to get in close enough to feel the detonation in your bones.

Dimitry wondered what it was like for a Gray, thousands of years old, to go into combat. Did they crave a break from their endless existence or did they think they had more to lose? He shrugged mentally. *"Chto delyat?"* The question was entirely rhetorical; he knew exactly what he was going to do.

He judged his moment and sent a three-round burst toward the alien attack craft. They all impacted, shutting down the rounds' internal containment fields and allowing the antimatter cores to react with the matter in the casings.

Though most civilians assumed the antimatter reacted with the enemy ship, the concept was mostly untenable. Most enemies had energy shielding, effectively preventing the antimatter from reacting in much the same way the rounds' own *internal* shields kept them stable until deployment.

The round reacted with its own casing, unleashing incredible destructive power.

The Hichef remained intact, protected through some minor miracle by its shielding, but the crew were undoubtedly dead. The small craft had been thrown several kilometers in the space of a half-second and no inertial dampening could negate that kind of force.

The Hichef continued along at the same speed on its new course which would take it straight into the largest of the system's three suns.

He accelerated and changed course, only to find there were no targets left. "Bravo Squadron, sector secure," he advised his pilots. "*Maladyets!*"

**P**aul brought his weapon halfway to the firing position as the Gray suddenly appeared behind Urbica. "Julia," he hissed, nodding at the projection.

She turned and, after a slight hesitation, waved her weapon through the hologram. It was detailed enough to make them wonder if the Grays had developed some kind of teleportation technology.

The alien jumped as her rifle passed through him. "Stop that!" he snapped.

"Or what?" she demanded. "You'll commit more acts of war against the Imperium?" She leaned the rifle casually against her shoulder. "Who the hell are *you*?"

"I am Prime-Spear Mthlok. Who are you?"

A prime-spear was roughly the equivalent of a colonel. Mthlok had been caught off guard. Julia doubted he would have opened a channel to Imperial forces and chatted if he could help it. It might very well lead to serious consequences down the road.

It would be harder for the Gray Quorum to write these forces off as rogue elements if there were recordings of Imperial forces actually interviewing them.

At the very least, the records from this battle would be more than enough justification for reprisals.

"I'm Colonel Urbica of his Imperial Grace's Marines."

A.G. Claymore

Mthlok's skin went from a misty gray to a light charcoal and his veins began bulging green. He showed no other sign of agitation. "You have much to answer for. Our ships were simple merchants..."

"At Carbon Well?" Julia offered him a look of disdain. "I was there. They were light cruisers selling attack vessels to secessionists. I kill anyone I catch trying to disturb the Emperor's peace."

"Your Emperor?" Mthlok gave her a slight head-tilt, the Gray version of spitting on the ground in disgust. "He's just a child." His voice showed no discernible emotion at all.

"And yet he kicked your bony little asses at Carbon Well, didn't he?"

Paul had been watching quietly until a message appeared in the center of his vision. "All personnel, this is about to go sideways. Take positions on starboard side of hull and stand by to board newly arrived Gray carrier."

"You will return our vessels to us immediately."

There was a glitch in the holographic Gray; he went from solid to a half transparent image. Julia began walking toward the nearest escape trunk, waving for Paul to follow.

He chuckled. She'd moved the prime-spear to a visual room in her CPU. Her systems would continue to project a version of her but it would extrapolate mannerisms and actions from the words she chose. The Gray would have no idea she was moving.

She'd also opened a side channel so her dragoons would know what was happening. They entered the trunk and closed the outer door.

"These vessels are legitimate prizes of conflict as defined by the terms of the Ceres Convention. They belong to the Emperor so I'm afraid I can't just hand them over without His Grace's permission."

She punched the controls and the outer door snapped open. They climbed out to find hundreds of dragoons already waiting.

161

"All personnel," a new message read, 'move to enemy carrier to our starboard and stand by for further orders at the entry ports."

"Nonetheless," Mthlok droned. "You will hand them over to me or they will be destroyed."

"You *do* understand, Mthlok, that you're moving from the realm of deniable incident to one of overt act of war?" She was halfway to Mthlok's ship, Paul passing her much more slowly this time.

"Bringing your warships into Imperial space was bad enough, but destroying Imperial property? If you destroy this ship, it enacts the emergency measures statute, allowing His Grace to bypass the Grand Senate and order any response he wishes." She had chosen her words carefully, saying *this* ship even though she had just landed on the hull of Mthlok's fast-attack carrier.

"All personnel," her next message read. "Commence boarding of the enemy carrier. Same drill – I want this ship intact." She led Paul and six dragoons through the carrier's escape trunk.

"Your Imperium lacks the resolve to press beyond the Rim," Mthlok insisted. "I will not give you another warning; surrender all captured ships immediately."

"Stand by," she replied, signaling that she wanted all six dragoons to come with her. "I'll give it some serious thought." She raced down a passageway toward the centerline of the ship.

Paul brought up a tactical display. Close to eight hundred dragoons were now aboard the Gray carrier. They were mapping the large ship as they moved through the passageways, their implanted CPU's working in hive mode to show the estimated positions of bulkheads and compartments.

They reached the centerline and found a riser. The Grays used vertical shafts with no grav-plating to move between decks. It was simple enough to move personnel or equipment up or down through the shafts and it reduced unnecessary complication.

## A.G. Claymore

They reached the command deck and slowed to peer over the edge of the deck plating. They found another two Marines on guard. Their helmets were still retracted, indicating Mthlok was unaware of his predicament. She signaled two of her dragoons to fire on her mark.

They settled the muzzles of their weapons on the edge of the deck and took aim.

The tactical display showed the vast majority of the dragoons had made it on board and several hundred had set up for a surprise rush on key targets.

"I've reached a decision," she advised Mthlok.

"The right one, I'm sure." His voice still showed no hint of subtext, but that was the Grays.

"I'm sure of that," she said. "All units, engage."

"You'll regret this for a very short time," Mthlok told her. He turned to nod to someone behind him. They were so close that expanding gasses and debris from the stricken cruiser hammered against the shielding of the carrier, causing the shield generators to shake on their mountings. The vibrations made a good approximation of the original explosion.

The self destruct on the first prize had been detonated.

But there was a far juicier prize to be won.

Mthlok's holo image turned in alarm as he heard two shots followed by the Marines crashing to the deck in their heavy armor.

The first two dragoons made their way onto the decking and started hauling out their comrades as quickly as they could. Urbica led them onto the bridge and they put down fifteen Grays in half as many seconds. She raced up to a Gray standing in the middle of a holo display and knocked him down with ease.

"Your days are numbered, you…" Mthlok's final sentence was cut off as Urbica put a boot on his chest to hold him still and fired a

# Rebels and Patriots

burst between his eyes. His own transmitter, located in his sinuses, wouldn't be sending any dead-man signals to the self-destruct.

"You sure that was him?" Paul asked her.

"Ship hasn't blown yet," she replied, breathing heavily from the frantic burst of violence. "And they only allow captains to use dead-man protocols so, yes, I'm pretty sure that was him."

She nodded. "Good work, boys. Stand by to land your squadrons aboard the Gray carrier. I'm going all-in for this one and I need every trigger finger we have to clear this beast."

She moved around the bridge, looking at the screens. The third one caught her eye and she pecked away at it for several minutes uttering a few juicy curses to keep things interesting.

Finally she stepped back with a triumphant expression. "Eddie, start bringing your guys on board; the combat shield is down at the hangar entry."

"Alright…" She turned to the dragoons on the bridge. "Any of you got a bridge rating?"

"Ma'am." One man nodded.

"Good! The rest of you, get busy clearing this deck. It only takes one Gray at a data node to destroy this ship so kill anything that isn't a dragoon."

"Or an ICI inspector," Paul called after them.

She chuckled as she turned to the remaining dragoon. "What's your station?"

"Navigation, ma'am."

"Excellent, good man. Find the nav console and figure it out. I want us able to bend space out of here if we need to."

She took a deep breath and blew it out as she looked around the bridge. Paul saw an icon for a virtual room and he opened it. Seconds later, Tony appeared between them.

"How's it looking out there, Major?" she asked.

## A.G. Claymore

"We're holding it together for now, ma'am. The *Dauntless* is secure enough for the moment, but she's got a hornet's nest of angry Marines from the 538. We've got 'em contained for now, but we might be forced to vent atmo from their sections to calm them down a bit.

"They lost a few of their ships in the fight when the Grays couldn't tell who was who and the ones that remain are barely able to keep station since they have skeleton crews.

"All other hostiles have been neutralized for now."

"Good." She ran a hand over her scalp. "You'll need to secure the area while we clear out the Grays and sort out the critical systems."

"You're going to use the carrier, ma'am?"

She grinned. "Know how we got the *Rope a Dope,* Major?"

Tony shook his head.

"We got her from a nest of raiders out by Hagensborg. With a few modifications, we gave ourselves a reach nobody expected. The SDF aren't allocated carriers by CentCom, so we decided to write our own allocations." She held out a hand to indicate the Gray ship. "Having a proper carrier will do wonders for our effectiveness. And it's going to help us in the next phase."

"Santa Clara." Tony nodded.

"Not quite yet, Major," she corrected. "Our next target is Agash."

He stared at her in shock. He looked to Paul but got nothing more than a shrug. "Ma'am, how far into Gray territory are we planning to go?"

"As far as we have to," she told him. "We can't let them get away with cruising into our territory with armed ships. If we didn't punch them in the face for that, aliens would be swarming through the Rim within a couple of years, and I don't trust CentCom to authorize a punitive mission.

"We have the momentum right now and I'm not inclined to waste an advantage. We're going to disrupt their ability to coordinate operations beyond the Rim first and *then* we'll go deal with Santa Clara. Chances are any Gray forces at Santa Clara will be recalled to deal with the threat we're about to present."

"And by the time they get to Agash…" Tony began.

"We'll have moved on to their logistics depot at Irsulian," she finished for him.

He gave her a fatalistic grin. "I'll put my best techs on a shuttle and send them over," he offered. "We'll need to get that auto-destruct pulled apart before we run into any more of those *goucàode húndàn*."

"Thanks, Tony. I'll…" She trailed off, standing in silence for a second. "Not bad," she muttered to herself.

"Uhh… ma'am?"

She shook it off. "Sorry about that, but you just gave me an idea. We don't exactly want to leave the *Dauntless* just sitting here when we bend space for Agash so I was going to leave them with you at the rendezvous point to scare the hell out of any pursuit. The *Rope a Dope* will stay here for now with just an anchor watch."

"Makes sense." Tony's tone indicated he expected more and his boss didn't disappoint him.

"Put your best barrel-bashers on a shuttle with a protective detail and get them over to the *Dauntless*. I've got a project that'll help restore the old gal's reputation.

"She's about to make a donation to the cause."

A.G. Claymore

The assault commander walked into the situation room, a large glazed space on the starboard side of the *Dauntless'* bridge. The sixteen bridge operators were standing against the back wall with a squad of dragoons aiming assault weapons at them.

"Listen up, you useless chair-warmers," he shouted. "We have no way to tell how many of you were active participants in this rebellion so you've all been awarded a blanket conviction for treason."

He gave them a few seconds to lose the color in their faces. They would all be dead within the next sixty minutes and he allowed the full realization to set in before moving on to the carrot.

"We need this ship ready for action. Your scheme has been neutralized but your little Gray sweeties have revenge on their minds. Inspector Grimm has authorized me to offer amnesty to anyone in this room who's willing to serve.

"We're gonna go into Gray territory and teach them a lesson. I'd say your futures will look a lot better if you have green blood on your hands." He waved a warning finger at them. "If you pull any tricks, your corpse will spend eternity floating out beyond the Rim. Only take this offer if you truly intend to regain your honor."

Unsurprisingly, none of them chose execution.

Rebels and Patriots

168

# ESCALATION

## *Agash*

Secondary-Javelin Mindar blinked his translucent third eyelid in surprise. He was only thirty hours into his shift as duty officer in Agash orbital control, and there was already an irregularity. He tilted his head backward a couple of degrees.

He realized he was making a spectacle of himself and fought to bring his histrionics under control. Those short-telomere degenerates in operations were always changing plans without filing the appropriate notifications.

Well, Mthlok might be a prime-spear, but he was in one of Mindar's orbital paths now, so he was going to obey commands or live with a note to his file. He might just get one anyway for letting his ship drift in such a sloppy fashion. It looked as though the fool was preparing to ram his ship into the planet.

Mthlok was about to get a blistering tirade.

He opened a projection in the middle of Mthlok's bridge. "Prime Spear, I did suggest it was folly to take experimental equipment into the Imperium. Do you require assistance with…" his inflammatory question trailed off. He could feel the pulse hammering in his frontal temporal cortex.

Perhaps now was a good time to indulge in panic.

**U**rbica smiled politely at Mindar's image. "So," she began, "Mthlok was dispatched to Imperial space from this particular rat's nest? You did warn Mthlok after all…"

The charcoal-colored alien lifted his chin. "You will return our vessel to us immediately or face the consequences of theft," he droned.

She chuckled. "Calm your self. Such a display is unseemly."

"You leave me no choice." The Gray turned away from her and issued a curt command. He turned back to her and waited.

And waited.

A buzz of rotary rail-guns echoed through the ship.

His third eyelid flicked a couple of times.

"I'm assuming, from your obvious confusion, that you tried to activate our self-destruct." She tilted her head back, ever so slightly, to show her disgust. "Did you really assume we'd leave such a device intact?"

She grinned. "We *did* leave the transmitter intact because I have a healthy sense of irony, but it's been connected to a new circuit." She leaned toward the holographic Gray. "You *did* manage to destroy something, but it will take time for the ordnance to reach you…"

**P**aul was in the main hangar, led there by a dragoon provost captain who didn't know what to make of his discovery. The firing of the external gunnery drew their attention away from the mystery. The two cops walked over to the cluttered mess of jury-rigged transformers and capacitors.

As they approached, a cluster of naval personnel in red vests closed their helmets. Before Paul could do the same, a vicious buzz

## A.G. Claymore

was torn from the massive trio of rails sitting between the power equipment and the bridge opening.

His helmet closed just in time to seal in the chlorine stench of the heavy weapon. The carbon dioxide nozzles came on, cooling the rails for the next firing, but they wouldn't be able to cycle the borrowed weapon very quickly.

Without the closed systems used aboard the Dauntless, the cooling gas would quickly run out. And it took time to generate more.

The white mist was cut off and the weapons techs ran away from the rails. A second buzz announced the main round's departure.

"Bridge, Gunnery. Rounds complete," a voice announced over Paul's open channel.

The first hail of external gunnery was a screen intended to distract defensive fire, not that the Grays bothered much with defensive fire. The first shot from the heavy naval rail gun had been filled with antimatter sub-munitions, each one capable of destroying the planetary capital below.

The final round had been a full 255mm antimatter warhead. Big enough to turn the rubble into a smoking crater. It would take just under a minute for the first rounds to impact.

Paul walked around the jury rigged mess to get a clear view of the doomed city below. The definition of an honorable military target was far simpler when fighting the Grays. Their cities had no children because the species were all clones.

They'd all lived a full life, several times, and they could use a rest. The Human invaders were more than happy to offer it.

The first rounds began impacting beneath the heavy, swirling cloud cover. Bright flashes lit the growing storm from beneath, and then the first antimatter rounds struck home.

The force of the AM detonations was enough to affect the shape of the weather system, creating new eddies in the pattern.

Then the main round hit, radiating tendrils of cloud vapor out from the point of impact. The storm, several hundred kilometers in diameter, had been killed along with the city beneath.

**C**olonel Urbica watched as the Gray in front of her was suddenly swept away in a hail of debris and then the image failed. "Bring us around," she ordered. "Bend space for the rendezvous as soon as she bears."

"At least six inbound Gray ships," the sensor officer warned. "Patrol frigates."

"Good," she replied. "They're welcome to come along."

The Gray carrier was far more nimble than any of its Human counterparts. She shimmered out of sight before the enemy could come into effective firing range.

"Counter is set," the navigator announced. "Reaching the rendezvous in ten minutes."

"How's that rail gun looking?" she asked the gunnery officer.

"All readings are nominal," he replied. "Carbon dioxide levels should be replenished by the time we drop out. Rails have minor damage from alignment issues but nothing serious."

"**A**lright, look alive!" Tony shouted as Urbica's new ship, the *Sucker Punch,* blasted her way back into standard space. The *Xipe Totec* and the *Dauntless* stood ready to fire on any pursuit vessels and all attack craft had been launched from the LHV. The *Sucker*

## A.G. Claymore

*Punch* cruised past in front of their bows and executed a hard turn to port.

The carrier was just coming onto the firing line when seven blasts of plasma announced the pursuit. Every gun in the small Human flotilla opened up on the Gray frigates, taking them in the flank.

The four lead ships were destroyed before they could get their shields up. The remaining three raised combat shielding and turned to face the threat, but they were hopelessly outgunned.

The closest frigate was taking an incredible pounding from AM rounds and her shield generator must have shaken apart. The blue haze suddenly disappeared and the ship it had been protecting quickly followed suit. At least a hundred rounds had detonated inside the small hull before the gunnery officers could re-focus fire on a new target.

The farthest frigate suddenly began to shimmer and Urbica ordered all batteries to concentrate on the closer one. "We want one of them to get away," she explained over the fleet-wide channel. "We came here to make a statement and to draw them away from Santa Clara."

The fleeing Gray ship disappeared into a distortion envelope and her abandoned comrade simply detonated, taking two assault craft with her.

"All call-signs, this is Colonel Urbica. Commence recovery operations and stand by to bend space for Tel Qatshin. Maintain general quarters until we enter distorted space."

She nodded to Paul as he returned from the hangar.

Paul returned the nod and moved over to study the holographic situation map. An icon appeared in his vision and he opened the message.

*"How are your quarters?"*

Rebels and Patriots

He forced himself not to laugh. He composed his response. *"Not bad, a little cramped and the bed is a bit short. The biggest adjustment from the* Rope a Dope *is the showers."*

*"What's wrong with your shower?"*

*"There isn't one. Grays don't shower more than once a month so there's a few communal shower rooms for everyone."*

She looked away pretending to study a holographic readout from engineering. Her ears were a little darker than normal. *"Not quite everyone. The captain's quarters has its own shower. Feel free to make use of it."*

Paul took another look around and then, with a polite nod to Colonel Urbica, he walked off the bridge and headed aft. He stopped and frowned. Where the hell would the captain's quarters be?

He had to assume it would be close to the bridge and almost certainly on the same deck. He began poking around in the central passageway, checking every door but finding nothing but offices or smaller officers' rooms. Finally he looked forward.

There was a pretty large area, just aft of the bridge with one door. The passageway curved around to the starboard side and led into the busy control room. On the port side, the passageway ended at a single portal.

He approached the door and it slid open. A large space inside had a seating area with three leather couches near the door and a double bed near the window. The Grays weren't big on furniture but a quick shuttle ride had brought a few comforts over from the *Rope a Dope.*

He approached the bed, looking down at an open black duffle bag. A stencil on the side declared 'URBICA, J. M-686-347-231. So he was in the right room.

Then why did it feel so odd? He realized it was partly due to the alien ship. Humans never traveled in anything other than Human ships, believing alien craft to be second rate. The Gray ship, however, was far better suited to combat operations than the old *Rope a Dope*.

Human ships, like Human software, always followed the same basic patterns and philosophies. The *Sucker Punch* had protrusions from the floor, ceiling and walls that made no sense to Paul but must have seemed normal to its previous crew. Controls were in counter-intuitive locations and the lighting was a slightly odd shade of red.

He found the door to the captain's washroom. It was a bare room with carbon matrix walls, a drain hole at one end and, at the other end, the same foot plate he'd seen in the crew washrooms. It had tread-plates for the user's feet with a self explanatory hole between.

He was about to deactivate his armor when he finally acknowledged the *real* reason why he felt odd. The frenzied encounter down in the ruins had been a spur-of-the-moment thing. He certainly had no regrets, but there had been almost no conscious thought involved.

Now here he was in the room of a woman who was far above his station, helping himself to her shower. The Urbica family may not be very prominent, but they'd produced eight Grand Senators. She was the daughter of a planetary governor.

Paul was the son of a deceased mine laborer. He represented the high-water mark for the Grimm family, but he still came from the wrong end of the wormhole.

He felt a sudden surge of anger at himself. It was bad enough living in a society that constantly tried to remind him he wasn't quite good enough. What purpose would he serve by telling himself the same damned thing?

He backed over to the wall between the washroom and the couches and opened the suit. He stepped out, pulled off the under-armor suit and walked into the shower.

# Rebels and Patriots

Once again, the weirdness of an alien vessel came into play. He felt like an idiot, standing naked in Colonel Urbica's shower trying to figure out how to turn the damned thing on. He finally noticed that the drain plate was the only thing in the room that stood out, aside from the foot plate at the other end.

He tapped the drain plate with his foot and jets of hot, heavy mist suddenly came at him from every direction. He hadn't had time for a shower since leaving the owner's suite on the *Pulsar Intrepid*.

It felt absolutely magnificent.

He stood in the middle of the room, letting the heat soak into his bones. His entire body was constantly coated with a running layer of hot water and he closed his eyes and let his mind wander.

What he'd found on the hangar deck had been disturbing. The reaction from the provost captain had added a new layer of concern as well. When word got out, the dragoons would demand immediate action and he knew they might end up going deep into Gray territory.

He opened his eyes as his augmented hearing caught the sound of the cabin door. Footsteps approached the spot where he'd left his armor and he heard the whirring sound of worm gears as another suit opened.

His pulse quickened as he heard the sound of under-armor fabric sliding on skin. He was no longer conflicted about being in this shower.

Footsteps crossed the room followed by the sound of someone rooting through the duffel bag. The sound ceased and nothing happened for a few seconds.

Finally, the steps approached the washroom. He could see a shadow through the thick mist. The form slowly took shape as she approached. Her electro-chromatic tattoos had been turned off and she looked much younger. She also seemed a bit nervous.

Paul was relieved that he wasn't the only one.

## A.G. Claymore

She held up a container. "There *was* soap in my bag," she chided him with a smile.

"I didn't want to invade your privacy."

The smile trembled, but didn't fade. "Privacy is a relative concept," she told him. "For someone in my position, there's often no such thing as privacy." She stepped closer. "I hadn't given much thought to the need for privacy until you joined us on the *Rope a Dope*."

"And now?"

She poured soap into her hand. "Ever notice, sometimes, that you don't realize you're thirsty until you have a drink?" She made a circular gesture. "Turn around and I'll do your back."

Rebels and Patriots

# *A New Target*

**P**aul looked up at his mother. *"You don't have enough for the three of us,"* he insisted. *"If you don't have to worry about me, you and Emma might have a chance."*

*Sarah Grimm wiped the wetness from her face and dropped to her knees to hug her little boy.*

*Paul felt her hot breath on his neck and water welled up in his own eyes. He knew he'd never feel that comforting sensation again.*

*"You're so like your father,"* she said, struggling to keep her voice steady. *"So ready to sacrifice yourself for the rest of us."*

*He pulled away and looked into her face for the last time. "Use the company bounty to get yourselves somewhere decent,"* he urged.

Paul woke before he could hear his mother's reply and he stared up in confusion at the ceiling.

He felt Urbica's hot breath on his neck. He reached his hand up to wipe his face and she began to stir.

"Mmmm, did I miss anything important while I was asleep?" she murmured.

"Not yet," he told her, "but the questions are bound to start hitting us soon. I have a few already."

"Like what?"

"What should we do with Kinsey?" Paul asked her, running his fingers lightly up and down her back. "I suppose we need him as a witness…"

"Hmmm," she replied helpfully. "Witness, sure. Sounds like a plan."

He chuckled, reaching up to trace a finger along her jawline, his finger following the line where implant met skin. "So I'll take that to mean you don't care at the moment."

A.G. Claymore

She reached up to move his hand away from the implants on her jaw. "We do have a few loose ends to tie up, but he can wait for a while." She frowned. "What I'd really like to do is go eight rounds with him in the arena. I know what he's been saying about me."

"That you have a Zhan-Dark complex?"

"We should have an equivalent name for men," she grumbled.

"Well, it would never be used on Kinsey," Paul asserted. "He has the good taste to show no competence whatsoever, so it's unlikely anyone would ever feel threatened by him."

She giggled.

Paul marveled that this could be the same woman whose very presence had subdued a train-full of sailors into silence. "You know, I heard a theory about the name."

"What name? Zhan-Dark?"

He nodded. "I heard she was a peasant maiden who saved her emperor. She claimed God was talking to her, telling her to lead the army against overwhelming odds."

She rolled over and sat up. "And I suppose she ended up married to the emperor and had lots of little emperor babies?"

"No." Paul paused, watching as she walked across to where she'd thrown her duffel-bag a couple of hours ago.

She caught him looking and rewarded him with a slightly embarrassed smile. "Well, what happened to her?" She pulled out a fresh under-armor suit.

"He betrayed her to the same enemy she'd *saved* him from."

She stopped, halfway into the suit and stared at him. "Seriously?"

He nodded.

She finished shrugging her way into the suit and its seams began to seal themselves. "Typical male bullshit," she muttered. "Where did you hear that?"

"Narbonne."

"Hah!" She picked up a spare suit and threw it at him. "So some little trollop with big eyes and even bigger…"

"Did you have a spare suit," he cut her off hastily, "because you knew I'd end up in your room?" He adopted what he hoped was a roguish grin.

She abandoned her attempt to tease him about Narbonne. It wasn't a big deal for her; she'd taken leave there herself, after all. "Chance favors the prepared mind, Marine. Assume each mission will be a success and plan accordingly."

"Why, Colonel…" He adopted a scandalized tone. "Was I a conquest?"

Another giggle. "More like a pacification." She backed into her armor and it started wrapping around her body. "Resistance was negligible."

He struggled into his under-armor suit. "The resistance never had a chance; there were collaborators controlling all key targets."

She chuckled and Paul wondered if she'd found some way to put on the warrior with the suit. He'd been hoping for another giggle, but it seemed he'd have to wait for the next 'shower'.

He backed into his own armor. "We've got something really disturbing down in the hangar bay," he told her. His suit closed and he turned to see her dark eye tattoos were back on. He definitely felt he was talking to the warrior now.

"At least you aren't telling me I have to rush down there and look at it," she allowed. "I have MacGregor telling me I need to look at some weird thing down in the engine room — as if a combat officer is any help figuring out alien technology — the ordnance officer is insisting that I need to inspect the forward ammunition lift and the cook is screaming green bloody murder about the rations."

## A.G. Claymore

She gave him a wry smile. "At least you're just *telling* me what you've found rather than dragging me down there." She tested her helmet snapping it shut and open. "If I can stop complaining long enough for you to get a word in, that is."

"We've got a couple thousand empty stasis pods down there," he told her. "There were DNA matches to some of the missing Vermillians."

"They took the missing citizens?" She test-flexed her joints. "What the hell for?"

"Well, I figure getting them out of the Imperium would tie up a loose end, but I think it has to do with the fact that the Grays are all clones. They've been body-hopping for thousands of years. They must have run out of original cells a long time ago."

She nodded. "We were briefed on that before coming out to the Rim. They're probably several copies removed from the original material. They're staring down the barrel of a whole lot of genetic problems."

"And those problems are accelerating," he added. "Each new iteration has shorter telomeres, meaning all the bodies in the series have shorter lifespans. The rate at which they depart from the original copies is increasing."

"So are you suggesting they're using our people for research?"

He took a deep breath. This might lead them down an even more dangerous path than the one they were already on. "Yes, I think they're hoping to find answers from a younger species."

"Hang on," she put a hand on his shoulder. "Stasis pods... Our people may still be alive, or some of them, at least." She shuddered. "Agash, what if..." She shook her head. "No, they wouldn't conduct that kind of research right on our doorstep. It's unlikely we killed our own people."

# Rebels and Patriots

"Tel Qatshin is unlikely as well, except as a transshipment point," Paul added. "It's a logistics center, right?"

She nodded her agreement. "We need to figure out the most likely place…" Her eyes suddenly flashed in triumph. "I don't know if I'm a genius for thinking of it or an idiot for taking so long!"

"What?"

She grinned. "Guess what that makes you?" She started for the door. "Come on. We can get the *ship* to tell us where they were taken."

They entered the bridge and she took a quick look around, settling her gaze on a young blond officer leaning over the navigator's shoulder. "Lars," she called out.

"Ma'am?" The young man came over.

"Inspector Paul Grimm, this is Lieutenant Lars Nielson." She waved a hand toward the young man. "When he's not serving with the dragoons, he's a trader. A lot of the Gray material you find in the Imperium was imported by his family."

Paul had an idea where this was going. "You can read Gray, Lars?" he asked.

A nod. "Passably, which is why I'm up here instead of down in the hangar." He nodded at the bridge terminals. "We're programming menu translations into the implant displays. Once we hive link them to everybody, we can have translations for all the action stations."

Julia stepped in close to the young man and lowered her voice. "Lars, we need you to get into the records and find out if they brought large numbers of Human bodies or prisoners aboard. Can you do that?"

"Yes, ma'am." He gave her a guarded look, then shrugged. "Shouldn't be too difficult." He activated a holo-screen and started entering commands in Gray glyphs. "Just setting up some guiding

A.G. Claymore

parameters and we are… searching." He pressed a green icon and lines of data began scrolling past. Several thin windows began popping up.

"Whoa," he muttered softly. "Folks, we've got more than just a few Humans being carried on this ship."

"Pick one occurrence and run the bridge records from the moment they're brought aboard," she ordered.

A holographic crew appeared on the bridge. Urbica's dragoons jumped back in alarm at the sudden resurrection of the Gray bridge operators.

"Sorry, folks," she called out. "Just looking through the logs." She opened a visual room and moved the log projection, restricting it so that only Lars and Paul could see it with her.

"Speed it up," she ordered.

The Grays' actions became almost comical as they flitted around the bridge.

"Wait," she hissed. "Stop the playback and reverse at normal speed."

The projection resumed in reverse, though it was hard to tell when looking at Grays.

"There," she said excitedly. "The star-field. It changed. Run us forward again." She shifted the display to put the helm station in the middle of the real bridges open area.

The three clustered around the projected Gray, looking over its shoulder.

The projection stopped. "That line means 'Transit Portal'," Lars whispered, eyes wide with the enormity of what he was saying. "They're also reading the beacon at Narsa, after the transit portal goes active, but the ship picked up the Human cargo through a ship-to-ship transfer in orbit around Agash."

# Rebels and Patriots

"*Wo de tian a!*" Paul hissed. "They have wormhole technology, and they figured out how to build it into a ship?"

"But nobody outside the Imperium possesses that kind of technology," Lars whispered back.

"And don't you forget it," Paul warned him. "Not a word of this to anybody, understand?"

Lars nodded, eyes wide. "You don't need to tell me twice, Inspector. I understand what this would mean if it gets out."

"Good man!" He turned to Urbica. "Maybe we should go down to engineering and have a look at the weird thing they found after all."

It took them longer than they expected to find the engineering department, but they finally located the engine room. A slightly hefty man with a bushy mustache hurried over. "Thanks for coming down, Colonel. I know it may sound like I'm making a big fuss over nothing, but I can't shake the feeling we're looking at something important."

"Inspector Grimm," Urbica gestured to the heavy-set man, "this is Daffyd ap Rhys, best engineer on the Rim."

"Daffyd." Paul nodded politely. "What's your concern?"

The engineer squinted at Paul. "Pardon my lack of comprehension," he said slowly, "but do we really need an inspector from the 'Eye' for this?"

"We might," she told him. "Show us what you've got and we'll decide whether it warrants the inspector's presence."

Daffyd nodded toward a portal. "First noticed it in here," he said as he led them through the opening. He put his hand on what looked like a five foot thick tube that ran through the top corner of the small room.

"Curvature seemed to mean it ran all the way around the ship; just inside the hull," he explained, "so I took a look at the on-board

# A.G. Claymore

schematics and…" he opened a holo and it showed a cross-section of the Gray carrier. A massive, five foot thick ring ran around the inside of the hull and two thinner rings were mounted fore and aft at the same diameter.

Paul turned and shut the compartment door.

"Daffyd," he began, "I'm invoking the Official Secrets Act. You signed a copy when you accepted the Emperor's commission so I shouldn't have to explain what this means, right?"

Daffyd simply nodded.

"Daffyd, I need to hear you respond with either 'yes' or 'no'," Paul demanded.

"Yes, Inspector," Daffyd answered, still sounding a little incredulous. "I understand that I'm constrained by the Official Secrets Act."

"Good. Then you understand that you're never to repeat a word of this conversation to anyone unless ordered to do so by myself or one of my superiors. Nobody in the military is authorized to give you that order."

A nod, followed by a slight expression of annoyance. "Yes."

Paul nodded. "Daffyd, we have reason to believe this is a wormhole generator."

"*Cái bù shì!*" Daffyd stared at Paul in disbelief.

"No, we're dead serious," Paul assured him. "This ship went from Agash to Narsa in the blink of an eye."

Daffyd's eyebrows dropped in the middle as he looked back to the schematics. He walked through the projection to look at it from the other side. A look of pure admiration dawned. "*Jingcai!*" he whispered approvingly.

He reached out and put a finger on the main, central ring. "This'd be the pincher," he said. "I'm not a wormhole specialist but I understand some of the basics. This ring is probably what creates

185

the fold in space, but I tend to think of it as more like a pinch than a fold.

"The really brilliant thing, if I'm right about this, is they're using the other two rings to focus the hole. Putting a wormhole generator on a ship is pretty impressive, but the thing that's raising the hairs on the back of my neck is the fact that they can create and focus a wormhole from the *origin* point."

He looked up at them. "This would free them from using gates. They don't need to open a hole between two gates in an existing system; they can just create a pinch and move the destination end to where they want to go."

"The phrase I'm looking for here," Urbica cut in, "rhymes with 'clucking bell'." She walked over to put a hand on the section of ring.

"This is a huge strategic advantage for them." She shook her head. "How many ships might have this?" She turned to look down at the projection. "We saw no indications of this on the cruiser we captured, did we?"

"I wasn't aboard her for very long," Daffyd admitted, "but we didn't notice anything."

"That orbital controller mentioned 'experimental equipment' when we showed up at Agash," she added. "We might have the only one."

"And it might have a few bugs left in it." Daffyd scratched the back of his head. "I know we need to keep this under wraps, but I need Lars down here to help me figure this out. I can't read these Gray scribbles."

"He's helping on the bridge right now," she told him. "We don't want them steering us into a black hole by mistake, but as soon as he's done up there, I'll send him down to you."

186

# A.G. Claymore

"Remember, not a word," Paul said. "Only Humans possess wormhole technology."

"I'd say you might want to re-assess that," Daffyd advised him, "in light of what we've…"

"Only Humans possess wormhole technology," Paul insisted. "Billions of Humans go about their daily lives, secure in the knowledge that the Emperor protects them. If word gets out that a fleet of Gray ships could show up without warning and reduce home-world to radioactive dust, we'd have anarchy."

"Look, Inspector," Daffyd held his hands up, "I hear you. I understand why I need to keep my pie-hole shut but, sooner or later, one of these ships is going to pop up in front of a planet full of honest citizens and the party line is going to look pretty thin."

"*Jiàn ta de gui!*" Paul cursed angrily. "Why is it every time we end up having to escalate this *goucàode* errand we have multiple reasons 'why' and none for 'why not'?"

He jabbed a finger at Daffyd. "Now look here; you're going to crawl all over this thing and tickle out every secret. If we get this heap back to Home-world, the Imperial Engineering Corps will pull her apart and study every angle, but we'll be presenting *you* as the inventor, got it?"

"But I…"

"But nothing, ap Rhys," Paul cut him off. "We can't have citizens thinking aliens are smarter than us, so you'll do the interview circuit for a few months, refusing to go into technical details for security reasons…"

"And because I don't understand them," Daffyd added.

"And then, you'll probably be made a colonel in the Life-Guards, which comes with an obscenely huge pension."

"This is buggered," the engineer whispered.

## Rebels and Patriots

"And always remember," Paul warned, "you need to keep this secret. If you *ever* tell anyone, even your cat, you'll suffer such a bizarre death, nobody would ever suspect it was a government hit. A freak poultry incident or something like that. If we use this generator, some of the crew are going to figure it out, but we'll just keep pointing to you and saying it was your invention. The public will believe the lie because it's prettier than the truth."

"Come on," Urbica opened the door. "We need to find out where this ship was put together."

"What are the chances we can make Daffyd the 'father' of shipboard jump engines?" she asked as they walked back to the bridge.

"Fifty-fifty." He grimaced. "I'm rooting for the whole happy-and-rich-Daffyd plan, since the other probability is they kill all of us, destroy the ship and then stuff their heads back in the sand. We're talking about CentCom and the Grand Senate, after all..."

He realized his focus was starting to shift. He'd always been primarily concerned with the machinations of the Nathaniel family but they'd practically ceased to exist, except for Tony.

Now he found himself forced into bigger issues. The fate of the Imperium now dangled in the balance and he suddenly felt the weight of billions of Human lives hanging on his every decision. If they screwed this up, the Imperium might just tumble down into anarchy.

They found Lars, still on the bridge, and pulled him aside again.

"We need to know where this ship was built," Urbica told him. "We're pretty sure this is an experimental engine so chances are good they're only making them in one place."

Lars nodded. "Something tells me we won't be doing a whole lot of trade with the Grays anymore." He started working his way through the main menus. "I wonder what the Snakes are like in negotiations...

## A.G. Claymore

"Hey, this might be getting close." He enlarged a screen. "Congratulations on your purchase of a *lightning class assault carrier*. This vessel has many adequate qualities…" He grinned. "Looks like standard copy and they just paste in details. Here we are — 'please direct any queries to the Tel Ramh shipyards for efficient and acceptable remediation'."

"Holy Hell." She was nearly laughing. "What a bland species. *Many adequate qualities?*"

"I'll have you know it's a veritable *font* of adequacity." Paul asserted huffily.

The three of them broke out laughing.

"Oh, dear me," Paul finally wheezed. "We're starting a full-out war out here, aren't we?" His tone didn't really cast it as a question.

She nodded. "It would be irresponsible not to. If we give the Grand Senate any wiggle room, they'll make peace and the Grays will throw everything into building a war-fleet of wormhole-generating ships. We need to disrupt their program at Tel Ramh, find our missing people at Narsa, save Santa Clara and then go home to scare our leaders into crushing the Grays."

"Easy enough," Paul quipped, "aside from the fact that they'll be throwing everything they have into destroying this ship."

She took a deep breath. "That's why we need to move fast."

## See, the Maintenance is How They Get You...

"**Y**ou've got to be kidding me!" Tony turned from Urbica to see if Paul was laughing, but no luck. "*Kuángzhede!*"

"Crazy maybe, but it's no less true, for that," Paul assured him.

In the interest of security, they'd brought Tony over to the *Sucker Punch* as soon as they reached the rendezvous. They were looking at the ship's schematics in Urbica's quarters and Paul was surprised to feel a little resentful of Tony's intrusion into what he considered to be a private space.

"We need to figure out how we're gonna bring this back to the Imperium without being killed for it," Tony asserted.

"We're working on it." Paul waved at their chief engineer. "This here's Daffyd ap Rhys, the man whose inspiration will lead to the development of point-controlled wormholes."

"Got a fever from eating at a dodgy walk shop down in Vermillion," Daffyd offered. "It came to me while I was losing weight from both ends, if you follow my meaning…"

"Oh… that's great, Daffyd." Tony wrinkled his nose ever so slightly. "Thanks for that."

"So, we need to put this engine to work," Julia announced, "and go smash the hell out of the shipyards that made it."

"It's clear across the other side of Gray territory," Tony ventured. "Does that mean we wait here with the *Dauntless* again?"

"No reason why you have to," Daffyd declared.

Everyone turned to look at him.

"That portal engine creates a wormhole and positions each end," he explained. "We just need to move the entry point a little farther out and you can take the other ships through first. That LHV is a bit smaller than this beast so no problems there…"

# A.G. Claymore

"But what about the *Dauntless*?" Paul asked. A super-dreadnaught was massive. "Can we make the opening any bigger?"

"We could but it would take an incredible amount of energy, and anyway..." he waved a dismissive hand, "super-dreadnaughts trick the eye. Sure, she's five times the displacement of this ship but she's six times the length overall. She'll fit through just fine."

"That changes things considerably," Julia noted. "Especially when we go to Narsa. We're going to need some serious orbital superiority if we have any hope of finding our people."

"There's your *casus belli*," Tony said. "Thousands of Humans saved from a Gray experimental facility? We get them back to Vermillion and stand them in front of the media and there's no way we could stop a war. Any senator who tried to downplay the situation would end up impeached."

"So do we go to Narsa first or Tel Ramh?" Paul asked.

"Tel Ramh," Julia replied. "Attacking their wormhole program is our priority. We hammer them flat, then bend space for Bish."

"A bit of misdirection?" Tony asked.

She nodded. "We bend for five minutes, then drop out and line up a wormhole for Narsa. And here I was planning to be all clever, pretending to show up at Tel Ramh for maintenance. Though I do like the idea of just kicking in the door."

"The maintenance is where they get you," Daffyd said with a chuckle. "Sucker you in with a good price then soak you on the repair bills."

"You see?" Paul nodded at Urbica. "I told you he'd do fine on the interview circuit when we get him back home."

"Anyway," she said, raising an eyebrow at Paul, "that might draw forces to Tel Ramh and Bish, making it easier to pull off a rescue raid at Narsa."

# Rebels and Patriots

She looked at Tony. "Get back to your ship. I'll brief Commander Schatz. I want her to take the *Dauntless* through first. She has the most firepower and can soak up a hell of a lot more damage."

"Now, wait a minute," Tony protested. "The *Xipe Totec* is packed to the gunwales with assault craft. With the element of surprise…"

"This is not a debate, Major," Urbica cut him off. "I need to consider the possibility that the enemy might anticipate our next move and have forces waiting for us. Hell, they may even be able to track this ship, for all we know. The super-dreadnaught goes through first."

"Ma'am!" Tony nodded curtly and left the room.

She headed for the door. "Daffyd, get down there and make sure we don't run out of magic wormhole fuel or whatever the hell that thing runs on." She followed the curving passageway to the bridge, talking to Commander Schatz along the way.

Paul sincerely hoped life didn't get any more interesting.

# A.G. Claymore

## *Tel Ramh*

**Q**edna had been on station for seventy-two hours now. Another forty-three and he'd be able to land his squadron on Tel Ramh and hand the next defensive shift over to Birin's squadron.

He had faith in his superiors' orders. The Humans would almost certainly come here if they managed to figure out what they'd stolen but that was a very big 'if'. Humans were all bluster and brute force; they lacked the subtlety to see technology that exceeded their own.

No matter. If they did come to Tel Ramh, one squadron of ship destroyers would be more than enough to hold them while the cruisers closed in from the other side of the planet. Unlike Humans, the Grays knew how to respond appropriately to a threat. One squadron was an elegant display of cool tactical thinking.

An entire combat wing would have been… vulgar.

He suddenly blinked as a portal opened to his front. Somehow, those hairless apes had figured out what they were sitting on. He touched his control panel, ordering a firing line perpendicular to the portal's axis. The bow was coming through now, but he would wait till the ship was halfway through.

He didn't want to waste his opening shot on just any part of the ship. He wanted the first, disciplined salvo to strike at the flank, where the rings came closest to the outer hull.

He blinked again in confusion. The ship just kept coming. It was massive and brutally ugly. This was no Gray carrier…

"First-Wing Qedna," one of his pilots droned, "it's a super-dreadnaught."

"Calm yourself," Qedna replied. "Whatever it is, we must engage the enemy. All units, open fire."

Too late, his sensors began calmly notifying him of a hail of antimatter rounds.

"Nothing else?" Commander Schatz turned her head to look at the sensor officer. "Just one squadron?"

"There are five cruisers approaching from the far side of Tel Ramh, ma'am, but I doubt they'll pose us any trouble."

"Well, you never know what kind of shenanigans they might be cooking up," Schatz muttered. "Get us off the entry axis, just in case they do something that's actually dangerous. I don't want to plug up the doorway."

"Aye, ma'am," the helmsman replied, "turning us toward the primary target." The massive orbital framework of the Tel Ramh shipyards slid into view.

"All batteries, weapons free," she ordered. She frowned, touching a hand to her right ear. "Roger that." Her face was suffused with anger. "Now hear this," she spoke and her voice echoed into the bridge from the nearby compartments. "This ship is now in a combat situation, responding to an act of overt war by the Gray Quorum.

"I will no longer tolerate any acts of mutiny aboard my ship. I am speaking specifically to those Marines of the 538 who have not taken amnesty. We can no longer afford the time or lives to suppress your activities. Compartments under your control will be vented to space in thirty seconds. If you wish to surrender before your suits run out of air, you may present yourselves at the firewall airlocks."

She nodded at the life support officer.

He turned to his screens. "Initiating a gas dump on all Marine EVA gear. All assault craft are venting their storage tanks as well." He turned back to her. "They're going to have two minutes to make up their minds when the compartments vent, ma'am."

She was quite certain the rebel Marines would view her earlier statement with scorn. They *preferred* fighting in vented compartments. They trained for it incessantly, but they would be hard-pressed to cook up trouble in two minutes.

She turned back to the tactical holo, surprised to see that the dockyards were already a complete mess. She enlarged the tactical display, forcing herself to ignore the distraction posed by a horde of mutinous Marines.

"Bring us around to face the approaching cruisers," she ordered. "Let's loop a few salvos around the planet at them."

**C**hirat knew he was too late to save the dockyards but the real objective was the destruction of the stolen carrier. His cruisers would clear the edge of Tel Ramh in a matter of minutes and he would have a straight shot at the carrier. He leaned forward slightly, positively frantic to join combat with the impudent invaders.

With the stolen ship destroyed, those idiot monkeys in the super-dreadnaught would be stranded and another force could be dispatched to deal with it. He doubted his force would survive against such a deadly vessel, but at least the Humans would know they'd been in a fight. He was amazed they'd figured out how to bring the cursed thing along with them.

"Prime-Spear," the visor murmured, "we detect objects entering an orbital path consistent with our own. We may be under fire."

"Shields to full," he ordered. "Evasive…"

"Well, that was kind of an anticlimax," Schatz remarked. "Why did they think hiding behind the planet would help? They might have done a little damage if they'd been with that patrol squadron."

"Helm, position the ship for orbital bombardment," she ordered. "Fire control, stand by to open fire."

"Aye, ma'am," the fire control officer confirmed. "The trace is active and updated; looks like almost everything is where intel thought it would be."

"We're in position," the helmsman announced.

"The *Xipe Totec* is crossing the event horizon," the sensor officer advised.

"They're late to the party," Schatz replied. "Weapons free."

The distant hum announced the outgoing hail of antimatter rounds from the main batteries. For some unknown reason, their stocks of smaller-caliber AM rounds were mostly conventional and nuke munitions. Schatz suspected Kinsey may have been selling ammunition on the black market.

The outgoing ordnance headed toward the planet on trajectories calculated to pull them into the gravity well of Tel Ramh and strike cities all over the planet. The Humans had come here to eradicate the Gray wormhole program and it was entirely probable they were doing research and development on the surface.

There might be facilities elsewhere, but bombarding Tel Ramh should prove a serious setback in their plans. Of the ninety million clones estimated to be down there, quite a few must be wormhole physicists.

# A.G. Claymore

"**W**e've cleared the event horizion," the helmsman announced.

"Very well," Urbica replied. "Seeing as there's nothing left for us to do here, let's move on. "Engineering, Bridge. Restore standard geometry and secure the generator."

"Restore standard geometry and secure the generator, aye, ma'am." Daffyd replied.

She opened a fleetwide channel. "Well done, Commander." She reached out and rotated the projection of Tel Ramh. "Not a stick left standing down there."

"Well done indeed," Tony added. "But I think we can reduce our intervals next time we jump."

"Not to worry, Major," she assured him. "You'll see plenty of action when we reach Bish."

The status board, programmed by Lars, showed the wormhole generator had gone to secure mode.

"All vessels, lay in a course for Bish and bend space on my mark." She rolled her eyes at Paul. It was unlikely anyone on the surface was listening, but they were probably being heard by a satellite or two. It wouldn't hurt to mention Bish a few times.

"Three, two, one… Mark."

The three vessels shimmered as they slipped into pockets of distorted space.

And then they were gone.

## *Nilak*

The stars in front of the *Sucker Punch* shimmered, like a pond disturbed by a pebble. Instead of fading, the ripples grew in strength until the center suddenly snapped away from the bow of the carrier. The hole stabilized, growing to the edge of the ripples and a cloud of blue gas came boiling out.

The gas quickly dissipated into the vacuum but a constant supply was still flowing through from the other end. The constant eddies of vapor made the event horizon look like a witch's cauldron.

"Searching for better weather," Daffyd's voice advised them over the internal channel.

The light eddies suddenly became a blast of blue vapor, wreathing the *Sucker Punch* in dying tendrils. As suddenly as it increased, the flow cut off almost entirely.

"Found a belt of flow in the other direction," Daffyd advised. "Looks like our best bet. Atmospheric flow is less than sixteen hundred kilometers per hour."

A brilliant flash of lightning from the other side bathed the small fleet in harsh light.

"Why is it," Paul asked, "that military plans seem so clever when you come up with them but so incredibly risky when it comes time to put them into practice?"

"Could have something to do with our plans being so incredibly risky," Urbica replied, smiling cheerfully. "Combat is usually a risky job.

"Alright, Daffyd, that's good." She walked over to the signalman. "Hold it right there."

She put a hand on the signalman's shoulder. "Send the go-ahead, Rishon."

## A.G. Claymore

All ship-to-ship signals would be sent using the optical arrays. There would almost certainly be harvesting operations in the gas giant, and that meant antennae on its satellite world, Narsa, would be aimed in their general direction.

It was unlikely the optical signals would carry far enough in the dense atmosphere to be picked up on Narsa. That limited range was still a calculated risk, however, as the three ships would have a hard time coordinating without access to anything more than infrared laser.

"*Dauntless* confirms, ma'am." Rishon reached up to touch an icon. "*Xipe Totec* standing by for her turn."

The super-dreadnaught lined up in front of the opening, flanked by three of her assault craft. She pushed into the event horizon, eddies of blue gas tumbling along her hull as she drifted out of sight.

The two assault craft followed and the wait began. Despite the original inclination to pour all three ships through with minimal intervals, the expected wind shear at their destination had forced a new plan on them.

The *Dauntless,* having the most displacement and mass, would go first. Once through the wormhole, she would pull ahead rather than off-axis. The *Xipe Totec* and *Sucker Punch* would follow, slipstreaming behind the massive battleship.

One of the smaller craft re-appeared.

"*Dauntless* in position, ma'am," Rishon announced.

The Marine assault carrier went through next. The other assault craft came back to signal the go ahead before landing in the *Sucker Punch's* hangar bay. The horrific winds were at the upper limits of the small ship's capabilities and it was better not to use them in the atmosphere any more than was absolutely necessary.

"Take us in," Urbica ordered.

# Rebels and Patriots

"Taking us through, aye, ma'am," the helmsman confirmed. He was one of four officers kept on the bridge for the jump.

So far, only sixteen bridge officers on the three ships had been told that the small fleet possessed a mobile wormhole generator. Even that small number made secrecy all but impossible. Someone was bound to talk, but they'd been warned of the consequences. If they talked, they would become drug addicts and die on the streets of Vermillion in surprisingly short order.

They still had to deal with the problem of launching the actual rescue raid, but Paul was already working on that. With the new plan, they would have to abandon secrecy and rely on speed and aggression.

As they approached the bubbling, vaporous event horizon, a sudden blast of blue erupted, bathing the *Sucker Punch*.

"Collision alert," the sensor officer shouted.

"All hands brace for impact," Urbica announced over the ship-wide system.

The object was far too small to be the *Xipe Totec*. It struck the side of the Gray carrier's hull and broke apart.

"One of the Marine assault craft," Urbica said quietly, looking over to the sensor officer.

The man shook his head. No life signs.

They'd known there was a risk in deploying the small craft in the fast winds of the gas giant, but they needed them as go-betweens. They had to know if it was safe to feed the next ship through the hole, but now they were flying blind.

"Like I said," she told Paul, "risky." She took a deep breath. "Helm, keep us moving."

A quick glance darted her way. "Aye, ma'am. Steady as she goes."

# A.G. Claymore

They could feel the turbulence as soon as the bow crossed the horizon. It continued to grow as the ship slipped from relatively empty space into a dense, violent atmosphere.

"We have the beacon from the *Dauntless*," Rishon advised. "No sign of the *Xipe Totec* as of yet."

Paul felt the sudden grip of fear. Having those Marines gave them a much higher probability of success but, more importantly, Tony was the last of the Nathaniels.

He may not have a very high opinion of the upper class, Urbica notwithstanding, but the Nathaniels were one of the rare exceptions. He suddenly realized how much he'd been counting on Tony resurrecting the Nathaniel dynasty.

Paul wasn't family, but his relationship to the Nathaniels had come to define him and now that definition may have been blown away by a sudden, moon-sized eddy in the giant's atmosphere.

Urbica eyes looked darker. "Rishon, do we have enough bandwidth to the *Dauntless* for voice?"

"Aye, ma'am. The gas is pretty dense down here but the light's getting through. The holo would be a bit spotty, but we should be able to conference them in."

Commander Schatz ghosted into existence in front of them.

"Commander, what the hell just happened?" Urbica demanded.

"We experienced a sudden lateral wind shear," Schatz replied. "Pushed us to starboard a bit and the *Xipe Totec* went out of comms range entirely. We don't know if she managed to recover that assault craft before it hit."

"No. It came through and hit us." Urbica brought up an order of battle list, opening a header labeled 'Assault-Support-Logistics'. "You have some heavy logistics vessels aboard, I see."

"Yes, ma'am," Schatz confirmed. "But the ASL's are for supporting a ground assault."

Urbica nodded. "Get their water tanks installed and fill 'em up. The extra weight should help minimize the effect of wind shear."

"You want me to send *more* ships out in this?"

"Commander Schatz, you were the second engineer before we boarded your ship, right?"

"Yes, ma'am."

"Then tell me why the *Xipe Totec* was pushed off station instead of the *Dauntless*."

"Well…" Schatz paused for a moment. "Our density is a lot higher. Our hull is five meters thick in some places 'cause she was built to survive a direct hit from a high-yield nuke round, back before the AM rounds started circulating."

"And the *Totec*, by comparison, is a huge, light-weight sail," Julia stated. "A small ASL, filled with water, will be easier to handle."

"I'll get on it right away," Schatz promised.

Commander Schatz approached the logistics bay. A very young-looking ensign crouched next to a very old-looking petty officer. Their security team were in positions of cover to either side of the large entry-portal. He noticed her approach and she was pretty sure she could recognize the mix of relief and apprehension the young man felt at seeing someone more senior.

The petty officer turned to see what the youngster was looking at and gave her a curt nod of respect. "Ma'am."

"Gentlemen," she greeted them together, not wanting to make it painfully clear to the ensign that she knew who was really in charge of the situation. "What's going on in there?"

A.G. Claymore

She managed not to smile as she caught the reassuring nod from the petty officer. The young officer was probably terrified and she forced herself to keep a straight face.

"Ma'am, we've still got most of the 'lunch luggers' in there. They managed to hack into a life support junction and recharge their suits."

It was hardly a surprise to Schatz. The logistics arm of the Corps had its own combat engineers. "Has the bay been re-pressurized?"

A nod, followed by an awkward pause. "Sorry, ma'am. Yes, it has."

"Good, weapons on safe. Pull your team back around the corner."

"But…" the P.O. started to object.

"It's alright, P.O.," she reassured him, hoping she was right. "We need to end this right now or thousands of people are going to die. Get your team back."

She walked up to the entry portal and pounded on the hatch.

After half a minute, the speaker on the wall startled her.

"Who's knocking?" a female voice demanded.

"This is Commander Schatz; I'm serving as the acting captain until we can get back to Home-world. Who are you?"

"You think I'm nuts?"

"We can get to that later," she told her. "Right now, I need you to let me in so we can talk."

*"Now* who's nuts?"

"I'm unarmed," Schatz assured her, "and the security team is back around the next corner. I need to talk to you and I'm not doing it till we can talk face to face."

There was a long pause and she was starting to think they were just ignoring her.

She was just deciding to hammer on the hatch again when it hissed and slid open. A Marine pilot stood there with an armed ground-crewman behind her, aiming at Schatz' head. Even Navy EVA armor could give their rifles a hard time.

The pilot was medium height and slender with dark hair and eyes.

"Well, 'Captain'," she said, stressing her title just enough to indicate what she thought of a second engineer running a super-dreadnaught, "you said you wanted to talk." She held out a hand toward the interior of the logistics bay.

Schatz fought the urge to take a deep breath, not wanting to show nervousness in front of the mutineers. She marched boldly into the cavernous space to find herself surrounded by the men and women of 538 Marine Logistics Group. They were standing behind rows of pallets or on top of their large cargo craft.

"Who do you serve?" she shouted.

There was a bit of confusion at this. Clearly they hadn't expected such a blatant question. The general gist of the muttering and shouts indicated that they served the Emperor.

"Who do you serve?" she shouted again, hope beginning to stir.

There was a great deal more unison in their response this time and she decided to press on. "Some of your senior officers have been serving someone else."

She activated a holo display. A pair of heavily armored Marines were being cut down by dragoons. The Marines around her growled in disapproval, their weapons inching back up to aim at her.

She paused the playback. "Take a look beyond the Marines and see what they were protecting." She walked over to stand in the image. "The bridge crew are all Grays," she said loudly. "Same thing down in engineering: Marines fighting Humans to protect a Gray warship in orbit around Irricana."

The noise began to fade. She activated a large view of the main hangar of the *Sucker Punch*. "These are stasis pods on the same ship," she told them, "built for Humans. So far, we've found the DNA of more than sixteen thousand missing Irricanans. People abducted by operators from the 538 to make it look like your activities out here were the work of secessionists."

It looked like there were many who thought she was flat-out lying, but enough were absorbing the message for her to move the agenda forward.

"I have no trouble believing you've been lied to by your superiors," she assured them. "I've met Colonel Kinsey but most of the bridge staff are more familiar with him." She grinned. "They say the trick to knowing when he's lying is to watch his lips. If they're moving..."

A chuckle rolled through the mutineers.

"Right now," she continued, "we're in the atmosphere of Nilak, a gas giant orbited by the world where our people have been taken. We're going to sit down here and listen in on local communications until we figure out where exactly those folks are.

The *Xipe Totec* came with us, but she was blown off station and we need those cargo carriers," she jabbed a finger at a row of heavy-looking, armored ASL's, "fitted out and ready to go look for them. We've got close to forty thousand of his Majesty's subjects waiting for us to come to the rescue and we need the *Xipe Totec* if we're going to save them.

"Make no mistake, folks. The Grays think this is their time to shine. They're up there right now," she aimed a finger toward the ceiling, "experimenting on our people and they know where to find lots more when they've used up the first batch.

"Who do you serve?" She barely raised her voice above a normal speaking volume this time. The room had grown very quiet.

## Rebels and Patriots

"The Emperor!" they shouted in near-perfect unison.

"Well, there are thirty-seven thousand Humans up there on Narsa, and they're counting on their Emperor to save them." She jabbed a finger at the row of ASL's. "Get every single ASL prepped for launch ASAP and install the water bowsers. We need every extra ounce to boost your resistance to the winds out there. We need to find the *Totec* as quickly as possible."

They slung their weapons and got to work. Schatz allowed herself a relieved sigh. There was no guarantee they'd ever find the *Xipe Totec*, but at least she'd found a way to clear up the last vestiges of mutiny aboard her ship.

"Ma'am?"

She turned to see the same pilot who'd let her in. "Yes, Major…?"

"Major Indah, ma'am. I'm the senior pilot of 538 MLG, unless some missing folks happen to turn up."

"What is it Major?"

"Just wondering what exactly you have in mind for our deployment. We'll just get lost ourselves if we get out there and scatter like cats."

It was a blow to the ego. Schatz was still patting herself on the back over ending the rebellion but she didn't really have a concrete plan for using the Marine ships.

Indah must have read her captain's expression. "If I may," she offered, "we can string out like an old-fashioned EVA rescue chain. Each ship extending the comms range and, hopefully, we can reach out far enough to find the *Totec*."

"It really is the only thing we can do," Schatz agreed, "but we can only use our optical arrays. We can't risk being picked up by the locals until we're ready to start killing them."

Indah tilted her head, frowning. "That certainly reduces our range," she said. "We'd better cut the safety margin down to five percent and hope to find them fast. There's a good chance they're trying to find us. Are we all running on inertial navigation at least?"

"As long as we're hiding down here."

Indah nodded. "Then they may not be very far. We'd better make sure they don't ram us in this soup."

"Just get out there as fast as you can." Schatz started for the portal but stopped. "Major?"

Indah stopped and turned. "Ma'am?"

"The amnesty ended a while ago but, if Inspector Grimm doesn't extend it for you, *I'll* offer one as acting captain. Let your people know."

Indah came to attention, the proper form of salute for personnel not wearing a head-dress. As this was a flight deck, nobody would be wearing their cover. "Thank-you, ma'am!" She understood the potential trouble such a stance posed for Schatz.

There were very few instances where a captain offered clemency to mutineers and managed to keep head attached to body after reaching CentCom. Mutiny was one of the most dangerous words in the military. Any captain who failed to ruthlessly execute a mutinous crew was seen as encouraging others to rise up against authority.

Schatz stepped back out into the passageway. "It's Schatz," she called out. "Mutiny's over, you can stand down your team and get some rest."

The ensign and the petty officer came around the corner, looking rather bemused. "Shouldn't we collect the prisoners, ma'am?" the ensign asked.

"There are none," she told him. "We need them flying those ASL's, not warming cots in the brig."

The petty officer, an old hand, nodded his approval. "Ma'am," he said quietly, "if you'll pardon the liberty, I'm damned glad to see we've got a captain willing to do what needs doing."

She knew she shouldn't be allowing an implicit criticism of the previous captain, even if the man had been in Kinsey's pocket, but the feedback was an enormous boost to her morale. This old-timer had been through a hell of a lot of senior officers. He knew what he was talking about.

And he deserved respect.

"Thanks, P.O." She dropped a hand on his shoulder. "Get your boys some rest. Never know when I'm going to need you again."

She headed back toward the monorail.

"There's the ASL's," the sensor officer announced. "Let's hope they find the *Totec*."

"For their sake, they'd better," Urbica replied. Her tone wasn't as dark as the apparent gist of her statement, but curious faces turned her way.

"If the *Xipe Totec* was blown off station," she explained, "it can happen to us as well. This ship is everybody's ticket home so we need to keep track of everyone."

She strolled over to the sensor section. "Anything coming in, Lars?"

A nod. "Quite a lot, actually. We've got a gas mining platform within a few hundred kilometers of our current position and we're piggy-backing off their connection with Narsa.

"They've got a high-bandwidth link and I think I can sneak a few queries through the pipe without anyone being the wiser."

"Are you sure?"

A.G. Claymore

A shrug. "Nothing's ever sure, Colonel..."

She sighed dramatically. "Alright, 'Trader Lars', would you put money on it?"

He grinned. "Ma'am, I'd liquidate assets to put money on it."

"If you'd risk money on it, go ahead and run a query," she ordered. "I don't want us sitting down here any longer than we need to. This plan is a disaster waiting to happen."

"Welcome to the military," Lars muttered good-naturedly as he set up his query. "Hurry up and explode."

She opened a channel to engineering. "Daffyd," she began with a glance at Paul, "what's the status on your prototype?" She was putting out the first hints for the bridge crew. From there, the rumor mill should take care of the rest.

"My protot... oh... yes, ma'am. The prototype. It took a bit of damage to the... field containment rings on the last hop but we're all good down here... How's everything with you?"

She rolled her eyes at Paul. "We're fine up here, Daffyd. Just keep your prototype working long enough to get us home."

"Aye, ma'am."

"A spy he most certainly is not," Paul whispered. "That was like watching a Gray in dark sunglasses try to sneak into a Humans-only lounge." He was pleased with the results of the performance, though. He'd caught a few bridge staff exchanging glances during the conversation with engineering.

The combination of dire threats and a juicy story practically guaranteed someone would spark the rumor. Daffyd, the clever bastard who'd managed to turn the *Rope a Dope* into a lethal, undercover raider-killer, had cooked up some kind of wormhole generator.

But mum's the word...

## Rebels and Patriots

It was always easier to force a disruptive innovation on the government if you'd already started the lies for them.

"You should get some sleep, Colonel," a major urged. "By my count, you've been up for thirty hours. Won't do to have you falling asleep during the rescue operation."

Urbica stifled a yawn. "Can't argue that, Major. You have the conn." She headed for the door but stopped halfway and turned.

"Inspector, can you head down to engineering and make sure Daffyd's prototype is secure?" she asked.

"Certainly, Colonel." Paul followed her out.

He turned at the main intersection to head aft, but she grabbed his arm and dragged him back toward her own door.

"And you thought *Daffyd* was dense," she teased, closing the door behind them. "Paul, I have nearly forty thousand Humans waiting for us to save them, close to the same number of Marines lost in this *goushi* weather and I'm supposed to just lay my head on a pillow and catch a few hours of sleep?"

"Ahhh," Paul mused as she activated his suit release, "so you're planning to use me as some sort of sleep aid? Just a tool to help release some endorphins and get you to sleep faster?"

"Well..." she hesitated.

"Hey, I'm fine with that," he grinned. "Just trying to get into the role is all."

A.G. Claymore

# *Lost and Found*

**P**aul woke first. His arm was asleep after several hours of Julia sleeping on it and he was trying to figure out a way to extract it without waking her. He tried shifting it, hoping to restore some circulation but she stirred and mumbled something unintelligible.

His attempt managed to restore just enough circulation to send pins and needles of agony through the trapped limb. He flexed his hand, gritting his teeth against the increased pain, but the movement was helping to force blood through his veins.

It also woke Julia. "Mpff…" She lifted her head from his chest and cuffed the back of her hand across her mouth. *"Zaogao,"* she exclaimed. "Sorry I drooled on you."

"I have that effect on women," he replied airily.

She giggled. "You get a lot of fan-girl drool, do you?"

"Practically have to carry a towel around with me." He grinned at her. "You slept well."

"Oh God!" She reddened slightly. "Were you awake the whole time listening to me snore?"

"Only for the first hour," he assured her. "Y'know, they say beautiful women always snore. Nature has to balance itself, after all…"

She made a face and sat up to look at the clock by the couches. "I've been out for nearly four hours."

"That's right," Paul asserted. "And, evidently, if I hadn't been here, you'd still be trying to fall asleep." He stretched. "Never before, in the service of the Imperium, have so few been so happy to give so much…"

He gave up as she threw a suit at him.

"Get dressed, Hero." She was already halfway into her own suit. "Sneak down to engineering and put in an appearance."

## Rebels and Patriots

"I'll spread the fire and brimstone speech," he said. "That should get the rumors flying."

Daffyd wasn't there when he got to engineering. He probably had the sense to sleep while he had the chance. Paul settled for a quick chat with the second engineer, warning him that Daffyd was involved in some very highly classified work and that everyone was to keep their pie-holes shut.

He arrived on the bridge to find Julia looking at a screen with Lars.

"Inspector," she greeted him politely, "Lars may have found something."

He'd noticed a slightly raised eyebrow on Lars' face as she called him 'Inspector'. Were there rumors floating around the ship beyond the one that he'd started to give Daffyd credit for the wormhole generator?

"I've found a document on their data hive," Lars explained. "It's basically an investing prospectus. This company is pointing to their recent contract with the Gray Quorum as a major source of future revenue. They're supplying a research facility on Narsa with an initial run of eighty thousand pairs of coveralls and footwear."

"And what makes this stand out?" Paul asked.

"They attribute the contract to their adjustable equipment. They also take aim at their competitors, claiming they would need to bring in new production equipment to make 'such large' items."

"You clever bastard!" Paul grinned at him. "Any idea where they ship their large clothing to?"

"Not yet," he admitted. "We'd need to get into their systems but I don't know if the hive on this ship will trip an alarm if I actively link it in. What I need is one of the quantum cores on the *Xipe Totec*. That garbage they have on the *Dauntless* is too old."

A.G. Claymore

"Well, we're going to have to wait," she told him. "When we find them, I'll put you on a shuttle and…"

"I can give you access to a quantum core," Paul offered. "My implant is at least as new as the equipment on an LHV carrier and we can avoid the dangers of flying between ships in this weather."

He swiped his hand in front of his head to open a blank holo-interface and linked into it. "Here," he said, turning the screen to Lars.

"Hell," Lars cursed softly as he set up the interface for the attempt. "This is worlds better than military gear. We could probably hook you up to the bridge on an LHV and you'd be able to run it yourself."

"Yeah, well, just stay out of the data files. I've got some classified stuff in there," Paul warned. This time he noticed raised eyebrows from both Lars and Urbica.

"You been making hive-porn, Inspector?" She teased.

Lars tried, unsuccessfully, to stifle a laugh as he turned his attention back to the screen.

"Sorry, Colonel." He shrugged. "I'd share if I had any, but it's just case files in there; nothing racy." He raised his eyebrows, tilting his head in thought. "Well, the case file that broke this whole mess open is actually a bit pornographic but… um…" He scratched at the back of his head.

"How're we doing there, lars?" He asked brusquely.

"I should be able to crack any security blocks by brute force with this core," Lars muttered as he finished his setup and held a finger over an icon. "Ready, Inspector?"

Paul nodded and fell down the rabbit hole.

He could see millions of data nodes. His mind automatically directed the CPU to arrange it in physical format so he could understand it better.

Rebels and Patriots

"They've got more than eight hundred shipping destinations on this world alone," Lars complained. "None of them are jumping out at me. Maybe if we search for large or over-sized goods…"

"Maybe we can link them up with cameras," Paul suggested. He waved at the holo projection of data nodes, spread around a three-dimensional representation of Narsa.

He selected the camera layer and hid the rest. "Shoot me your shipment destinations, Lars."

He ghosted any cameras that didn't have a company shipment within a hundred-meter radius. It was still a couple hundred. "Let's eliminate any cameras with no security on them."

That took them down to twenty-three cameras. Paul added them to a new layer and reviewed each camera, adding nearby cameras to the layer.

They were looking at nearly ninety cameras, spread around the world in tight clusters. "We could automate the search if we had facial images showing some of our missing citizens," Paul muttered. "Colonel Urbica, can you see if…"

Lars thrust a small polymer sheet into his hands.

Paul looked down at a young woman. The facial structure was very similar. "Your sister?" he asked the young trader.

A nod. "Bjorghildr. She's only fifteen." His voice trembled. "I signed up after she went missing a year and a half ago."

Paul touched the points on the lower right hand side and uploaded three images of the young woman. His ICI recognition algorithm identified the key facial elements and he set it to search the incoming feeds.

Once he was ready, he directed his CPU to crack the security codes on every camera in the list. In a matter of seconds, the quantum core had run through every possible combination of glyphs and opened the feed from each unit.

## A.G. Claymore

"How long will it take?" Lars asked.

"Hard to say," Paul told him. "We might get a hit right away or it might be days. I'm also searching for generic Human features but we still get false matches from a template, even with Grays. Frankly, I think it'll happen quickly, if they have cameras on our people."

"Are you just going to stand there till we find something?" Urbica asked him.

"No, I can carry on with this running in the background," he replied. "I only use the CPU for police work. If you let yourself get dependent on it to do your thinking, you can end up a complete basket case."

"Only police work, huh?" She looked mildly relieved. "I suppose…" She stopped in mid sentence, one hand reaching for her left ear.

"They've found her!" The sensor officer shouted. "They found the *Xipe Totec*!"

A cheer rang out on the bridge. People were smiling and slapping each other on the back. Urbica had to shout to be heard over the din. "Quiet!" She opened a channel, routing it through the *Dauntless* and her string of ASL's.

A very hazy Tony Nathaniel shimmered into view. "Colonel, it's sure nice to see you again," he declared. "We were starting to think we'd have to assault Narsa the old-fashioned way."

"And give the bastards a fair fight?" She shook her head. "You know the rule, Major."

"Fair fights fill graveyards," Tony replied with what looked like a grin. His image was growing stronger. "Have you picked up any leads while we were off touring?"

"We're closing in on a location. We might be sending you in very soon."

215

# Rebels and Patriots

"I like the sound of that, ma'am. We should be back on station in twenty minutes."

She closed the channel. "Lars, why don't you drop down to engineering? See if Daffyd needs any..."

"Whoa!" Paul exclaimed suddenly. "Looks like somebody just turned a light on. Folks, I think we have a hit!"

He changed the display from a rotating image of Narsa to a large room filled with racks of pods, three high. "I've discarded more than three hundred false positives from surprisingly Human-looking Grays since we started, but I think this is the real deal."

He moved toward the image, pointing at a pod. "Same pods we found here in the hangar bay, and those faces are really low resolution, but I think they're Human."

Lars moved forward on Paul's right, pointing at one pod with a reticule around it. "What's the target for?"

A deep breath. "The algorithm assesses a thirty-one percent chance of that being Bjorghildr."

Lars stepped right up to the pod, but the three-dimensional projection was hazy. With the camera at the far end of the chamber, it lost too much resolution to be certain of the faces. He shook his head in frustration.

"The location is about to pass into night," Paul advised. "By the time Major Nathaniel gets here with the 488, it will be a perfect time to hit them."

Lars looked up at Paul, eyes wide with excitement. "That *was* her!" he declared excitedly. "It can't just be a coincidence."

"What can't just be a coincidence, Lars?" Urbica asked him.

"My sister was named after an ancient goddess of the evening mist," he explained. "The name comes from the words for 'salvation' and 'battle'." He held out his hands to the sides. "Look,

## A.G. Claymore

I've never been a mystic or anything, but this is too much to be coincidence. It's fate."

Paul looked at Urbica. "We *are* about to hit them at dusk…"

"And we're going to be bringing a hell of a lot of mist," Urbica added. She shivered.

## *Narsa*

**N**'mid exited the transit module and ascended to the pedway level. He was several grades too junior to rate a personal transport, even though his work may well restore the future of his race. His chin raised a fraction as he walked.

He knew he was vital to the program. His methodologies were far more robust than those of his superiors. The subjects rarely lasted more than a few hours, but he'd unlocked more data about telomere degeneration in the last two years than the rest of the team had in a full body-span.

One day, one of his superiors would make a grievous error and there would be advancement available. Getting ahead in the Genetics Corps took a careful blend of caution and daring.

N'mid possessed just such a blend. His chin raised another fraction, but then he stopped walking and brought his blatant swaggering under control. It wouldn't do to walk into the institute like he owned the place.

Not for the next few centuries at least.

A shimmer in the night sky caught his attention and he looked up to find what looked like ripples in water. He blinked in fascination. The ripples hovered in the air, only a few cubits away. Even *his* weak arms could have thrown a small object with enough force to hit the anomaly.

As he watched, the center of the ripples was suddenly snatched away and a glimmering surface appeared in its place, growing to fit the outer edges.

His fascination suddenly turned to horror as an evil-smelling rush of gas came tumbling out of the hovering mirror, causing an intense, freezing pain on his skin. He tried to give voice to his fear but his vocal cords froze and shattered as the muscles of his neck flexed.

Before he could suffocate in the unbreathable gasses of Nilak, his body froze solid and he remained there, stuck to the pedway. His corpse bore witness to the arrival of the first heavy attack gunships of the Imperial Marines.

The second gunship swooped low to dodge an automated air defense beam and smashed his frozen remains to pieces. Its wingman took out the Gray weapon platform and they moved on.

"We've knocked out the air defense systems in our target sector," Tony advised. "I'm taking the ground assault in now."

"Good hunting, Major," Urbica replied. "And come back in one piece."

The *Xipe Totec* was sitting directly in front of the event horizon. Any ships being launched or recovered would be spared the vagaries of flying through a sixteen-hundred-kilometer-per-hour slipstream.

Tony gave the pilot a thump on the shoulder. "Get us on the ground, Harrison." He headed back to lock in.

The heavily armored dropship lifted off the deck and moved forward. The rest of the transports would follow at regular intervals.

They hurtled out of the portal into a dark haze and Harrison pulled a hard turn to port, dropping between a row of buildings and accelerating to a terrifying speed. Tony had a great deal of respect for pilots like Harrison.

The fast assault pilots got most of the glory, but guys like Harrison often faced just as much danger but with less weapons and maneuverability. That was why he pushed his ship to the edge of its limits.

The red lighting in the troop compartment suddenly went to half illumination. Time for the equipment check. They all confirmed their ammunition load-outs and double-checked their data feeds.

The lighting dropped to one quarter illumination and they held their weapons to the sides, giving room for the ceiling-mounted restraints to retract on touchdown.

Tony felt the familiar old lurch in his gut as the transport reversed its forward thrust to begin the standard controlled crash of a combat landing. They seemed to drop like a rock and then slowed rapidly at the last second, rifle barrels hitting the deck all around him as the grav plating temporarily lost its fight against the small vessel's deceleration profile.

The landing points made contact with a thump and the restraints retracted. Without a word, the two platoons of armored Marines trotted down the back ramp and set up an all-around defense as the armored craft lifted off to circle overhead. The dropships would remain on station, providing aerial surveillance and limited fire support from their conventional weapons.

And hopefully they would be picking up passengers.

More landers were hitting the street to his rear, and Tony was glad to see that the lieutenant commanding the first platoon had decided to lead his men toward the research facility. Tony almost always approved of decisions that kept up the momentum.

The hollow echo of small arms fire began to reach them from farther back and it appeared the fifth platoon was meeting light resistance. First platoon pushed on, reaching a loading door where they placed a set of charges and pulled back a few feet.

They were fighting in full armor and they were running fully closed up. The blast effect on them would be negligible.

## A.G. Claymore

The door blew into the loading bay and the Marines rushed the opening. Dull thuds indicated the second assault group was entering the facility from the other side.

A Gray rushed into the room to investigate the explosion and died in a hail of 5mm rounds. The lieutenant started moving across the bay but halted, bringing his weapon up to fire.

He lowered his assault rifle, holding up a hand to warn his platoon to hold fire as well. The shadow in the hallway door was far too tall to be a Gray. "Imperial Marines," he shouted.

"What the hell is going on?" a Human shouted back. "Where are we?"

Tony grinned. The plan was working, and thank God; thirty-seven thousand stasis pods would have been a hell of a lot of lifting. They'd never pull this off if the prisoners were unable to walk on their own.

Paul had managed to hack the systems and get them moving in advance.

"This way," Tony shouted back. "We'll explain when we get you to safety."

He ran back out into the street and waved down a lieutenant. "Jackson, we've got evacuees coming out. I need you and your platoon to marshal them. Get 'em on the ships and keep 'em moving. If you need more men, grab whoever you need."

Jackson got his men to work, clearing debris and personnel from a stretch of the street. He soon had infrared beacons planted for five landing zones and his men were lining up the flow of escaped prisoners in groups of two hundred and forty.

Tony made a note about Jackson. The man had a good head for details. A dropship that could carry eighty armored Marines could, in a pinch, carry two hundred unarmored civilians with some mild discomfort.

# Rebels and Patriots

In a combat evacuation, two hundred forty civvies per ship was much better. Even with that kind of crowding, they were looking at more than a hundred and forty flights to evacuate the Humans. He was glad the ASL's were already loitering overhead.

A dropship hammered onto the carbon matrix of the street, the shock of the combat landing punching Tony in the gut. He knew he shouldn't love his work so much, but it was thrilling to unleash so much raw power on his Emperor's enemies.

A pair of ASL's landed next to the dropship and Jackson was already ushering the first group forward while his men were pushing four groups, combining them into two bigger ones. The ASL's should be able to take more than four and a half hundred each.

The dropship lifted off as another ASL and a dropship descended toward the last two beacons. Tony opened a channel. "Bridge, patch me through to the forward air controller."

A new layer of noise hissed in his helmet. "Connors, this is Major Nathaniel; I need you to prioritize the ASL's for evacuee pickup. I don't want us hanging around here any longer than we have to."

"Understood, sir." Connors replied. "We've got three pick-up zones running and the ASL's are at full utilization. We're just using the dropships to fill the cracks in the hangar cycle."

"Right," Tony hoped the tone of contrition made it through the comms system, "Good man, what's your time-line estimate?"

"Another forty minutes for the civvies," he advised, "and twenty more to get our grunts out."

Tony knew it would feel like an eternity but, in terms of planetary incursions, this was a lightning raid. If he didn't end up executed for stealing an expeditionary force, this operation would end up being taught to cadets at the academy.

## A.G. Claymore

Using every ship in the hangar, they were bringing in five loads of civilians every three minutes. That worked out to six hundred evacuees per minute and they were doing it deep inside Gray territory.

He looked up at the sound of a Gray auto-cannon. One of the loitering ASL's above them had taken a hail of rounds in its starboard flank and began to spiral down into the city. Marines holding the next intersection scrambled out of the way as the armored craft thundered into the carbon surface.

The Marines raced back in, climbing over the wreckage to search for survivors.

Tony bit back the urge to contact the FAC again. Connors would already be aware that a Gray Hichef had slipped past the cordon of Marine gunships.

A formation streaked overhead and he looked up to see the lightly armored fast-attack ships favored by Urbica's dragoons. They'd managed to slip through the gap between the *Xipe Totec* and the wormhole, and now they were lining up on the offending Hichef.

The throaty buzz of their guns caused everyone to look up. The Hichef yawed off course and then its shields failed. The Gray craft disintegrated and tumbled into the side of a tall building, raining debris onto the street below.

Some of the more recently-abducted civilians had recognized the markings and word quickly spread that the 1st Gliesan Dragoons had come as part of the rescue. The evacuees were screaming and cheering as their own fighters streaked off to plug the hole in the defenses.

"Keep them moving," Tony growled across the open channel. "They can celebrate once we're out of here."

The counter at the upper right side of his heads-up display showed the rapidly rising count of evacuees stepping out of rescue

# Rebels and Patriots

ships and into the scanning envelope of the *Xipe Totec*. It would be a lifetime before he could order the withdrawal.

A deep boom sounded from several hundred meters away, the force racing through the carbon roadway and rattling his bones before the secondary wave reached him through the air, causing his teeth to chatter.

Gray heavy-tanks, firing enhanced conventional rounds. He'd come up against the export version of Gray armor at the Susa rebellion and his experienced mind was able to place the vehicles from the delay between the two shocks.

He looked to the corner where the ASL had gone down. A squad of Marines came pelting around the corner, just ahead of a hail of debris from the road. Shards of carbon flew past behind them, torn up by the anti-personnel guns of the enemy tanks.

The mind-numbing hum of the heavy vehicles' suspensor fields grew louder as they approached. Tony looked back to see the civilians frozen in terror. Before he could say anything, Jackson grabbed an evacuee and shoved her toward a waiting dropship. "Keep them moving," he snarled over the open net, not caring if he was stepping on the toes of other platoon commanders.

No knowing if it would last beyond his return to CentCom, Tony accessed the personnel system and awarded the man a brevet rank of captain. It might never be confirmed but it should at least let his good sense carry the day if a conflict with another platoon commander should arise.

The automated notification fell into the queue and a computer-generated voice advised all ground units of the change, timed with an update to the rank display on Jackson's armor.

The hum from the tanks indicated they were close to the corner. They'd be in a position to fire on the landing zone in seconds.

A.G. Claymore

A series of loud chirps heralded the ignition of the hydrogen-based propellant of several Ice-Picks. The Ice-Picks were a close-quarters anti-armor and bunker-buster weapon that used a thermodynamic precursor warhead to bring the temperature of the targeted area close to absolute zero.

The relatively small main warhead could then shatter the frozen armor and send a stream of explosive gasses inside. The weapons were small enough for the grenadier of each fire-team to launch from a tube beneath the barrel of his rifle.

The hum began to lose its volume. At least one tank had fallen silent and the chittering noise told Tony that another had taken damage. A second volley of chirps put an end to the noise altogether and the Marines who'd played decoy got up and ran back around the corner to link up with their hidden comrades.

A smattering of rifle fire announced the death of the tank crews.

An auto-text message appeared from Connors. The FAC advised that they were facing increasingly heavy resistance as Gray ships were vectoring in from around the planet as well as from orbit. Their position was becoming untenable.

Another formation of dragoons screamed past overhead, unable to hear the cheers below.

Tony saw that the counter had reached thirty-three thousand and he turned to look back at the sprawling research facility. Very few Humans were coming out now. He took a look at the locater trace. The sweep teams had been through the complex, killing Grays and releasing bound Humans and they were bringing the last of them out.

Some evacuees were being carried but most were able to walk. The last of the stragglers were almost at the landing zones.

Somehow, though it had seemed like an eternity, the whole operation now seemed as though it had passed in the blink of an eye,

## Rebels and Patriots

and Tony was mentally scrambling to ensure his forces withdrew in good order. He activated the 'prepare to withdraw' icon, causing it to flash in the lower left corner of every Marine's heads-up display.

He looked at the overall image in his HUD. The last lifts were almost ready to return to the *Xipe Totec*. He opened a channel. "All ground units, disengage. Break contact and fall back to the landing zones."

The last of the civilian lifts ascended and they were replaced almost immediately by dropships. A series of detonations announced the start of the withdrawal.

The withdrawing units were blasting large chunks of the surrounding towers into the street to slow the enemy pursuit. The first of the withdrawing troops began streaming past him. He knew a few of the wounded would be running their armor on 'platoon flow', an algorithm that let the armor stay with the unit and board a drop ship even if it's wearer was unconscious or dead.

A few of the Marines raced past in no armor at all. They were the ones who'd pulled a wounded comrade out of his disabled suit and stuffed him into their own, setting it to platoon flow before closing it up.

It was a risky thing to do. Even a near miss from enhanced conventionals would generate enough force to kill if you had no armor on. Still, few Marines would hesitate to offer their suit to a wounded man.

He turned and ran with the last few men, boarding one of the last two dropships. His locater feed confirmed all living markers were off the surface. "All aerial units, ground withdrawal is complete. Disengage and withdraw to the *Xipe Totec*. All dragoon units, withdraw directly to the *Totec* as well. We'll find room for you somewhere."

The clatter of rifle barrels on the deck accompanied the rapid ascent of their ship and they swung around with sickening speed. The dropship accelerated, loose gear sliding aft to strike the rear ramp.

The ride was quick. The ramp opened and Tony retracted his helmet, glad to smell the hydraulics, the ozone and the stink of his fellow Marines. It was the smell of home. He stopped on the ramp, stunned by the cheering civilians crammed into every available spot.

"C'mon," a ground-crewman roared at him. "We've got to get this pig stowed to make room for the rest."

Tony jumped down and scrambled out of the way as the ugly ship lowered out of sight. A new elevator platform slid into place above it, closing the large opening in the deck.

The gunships started arriving, their crews climbing out to thunderous applause from the rescued Humans. They were absorbed by the crowds as their ships disappeared beneath the deck.

Last to come aboard were the dragoons. The automated storage system on the *Xipe Totec* wasn't compatible with their assault craft and so they'd be tied down on the main hangar deck while the ground crews serviced them.

Though the civilians had been through a harrowing experience, they still managed to muster enough energy to celebrate their hometown heroes. The dragoon crewmen were treated to a thunderous welcome. The Irricanans flowed onto the hangar deck, hugging, shaking hands and kissing the flight crews.

"**X***ipe Totec* confirms recovery of the strike team," the communications officer announced.

"Very well," Urbica replied. "Engineering, adjust geometry for phase two."

"Aye, ma'am," Daffyd responded.

"Telemetry confirms a high orbital exit point," the sensor officer advised.

"*Xipe Totec*," Urbica began, "you are clear to initiate phase two."

The revelry on the hangar deck was interrupted by the buzz of auto-cannon fire reverberating through the carbon and steel fabric of the *Xipe Totec*. Now that the Narsa end of the wormhole had been moved out into space, the ship could fire its deadly AM rounds without the blast coming back through the open gate.

It had nearly been missed during the planning session. No Human force had ever incorporated a portable wormhole generator into an attack plan before. Fortunately, Daffyd had been there.

He'd pointed out that, though the initial wormhole geometry would let them deliver the AM rounds with no warning to the defenders, the *Xipe Totec* would be destroyed by the resulting blast. The wormhole effectively meant the Marine vessel was sitting only meters away from her target, even though she was still in the atmosphere of the gas giant.

By moving the Narsa end of the wormhole out into space, they prevented the blast of their ordnance form funneling back through the opening and killing them.

The deep hum of the main batteries vibrated the deck plates and the heavy rounds streaked through the wormhole, following the lighter munitions.

The pattern continued as screens of lighter rounds preceded the heavy munitions, distracting the defensive fire and increasing the chance of complete destruction at each target. Even one of the smaller-caliber AM rounds would be enough to cripple a city. One of the larger ones would remove all traces.

**A** young woman stood with the crowd in the central passageway, touching the shoulder of each Marine and dragoon as they passed. Tears ran down her face. She'd been in a state of altered consciousness for the last year and a half. Somehow, boredom wasn't a possibility in the pods but she still knew she'd been locked away for a very long time.

Some of her fellow prisoners, among the more recent abductees, had recognized the dragoons as being mostly from Irricana and entirely from the Gliesan systems. It seemed almost inconceivable that the corrupt Gliesan Sector Defense Forces could have fielded such a unit, but she certainly wasn't complaining.

Some of her family might be standing here with her. They might even have died on that world and the thought had been a torment in her semi-conscious state. She looked to her left as a new group of dragoon pilots approached and her heart leapt with joy.

Stepping out from the crowd to block the path, she smiled up at a surprised pilot. "Lars!" She threw her arms around his neck.

The crowd cheered even louder as Bjorghildr found her brother.

### Rebels and Patriots

*"**X**ipe Totec* reports rounds complete," the communications officer announced. "Target destruction estimated at ninety-seven percent, planet-wide."

"Very well, signal both ships to stand by for the jump to Irricana." Urbica activated the channel to engineering. "Engineering, bridge. Restore geometry and configure for a transit to Irricana."

"Aye, ma'am," the 'father of mobile wormhole generators' replied.

# Irricana

"**T**hat's the last of them, Colonel," Lars said, waving at the heavily guarded docking portal.

Warships like the *Xipe Totec* almost never physically docked with a station, especially out on the Rim, but the prospect of ferrying thousands of rescued civilians had tipped the scales. Security would hardly be compromised any further by docking.

If anything, it was improved by getting them out faster, but it hadn't prevented the media from sneaking aboard.

Everything Urbica said was being listened to in real-time, down on Irricana, so she had to be careful. But it also meant she could use that publicity as a weapon.

"Good," she told Lars. "The sooner we can get back to Homeworld, the better. The threat has been neutralized out here for the time-being."

A small delegation arrived at the portal and they were directed toward Urbica. One man stopped, faced aft and came to attention. He was paying respect to the Emperor's person sigil.

Morgan. Old disciplines die hard.

Balthazar shook Urbica's hand. "Colonel," the governor boomed, "there's hardly a single family down on Irricana who doesn't owe you and your forces their heartfelt thanks."

The man was almost certainly one of the conspirators, but it was better to leave him in place for now. Far better an enemy whose sins you know.

"Well, Governor, your own police provided us with the key to cracking the mystery." Urbica nodded at Paul.

"That's right," Paul agreed as Morgan joined them. "Your chief here was the one who made the link between the missing citizens and the secessionist attacks."

# Rebels and Patriots

"He did?" Balthazar turned on Morgan in surprise. "How long did…"

"Operational security, Governor," Paul cut in smoothly. "Anyone in possession of that knowledge would have been in grave danger."

"Standard procedure," Morgan added, "when you do a joint operation with the *Eye*."

"Looks like someone's going to drink for free for the rest of his life!" The governor gave Morgan a slap on the back.

They took a quick shuttle ride and Urbica led the party on a quick tour of the captured ship. She wanted to make sure CentCom couldn't just kill them all and dispose of the ship. They had a tendency to favor the status quo and a potential game-changer like the *Sucker Punch* could easily end up scrapped. Knowing the Gray shipyard had been destroyed might give the military a false sense of security. It didn't take much to push strategic imperatives to the back burner.

Every senior officer at CentCom owed their position to a grand senator. Disruptive innovations like a portable wormhole generator might mean a huge shift in defense contracts. Entire shipyards might close, leaving some senators in political jeopardy.

Showing off the ship to the media, even without mentioning her jump capabilities, would help nudge the idiots at CentCom in the right direction. Morgan held back.

"You're so full of it," he told Paul, "you're sneezing brown." His grin took the sting from his insult.

"We never would have known to look for those missing citizens if not for our conversation. Of course, Balthazar's probably not very fond of you for helping to scuttle the scheme."

Morgan chuckled. "You're still an ass," he insisted, "but so am I, so it's not like I'm complaining."

A.G. Claymore

# *Santa Clara*

"**T**here it is," Eddie announced. "Lining us up for a straight transit.

He pulled the Salamander up and climbed away from the night surface of Irricana. The small craft rolled and dove straight down into the event horizon of a wormhole that gushed with icy water.

They emerged into an eerie, milky blue ocean teeming with life.

"*Wèi!*" Eddie exclaimed indignantly, throwing the armored sub into a hard turn to avoid a hanging block of ice the size of a heavy cruiser. "Who the hell put that there?" He made a fine adjustment to the sonar feeds.

"Let's go a little deeper, shall we?" The squadron leader angled them down toward the floor of the enclosed ocean.

Santa Clara was entirely encased in a crust of ice that averaged thirty kilometers in thickness. Beneath that layer, a ninety-kilometer-deep layer of ocean surrounded the rocky moon itself. It was kept in a liquid state by the energy resulting from tidal flexing. As the moon rotated, the rocky interior was constantly being deformed by the gravity of the super-planet it orbited.

They descended into the darkness without picking up any local ships. Though there were thousands of harvesting subs collecting silicon nodules from the ocean floor, they rarely ascended unless they were off-loading at the world's only factory sub.

The fishing vessels that kept the gigantic factory sub fed numbered in the hundreds, but they always remained within a hundred-kilometer radius. Encountering them in billions of cubic meters of water was extremely unlikely.

"Picking up an ELF beacon," Eddie slowed the small craft. "Looks like it has a data stream."

## Rebels and Patriots

The Extremely Low Frequency beacon system was a one-way transmitter. Requiring antennae as long as fifty kilometers, it was impossible to equip ships with their own transmitters, and the data rate was incredibly low.

Santa Clara used the system to let harvesters know when the factory ship would be in their area.

"Getting coordinates," Eddie said. "Got to be an easy job, running the ELF system. Takes an hour just to say where they are. Of course, they won't be there anymore by the time the signal completes."

"Maybe," Paul hedged. "The factory ship is almost the size of Vermillion. I'd imagine a ship the size of a city doesn't push through the water very fast."

Eddie shook his head in amazement. "Seems like an expensive way to set up a city. Why not just build on the outer surface of the ice?"

"They're practically immune to orbital bombardment down here," Urbica offered. "No chance of getting through that ice and hitting them at depth, even assuming you knew where to shoot."

"And it puts them closer to food and silicon," Paul added.

The Salamander banked gently.

"We've got the neighborhood," Eddie announced. "It's an easy, thirty-two-hour run."

A.G. Claymore

## *Hitting Rock Bottom*

"**P**icking up pings from the harvester," Eddie announced. "I'll go up and take the conn for the drop-off. We want to get close enough to get you inserted before they reel in their vacuum heads."

"Eddie…" Paul looked up from his meal, a frown of concern on his face. "… If we can hear their pings, doesn't that mean they can 'see' us?"

"Doubtful," the squadron leader told him. "We've got anechoic tiling to cut down on the signature. If they did get anything back, they'd think we were a whale or a shoal of fish."

"How long since you piloted a Salamander?" Paul raised an eyebrow.

Eddie didn't take it personally. "Six years since my demobilization date, but you know the old saying: nobody's ever heard of a pilot forgetting how to operate a Sally."

Urbica grinned. "Cause if they *do* forget…"

Eddie brought his hands together and made a crushing motion. "Nobody ever hears about it."

"Yeah, I remember that one from amphib training," Paul told him. "It's about as funny the second time around."

"It's all in the delivery." Eddie took a slight bow. "And speaking of delivery, we'll be dropping you in the nodule field, just outside of their active terrain-mapping sonar."

"The harvester has enough time to hit the end of that field before ascending to meet the factory ship," one of the dragoons offered. "Why not just drop us at the far end and avoid the risk of detection?"

Paul looked down, pinching the bridge of his nose. "Karl! Why did you have to ask him that? Haven't you heard enough?"

Eddie laughed. "Even with the two emergency fuel cells per team-member, your shields are gonna go through power a hell of a

235

*Rebels and Patriots*

lot faster than you would in space. Your suit's integrity field is going to be holding back twelve thousand atmospheres while you wait for that vacuum-head to come close. If you miss it at the *end* of the field, I'm not gonna have enough time to come get you."

"Are you happy now, Karl?" Paul sighed.

"Are you claustrophobic, Inspector Grimm?" Urbica grinned, her eyes flashing with mischief.

"No," Paul replied irritably. "I'm *crush*aphobic."

"I wouldn't worry about the crushing," Eddie said helpfully. "At this depth, your air supply would incinerate the instant the field gave out."

"Why are you still here?" Paul asked loudly. "Shouldn't you be piloting this abomination?"

Eddie grinned, sketched a salute and turned for the control room. "Dropping you in twenty, so get ready, kids."

Paul followed the team down to the escape trunk and put his suit back on, feeling like a condemned man. By the time they finished double-checking each other's external fuel cells, the green light by the hatch began blinking.

They closed the hatch and activated their helmets.

Water began flowing in around their feet, forcing the air out through a valve in the ceiling. The pressure steadily climbed, but Paul had turned off the display in his suit's heads-up display. He only knew he was already at a killing pressure by the time the water reached his ankles.

Somehow, it was less oppressive as the cold liquid passed above his head. He almost felt calm, but it was only a calm in comparison to his earlier agitation. The outer door finally opened and they let themselves drop to the ocean floor where they were surrounded by small fist sized nodules of mixed metal.

## A.G. Claymore

As the Salamander moved off, they activated buoyancy control and ascended to a height of ten meters and Paul's fears had some leisure time again. With nothing to do but wait, his mind kept mulling over the unforgiving weight of water and ice that sat above him.

He wondered how much the maintenance crews on the harvesters were paid. It had to be a lot. Paul would have needed a hell of a lot of money to do this for a living.

He had no idea why this should be any more frightening than a shield failure in space, but fear didn't always make sense. He tried to distract himself by thinking about Julia Urbica.

He'd been loyal to the Nathaniel family for a long time, but he'd never really had anything more personal. He wondered if that was changing. Julia came from a moderately well-placed family. Her father would likely frown on a match to the son of a miner.

Then again, the Urbica patriarch probably frowned on his daughter staying in the Imperial Marines beyond the standard contract. Few women joined in the first place, but for her to stay on and, even worse, to be incredibly good at it... Poor old Governor Urbica must have all but given up on brokering a decent, dynastic marriage for his daughter.

Paul almost laughed as he pictured an uncomfortable family gathering. The old man would disapprove of Paul's low birth, fear his authority and influence as an inspector from the *Eye* and wonder if that influence might be useful in some future scheme.

He realized with some surprise, that the harvesting heads were now in sight on his passive sonar display. He maneuvered to the left and turned to face away from the reinforced vacuum line of the nearest head. He accelerated to match velocity and then slowed slightly to drift back into reach of the maintenance ladder that ran up the line.

Rebels and Patriots

Now came the waiting game again, and his fears threatened to flood back in. He didn't want to obsess about Julia, so he turned his thoughts to a more concrete future. If they managed to thwart the attack here in Santa Clara, the next step would be Home-world.

They would need to present their evidence to the *Eye* and CentCom simultaneously. The media had already started the ball rolling after the interviews in Irricanan orbit, but they would reduce the chances of a cover-up by involving more than one government agency.

Both CentCom and the 'Eye' might have compelling reasons to cover up what had happened, but it was very unlikely they'd succeed if both were involved. A room full of cats would dance *Swan Lake* before CentCom and the *Eye* ever cooperated on anything.

He nearly lost his grip when the ship finally started reeling in the vacuum lines. The massive collector heads lifted off the floor and followed the team up into the bottom hatches of the harvesting sub.

Paul rode the line into the storage bay for the vacuum head and he hugged the ladder as the line passed through the small, pressure-shielded aperture. His suit shorted as he cleared the pressure-shield and he shuddered, barely remembering to step off the ladder as soon as there was a dry floor.

Though he knew it didn't matter now, he still hoped it had been the pressure-shield that shorted his suit and not just random chance. He retracted his helmet just before a worker came around the corner to check on the huge reel that held the vacuum line.

Paul knew, from long experience, how quickly the look of momentary confusion on the man's face would turn to suspicion. He headed off the transition.

"It looks good enough for now," he told the man as though he had every right to be there, "but you tell your idiot of a boss that he

# A.G. Claymore

needs to follow the proper schedules. I'm not going to be the one taking a hit if this line fails in the middle of a field."

The worker gave him a vague nod and carried on. Paul resisted the urge to smile. Everybody had an idiot above them in the hierarchy. A stern warning to said idiot was usually enough to get on somebody's good side.

He casually strode out of the massive room filled with vac-line reels. He'd had every intention of sneaking out of the reel room along with the other six team members, but he'd been found immediately. Now his best camouflage was to stay in plain sight and act as though he owned the place.

He found himself in the ore-straining room, where the water was separated from the incoming nodules. He could see workers moving toward a door three levels up on the starboard side. The room would be empty soon and he'd be able to reach the ore cars.

"Excuse me," an authoritative voice called, "can I help you?"

He turned to find another man standing to his left, between the supports of two vac lines.

"Yeah," he replied gruffly, "you can follow procedures." He stepped forward and jabbed a finger at the man. "I know what you're up to."

"Y – you… What?"

Paul nodded his head back, eyebrows up. "Oh, don't think we don't know this trick when we see it. You guys are skimming the preventative-maintenance budget and, when things get out of hand, you expect us to authorize a capital expenditure in order to keep the lines running."

It was a safe enough bet that somebody was skimming money from this department. It was so common in the Imperium that it wasn't even considered illegal. It only led to repercussions if you let it get out of control.

# Rebels and Patriots

"Whoa! Hold on now…"

Paul shook his head. "I don't want to hear it. You tell that moron to follow the PM schedule or we're bringing an audit down here."

He turned and stalked off, but he couldn't go through to the ore cars now, not with the nervous employee watching him. He ascended the stairs, hoping it didn't just lead to a break room.

He was relieved to find himself in a broad passageway. He took a quick look both ways to ensure nobody was approaching before he placed a hand on the emergency evacuation panel. A holographic display showed him the layout of the large harvesting sub and he stored it on his CPU.

There were boarding gates on either side of the sub, one level down from where he was. They were on the port and starboard ends of a single passageway that ran across the ship. He moved aft a few hundred feet and entered a stairwell, exiting one level down.

Moving a little farther aft, he came to the passageway to find a few dozen employees waiting at the port end and he simply joined them. There didn't seem to be anybody in charge of the small group. He suspected security might be somewhat lax between the vessels of the fleet.

That suspicion was confirmed when, after docking for the ore transfer, the portal slid open and the group flowed out past a bored-looking pair of security guards who paid far more attention to their dice rolls than they did the miners entering the factory ship.

The plan was a little light on details from this point. They knew the bomb was likely aboard this vessel because there was only one factory ship. The conspirators could blow up dozens of harvesting ships and barely make a dent in production rates. Take out the factory ship, however, and the Imperium would be on deathwatch. The Imperium's Military ships would turn into stationary gun platforms within months.

## A.G. Claymore

So they were reasonably certain the bomb would be here, but this was still a hell of a big submarine. They'd divided the ship into sections but, beyond that, it was going to take a miracle to find the damn thing.

And then he left the Arrivals lounge and saw salvation, right there in the middle of the off-duty market.

A falafel stand.

Rebels and Patriots

## *Follow the Falafel*

**W**hen Urbica spotted him sitting at a table eating his falafel, Paul wondered if he was reading too much into her expression. Still, she looked pretty damned happy to see he'd made it into the ship alive.

She moved past the table, putting a hand on his shoulder as she continued over to the food vendors. She fit in well enough, he was surprised to see. In a city that never saw the surface, items like soap were incredibly expensive and what people *could* afford was pretty harsh on hair.

Close to a third of the citizens of Santa Clara kept their heads shaved. Even her implants were unremarkable. This factory city only existed to manufacture high-tech components and a large number of citizens sported more extensive implants than hers.

She returned with a plate of fishcakes and sat next to him. "I thought I'd lost you," she told him before taking a bite.

He noticed she hadn't said 'we'. "Yeah, I got caught by a maintenance worker," he explained as two more members of the team joined them with their food. The agreement had been to rendezvous at this food market after getting aboard. It was the closest to the ore receiving plant.

"You got caught?" one of the dragoons asked. "How did you get away?"

Paul shrugged. "Gave him a stern lecture and called his boss an idiot."

"That worked?" the other dragoon asked, frowning.

Paul nodded. "Twice, actually. You'd be surprised how often a belligerent attitude can give you the upper hand."

## A.G. Claymore

They chuckled. One of them noticed two more dragoons searching the crowd with trays of food in their hands and waved them over.

"Anyone see Karl?" Paul asked.

"Lost his grip on the ladder when his line started to reel in," one of the men said quietly. "My suit was running on fumes when I came aboard. I don't know if he had enough to make the pickup with Eddie."

"Hell," Urbica muttered. "Alright, we need to make sure his troubles aren't for nothing. Kendricks, Hensen, take his zone and split it between you."

"I have a suggestion that might help save us some trouble," Paul said, looking past Kendricks to where two men sat at a table ten meters away. "We could try following those two shaggy-haired Marines over there. Don't look," he warned as Kendricks and Hensen both began turning their heads.

"One at a time, and not directly. They're at your six. When I point to your five, take a look, then give us a lewd gesture, as if I've just pointed out a good-looking woman."

They did as advised and everyone shared a good laugh. Urbica leaned in. "They're looking our way. I've just said something really obscene and amusing." She licked her lips as the team burst out laughing.

"Nicely done," Paul said calmly. "But I think they were looking at the three women sitting behind us."

One of the two Marines was now making a gesture that left little doubt as to what occupied his mind.

"Are you sure the colonel didn't get him worked up when she was licking her lips?" Kendricks asked, grinning.

"I'm starting to think you might be right," Paul admitted. Anyway, the falafel guy says they showed up about five months ago

Rebels and Patriots

dressed like civvies but they stood out like a sore thumb. Mostly keep to themselves. There's three of 'em but you never see more than two at a time."

"The falafel guy?" Urbica didn't sound convinced.

"One thing I've learned from this adventure is to always take time to talk to the falafel guy," Paul told her. "Now watch this."

One of the Marines got up, tossed his wrappers in the recycler and bought a new falafel. He returned to the table and waited for the second Marine to finish eating.

"That sandwich is going to lead us to the bomb," Paul said quietly.

Kendricks shook his head in amazement. "It's a damned good thing this place has a falafel hut."

"You guys wait here." Paul finished his drink. "It's too easy for them to notice if a small horde is following them. Just myself and the Colonel, I think, and we should get up now, before they do."

He led Urbica to the main exit and stopped, pretending to examine a necklace at one of the jewelry stalls. He held it for her to examine, but also at an angle that let him see the Marines as they left their table. "Coming our way," he said quietly.

He paid for the necklace and made a show of putting it around her neck as they walked past.

"Just so we're clear about this," she said, "the first time you buy me jewelry, it's just a cover?"

He rolled his eyes. "It does complement your eyes. If I do a cover, I do it right." He gestured toward the exit.

They moved off, flowing with the crowd. They kept several people between themselves and their targets as they walked, but the Marines didn't seem to be concerned about a tail. After several months in the factory city, they appeared to have grown careless.

# A.G. Claymore

The whole place had that old-ship smell. The metallic tang of the vessel itself held hints of bearing grease, ozone and accumulated corners of dirt and grime.

The people around them smelled of sweat, like they would anywhere, but the sweat was scented with acrid, bitter aromatics from dark kelp. The cheap seaweed grew on the ocean floor and it found its way into almost every dish served on board.

The two Marines split up as they reached the end of the business district. "Follow the sandwich," Paul said quietly, taking her hand and leading her after their target.

They were led deep into a residential zone of the submarine and they began to see children. They chased each other as well as the ever-present cats that lived on every ship in the Imperium.

There was hardly a world that didn't have some annoying little animal that would stow away on cargo or escape from an owner. Even the *Xipe Totec* carried its own unofficial pest patrol.

The Marine stooped outside an apartment door to scratch a battered old tomcat behind the ears. He straightened and put his palm on the lock-plate.

Acting on impulse, Paul closed the distance just as the door was opening. He shoved the man through the door, sending him sprawling on the floor. He leapt over him and raced into the main room as Urbica got a grip on the hapless Marine's hand and slid it up behind his back.

The third Marine was already halfway across the room before Paul set eyes on him and the man managed to get his hands on a small device. He spun around, determination on his face as he stared at Paul. Then his features faltered. He looked down at the trigger in his hand.

# Rebels and Patriots

Paul held out a hand, palm up. "I'm not going to move," he assured the man. "Just take a minute to stop and think about what you're about to do."

"I have my orders," the man said quietly, as if to himself.

"There *is* such a thing as an illegal order," Paul insisted gently. "Every Marine knows that."

"How the hell do you expect me to assess the legality of my orders when I'm stuck down here? What are we supposed to do, hire lawyers to follow us around and analyze everything our officers tell us?"

"Don't give me that bullshit," Paul replied calmly. "At your level, you're still responsible for your actions if you follow orders that are blatantly illegal or even treasonous."

"Hold on," the man looked annoyed. "Who said anything about treason?"

"Are you kidding me?" Paul stared at him for a few seconds. "You might be missing some pretty important 'big-picture' stuff here. What happens if this factory ship is destroyed?"

"Shipments from Santa Clara will stop." The Marine shrugged. "Other data-gear producers will have to pick up the slack."

"They can't," Paul replied. "The vast majority of data chip and circuit production takes place right here on this ship. The other companies can't make a dent in the loss. It would take half a year to get them ramped up for that kind of production."

"So the banking and porn industries will collapse," the man said with a shrug. "What do I care? I'll be dead anyway."

"It's not just that. Don't you have family?"

No response.

"I'll take that as a 'yes'," Paul told him. "They'll have to suffer through the effects of what you're about to do to them.

## A.G. Claymore

"Without this world's products, everything will start to fail, and not just banks.

"Everything from your assault rifle, to the ship you came out here on will grind to a halt as the circuits fail and there's no replacements available." Paul spread his hands out. "Why do you think we call every quartermaster 'Chip'? Do you seriously think the military sets aside anyone with the name and trains him as a store-man?"

"Well, no." The Marine shrugged in annoyance. "I realize they're always sitting in the armory, swapping out circuits, but I think you're just trying to confuse the issue with a load of bullshit."

"Let me catch you up on what's been happening on the other end of your particular chain of command," Paul offered. "Several days ago, someone walked up to Senator Hadrian Nathaniel in the rotunda and vaporized him with a body-bomb. With Nathaniel and the 488 out of the running, who do you think was the most likely man to lead a pacification of secessionists at Irricana?"

A shrug.

"Seneca," Paul told him. "Of course, he's not the type to lead from the front, so he's back at Home-world. He sent the 538 out to do the heavy lifting – easy work when you consider *they* are the secessionists anyway."

"It makes no sense," the Marine protested. "What does Seneca gain from destroying the Imperium?"

"Nothing at all," Paul agreed, "but he stood to gain a lot from having saboteurs placed to carry out the *threat*. If he'd been able to seize control of Irricana and Santa Clara, the threat of destroying production would have kept the military from walking in and taking both worlds back.

"He'd become the power behind the throne and the Grays would have been the power behind *him*. If the plan failed and production

## Rebels and Patriots

was destroyed, the Grays could have just waited a few months and then walked right over us."

Paul pointed at the Marine. "That's where you come in. Who do you serve?"

"W... the... the Emperor," he blurted in surprise, offended at having been asked.

"Not from where I'm standing," Paul told him. "As long as you're holding an armed trigger, I'd say you're serving the Grays."

The Marine looked down at the device in his hands. He took several deep breaths. Suddenly he looked back up at Paul. "Who the hell are you?" He demanded. "How am I supposed to trust you?"

Paul nodded. "Good man. That means you're starting to question everything, including me. Turn on your IFF transponder and I'll do the same."

The man frowned at Paul for a few seconds but, apparently seeing no trap in the proposal, he nodded his assent.

Paul saw the man's icon appear in his vision and he opened it. Lance Corporal Harry Clark. He looked past the data to see the wide eyes of the Marine.

"You're from the *Eye*?" Clark asked.

"That's right, Harry. Started out in the Corps as a military cop and you know that folks like us only betray the Imperium if we've been lied to." Paul nodded to Harry's left hand. "Why don't you disarm that trigger and show us who you really serve?"

Harry stared down at the trigger.

"They have someone, don't they?" Paul asked.

A nod. "My daughter."

"Pulling that trigger won't save her," Paul warned. "The entire Imperium will descend into anarchy until the Grays take over. Civil war, famine, disease, and then enslavement as experimental

## A.G. Claymore

subjects. Once they have no further use for us, the Grays will likely wipe us out. They're funny that way."

Harry's face was slick with sweat. His left hand was trembling. He was looking straight through Paul. "Shit!" he muttered.

"Just calm down, Harry," Paul soothed, "and think it through."

Harry shook his head, looked Paul in the eye and took a deep breath. "Just take it," he blurted, holding out the trigger. His knees collapsed under him as he let go of the device.

Holding the death of billions in your hand can be a draining experience when you aren't used to it.

Rebels and Patriots

A.G. Claymore

# CONSOLIDATION

## *The Eye*

aul walked into the wood-paneled office. A fireplace crackled away cheerfully at one side of the large room, showing any who entered that Chief Commissioner Maurice Tudor was wealthy enough to buy wood and set it on fire.

One didn't climb to the very pinnacle of the ICI through merit alone. The great man himself sat by the fire, grinning up happily at Paul. Sitting next to him was Bao Zheng, the Grand Magistrate, the legal balance to Tudor. The two could easily thwart each other but, when they worked in concert, there was very little that could stand in their way.

"Have a seat, my boy," Tudor waved at one of the deep chairs. "Sit, sit. You need a rest after all your adventures!" He leaned forward as Paul settled in. "Quite a little rat's nest you've kicked over out on the Rim," he declared.

"I should say so," Zheng agreed. "Thousands of citizens snatched away to Gray territory, Imperial troops suborned, treason… It's enough to put silk around quite a few necks."

"If we have the proof," Tudor leaned back and gazed at Paul. "So, do we have the necessary proof, Inspector Grimm?"

Paul took a deep breath and activated the case file on his CPU. "The data is open for you to review, gentlemen." He waited until both men connected and accessed the file before beginning the summary. "I believe we have more than enough for several quick convictions. Seneca and his cronies framed Julius Nathaniel and they murdered Hadrian.

"They conspired to seize his Majesty's territories, they planted weapons of mass destruction in Imperial cities and they used his Majesty's forces to attack Imperial citizens. They conspired with the Grays, handing kidnap victims over to them for experimentation and they were willing to give aliens a frightening level of influence over the future course of Imperial politics."

"Can we prove that last part?" Tudor asked. "You have more than enough for treason, but giving the aliens influence? That would ruin Seneca's entire family; we'd need a damned good argument."

A steward brought coffee and Paul took the time to savor a few sips while he marshaled his thoughts. He sat forward on the edge of his seat and set the cup on a side table. "Seneca planned to use threats to keep us all from touching him. Specifically, the threat of disrupting erbium production at Irricana and circuit production at Santa Clara."

The two older men nodded.

"That threat would have been sufficient to keep us all at bay while he dictated policy to us," Paul continued, "but Gray systems don't rely on Human circuits. They were perfectly free to attack Seneca's forces without any danger to themselves. They could have easily traded peace for influence."

"Effectively turning Seneca's own weapon against himself," Zheng declared.

Paul nodded. "And against us in the process. An enemy's greatest strength often turns out to be his greatest weakness as well. If the Grays ever tired of controlling the Imperium through Seneca, they could have simply attacked both worlds and triggered Seneca's threat scenario."

# A.G. Claymore

"There isn't much to stop them right now," Tudor added. "now they're aware of our weakness, and they're probably very perturbed by your incursion into Gray territory."

"Blinking mad, no doubt," Zheng added mildly. "We need to press for diversification immediately and beef up security at both worlds before they decide to come after us."

"I suppose we have Seneca to thank for pointing out this weakness in our society," Tudor mused, "but we'll still strangle the bastard." He raised an eyebrow at Zheng. "You've seen the data. Are you ready to render sentences?"

Zheng nodded. "I'm ready to transmit. I assume you want our man here to carry them out?"

"I do," Tudor agreed. He turned back to Paul. "Now look here," he began, jabbing a finger at Paul, "you've done very well so far. Really put a feather in our cap on this one, so don't bugger it up in the final stretch. Make sure it happens while the Grand Senate is in session. We want the public watching when you make the bastard's eyes bulge."

Rebels and Patriots

## *CentCom*

**U**rbica stood before a panel of two Admirals and one Marine General. If ever she'd needed proof that money could buy any rank, she need only walk into this room. Most senior officers were the dullard sons of their respective families, too dim to hold public office and too prone to drink to leave to their own devices.

In many ways, the Imperial military had become a daycare for rich adults. But these were adults who might well be ordering her execution for starting a conflict with the Grays.

"What did you think you were doing, Colonel?" Admiral Silenn demanded. "You can't start a war without consulting us, you know."

"It was hardly my intent to start a war, sir," Urbica countered. "I had reliable information indicating that thirty-seven thousand of his Majesty's subjects were being tortured on Narsa. The only way for us to reach our citizens and relieve their suffering was to take the Gray warship and travel directly there."

She smiled politely. "Perhaps it might be worth reiterating, with all this talk of provocation, that I seized that Gray warship in orbit around one of the Emperor's own planets. There were quite a few Gray warships in the area, *firing* at our vessels."

Silenn went red in the face, but he had nothing to say in response.

Urbica had no intention of letting him take cheap shots without having to endure any return fire. "What course of action would you have recommended, Admiral Silenn, to a commander under fire in Imperial territory? Perhaps I should've withdrawn my forces from Irricanan space and consulted with my superiors?"

"Perhaps," Silenn ventured. "Cooler heads might have prevailed."

A.G. Claymore

"And His Majesty's citizens on Irricana would have been left to the mercy of an invading alien force," Urbica countered. "I swore to defend the Imperium, not to simply report on its demise."

"Defending the Imperium is one thing," General Pfizen growled. "Invading Gray territory is quite another."

"Inflammatory!" Silenn declared.

"Treasonous," Pfizen added ominously.

"As the Grays had already invaded *our* territory, I felt quite certain that our own incursion would do little to incite further attacks. I had no intention of leaving our citizens in Gray hands." She was starting to believe that these fools may have had a hand in the scheme.

She might not leave this building alive.

She'd expected some alarm at her attack into Gray territory as well as a desire to see the captured Gray carrier disappear, but they seemed far too focused on criminalizing her actions.

Time to throw a cat amongst the pigeons.

"What's treasonous," she replied, "is Colonel Kinsey's close association with the Gray forces. We have proof that his Marines were equipped by the Grays and that they used that equipment to prey on law-abiding Imperial vessels."

"Yes, well, you can hand your evidence over to us and *we* will decide the truth of these allegations," Silenn ordered.

"I'm not the one in possession of the data."

A smug smile. "How *convenient*. I suppose you hid the data in a…"

"An inspector from the ICI has the data. It's been presented, along with Colonel Kinsey, to the Grand Magistrate."

The result was almost comical. Pfizen and Silenn exchanged glances but found no answers there. Their body language became erratic, twitchy. They were filled with the adrenaline rush of a fight

# Rebels and Patriots

or flight response but they were in no position to follow either course of action.

Admiral Halsey, on the other hand, simply raised an eyebrow at this news. Apparently, he had no reason to fear this development.

"I'm sure nobody faults your decision to assault Narsa, Colonel," He said. "But Agash and Tel Ramh?"

"Diversionary attacks," she replied. She had originally meant to attack Agash to draw forces away from Santa Clara, but it served as a diversion for the attack on Narsa just as well. "And, in light of the capabilities of our captured ship, we thought it wise to make our second diversionary attack at the world that built it."

A nod. "You understand our displeasure at your decision to give the media access to the Gray warship?"

She shrugged. "Sir, tens of thousands of our citizens had seen us open a wormhole to get back to Irricana, not to mention the records from Orbital Control and the civilian witnesses in orbit."

"We need to destroy that ship," Silenn urged.

Halsey glanced at the man out of the corner of his eye. "Not without sending in an appraisal team from Nordegg & Fishcher," he said. "The military would have to know how much prize-money to pay the Colonel and her intrepid dragoons before taking the ship from them. It would look very bad for us if the media learned that we'd robbed the saviors of Irricana."

Urbica was starting to feel she had an ally in the room. Halsey had remained quiet at the start, but he may have been giving her a chance to outmaneuver Silenn and Pfizen on her own. She sent a quick message to Paul. She'd never bothered much with the machinations of the leading families but now was a time when such knowledge would be incredibly useful.

*Admiral Halsey owes his position to the Thynnes.* Paul's quick reply gave her hope. The Thynne family was one of the most

256

# A.G. Claymore

powerful of the senatorial families. They believed in a strong Imperium and were unlikely to be tied up in a plot with Seneca.

"This business of seizing Irricana and Santa Clara," Halsey continued. "You're certain of the details as presented?"

"Yes, sir. They had every intention of destroying those production sites if they were losing control. The device at Irricana activated while I was disarming it, so there can be no doubt on that count."

"Activated?" Halsey's chin raised an inch.

"Yes, sir. I had to shoot the trigger."

A smile played around the corners of his eyes. "And I suppose the ICI has been presented with a conspirator who's willing to talk?"

"Indeed, sir. Kinsey's been outlining the entire structure of the conspiracy in exchange for his life."

"Excellent!" Halsey gave her a respectful nod. "You've done well, Colonel! We'd appreciate if you could keep your new ship here in orbit for the time being. The Imperial Corps of Engineers should take a look at her, but I'd like to keep them from taking her apart for the time being.

He grinned at her. "They might not be able to put her back together."

Silenn bristled. "Are you suggesting that Humans can't figure out an alien device?"

Halsey slowly turned his head. "I'm suggesting," he said as if to a child, "that the Grays have built a portable, origin-controlled wormhole generator and we haven't, despite the obvious advantages it affords. It must be kept as quiet as possible."

"But too many have already seen it," Pfizen protested. "You can't keep something like that under wraps unless we get rid of it entirely."

## Rebels and Patriots

Halsey waved a dismissive hand. "The right rumors can cover up just about anything. This Daffyd ap Rhys fellow…" He looked back at Urbica. "We can rely on him to take the credit?"

"He's a reliable man, sir," She assured him. "We can count on him to play his part in this."

"Good," Halsey thumped the table. "That's out of the way." He grinned at her. "Now, what shall we do with you, Colonel Urbica?"

A.G. Claymore

# *The Grand Senate*

Tony stood at the end of a richly paneled pedway. A page stood by the door, his sidearm tucked neatly away in a shoulder holster, but still easily visible to anyone who knew what to look for.

Behind the page stood two security officers. They carried submachine guns and always had a finger near their triggers. Nobody passed through those doors unless they had permission.

The page focused on a distant point for a few seconds and then nodded, looking up at Tony. "It's time, sir," he said simply.

The doors swung open and Tony marched out to stand next to the president of the Grand Senate. He'd been in this chamber many times as an assistant to his father, but he'd always been in Senator Nathaniel's balcony, never down here on the podium.

The balconies were spread out before him in a half-bowl arrangement. The farthest was more than a hundred meters away.

"Under Senate House Rule 3425, paragraph 234b, the house recognizes Anthony Nathaniel." The president stepped back.

It was the most expensive welcome Tony had ever heard, but he couldn't afford not to buy it. If this didn't work, he'd end up imprisoned for inciting dereliction of duty. It didn't matter that he'd helped save the Imperium, stealing an expedition force was not something CentCom could afford to go easy on.

He took a deep breath and swept his gaze around the room, just as his father had taught him to do. The senate chamber looked a hell of a lot bigger from down here.

"Thank you, Mr. President." Tony gave him a polite nod. "As the members of this august body are well aware, my father was vaporized by an assassin's bomb mere meters from where I now stand. I come here today because my father made a commitment to represent the people of sector two-eight-six-six.

# Rebels and Patriots

"As his only known heir, I offer to fulfill his duties until the next election for class seven." His only chance was to take his father's place in the Grand Senate. The law allowed an heir to take on the senatorial duties of a deceased parent, provided his colleagues voted their assent.

It was an efficient system. Senators almost always brought their children to work, grooming them to take on the job in their own time. Tony knew how his father operated, who his allies and enemies were. He would almost certainly be confirmed by the voters at the next election for class seven.

As a senator, Tony should be safe from military justice. They could ask the *Eye* to arrest him, but they would already be reluctant to punish him, considering what he'd accomplished with the 488. If this worked, CentCom would be able to point to his senatorial rank and look the other way.

The president stepped forward again. "In accordance with law and custom, Anthony Nathaniel offers to fulfill the duties of his deceased father, Grand Senator Hadrian Nathaniel. Are there any here who wish to speak for or against this offer before I call a vote?"

He looked down at a flashing icon on the surface of the podium. "The house recognizes Grand Senator Cicero Spectre-Vandenberg."

He stepped back once again and a shimmering hologram of the senator appeared. The senatorial balconies were designed to obscure the conversations within and it would take forever for speakers to walk all the way down to the podium, so the regular discourse of the house was conducted by holo-presence.

Spectre-Vandenberg was something of an oddity in the Grand Senate. He rarely wore the top hat common to his social order and his threadbare frock coat was something of a statement on aristocratic waste. Despite his shabby appearance and his thin voice, there were few who dared ignore his words.

## A.G. Claymore

"Many of you already know this young man," he wheezed. "He has spent many years in these halls, learning the family trade, and he has even spent many hours in my own offices. When my eldest was killed, young Anthony took leave from his military duties to assist me.

"He helped to train Mercurius, my youngest son, and he proved himself to be an able administrator. I have no doubt that the people of two-eight-six-six will be well pleased with his tireless service."

"That's a lovely story," a loud voice sneered from the tiers of balconies, "but it completely fails to consider recent events."

The president of the House stepped forward, raising a warning hand. "The House has not recognized the representative from sector three-seven-four-two."

Seneca ignored the president. He left his balcony and began making his way toward the podium. If the president wouldn't let him activate a projection, then he'd just do it the old fashioned way.

"You speak of his administrative skills," Seneca shouted as he approached, "but what about his character?" He pointed at Tony. "This man stole a military unit to avoid arrest."

Tony frowned at him. "You're not making any sense, Senator. There's no arrest warrant that I'm aware of. Can you provide us with proof of your wild allegations?"

The smug look had been knocked back a notch on Seneca's face. Technically, General Pullman had only ordered Tony's *detention* so he could play both sides of the fence. He could always claim it had been for Tony's safety, in the event the plot failed.

But Seneca kept coming. "You stole a military unit," he repeated, leaving out the weaker accusation this time. He reached the base of the podium and began the thirty-step climb.

Tony couldn't help but notice how dependent the Grand Senate was on technology. This chamber must have been built with holo

## Rebels and Patriots

technology in mind. If the flow of replacement circuits ever stopped, the senate would accomplish even less than it did now.

It would be his first mission, if he succeeded in filling his father's post. The production of optical circuits had been largely consolidated at Santa Clara through Imperial apathy. It represented a single point of failure. The Grays would almost certainly attack the planet if the Navy didn't deploy a major security force immediately.

The smaller producers would have to be given a bigger share of the contracts until they became viable rivals. He wondered how many other weaknesses were waiting to be exploited by an enemy.

Seneca's head appeared as he neared the top of the stairs and Tony decided to have a little fun at the man's expense.

"Senators of the Imperium," he announced, extending a hand toward the winded man, "Senator Seneca has come to reflect on all the accomplishments he's thwarted over the years."

Seneca mounted to the podium amid gales of laughter and his face reddened. He jabbed a finger at Tony. "Do you deny that you stole his Majesty's forces?"

Tony grinned. "Why Senator, I deny nothing. Of course I stole them."

The cheerful admission threw Seneca for a loop and he didn't seem to know how best to adjust his attack.

Tony, however, was ready to continue, and he timed his moment. As Seneca finally opened his mouth to speak, Tony resumed. "Those forces came with me willingly, but their hearts, as always, remained loyal to the Emperor.

"Had they not gone with me to Irricana that world would now be in the hands of the Gray Quorum."

He looked around the chamber. "Let there be no confusion about this. Those Marines engaged in combat with Gray warships in

## A.G. Claymore

Imperial territory. They then went deep into Gray territory and rescued more than thirty-five thousand of His Majesty's loyal subjects."

A general tone of approval filled the room. Hands thumped on railings and the approval counter on the podium surface was trending well into the green not only for the senators in the chamber but the viewing public as well.

"And this man," Tony added relentlessly, "would hand them back to their captors because I didn't possess the proper written orders, in triplicate."

Seneca was enraged. He was being made to look a fool in public by some renegade officer who'd come to beg for his father's job. He reached out to grab Tony's collar, intending to have him removed.

Though Seneca had served as a naval officer, he'd never deployed to a combat zone. His clan frowned on aristocrats who allowed their sons to receive implants and load combat algorithms. That was for the lower classes.

The Nathaniel family took a very different view. Tony's hand snapped out to trap Seneca's hand, bending it in toward the elbow and rotating the thumb away in the classic *kote gaeshi*. He applied just enough pressure to force his opponent into a deep bow.

*Now*. He sub-vocalized.

The pedway doors at the back of the podium were thrown open and Paul strode out to join them, a silk scarf dangling from his hand.

Seneca looked up from his undignified position and his eyes locked in terror on the red silk.

"Grand Senator Cyrus Millhouse Seneca," Paul said loudly, "You have been sentenced to death for the crimes of high treason, terrorism, and conspiring to betray the Imperium to the Gray Quorum. Do you have any last words?"

"No!" Seneca screamed. "Not here! Not like this!"

# Rebels and Patriots

"Your last words are duly noted," Paul replied calmly. He stood next to Tony and looped the scarf around Seneca's wildly twitching head. He rotated his right elbow as far as he could to the right and wrapped the scarf ends tight around his right hand.

"Witness now," Paul intoned, "and fear the Emperor's swift justice." He stepped to his left, rotating his body around Seneca's head, rotating his right elbow swiftly.

Seneca's eyes bulged, just as Chief Inspector Tudor had insisted. His one free hand clawed frantically at the expensive silk, the ancient execution device that served as the last concession to his exalted rank.

Cicero, still technically holding the floor and therefore still projected in the podium, looked down impassively.

It was in Paul's authority to end the condemned man's suffering with a twist of the neck. Many executions ended with such an act of mercy, but he was in no mood.

He thought of Hadrian, the man who'd plucked Paul out of obscurity and rewarded him with wealth, rank and respect. He thought of Julius, whose sense of duty and justice had brought Paul to Hadrian's attention in the first place.

He closed his eyes and savored the rattle of Seneca's expensive shoes against the citrus wood floor of the podium. His heads-up display informed him that the man was dead and he heaved the body over the edge of the podium steps.

The remains of Cyrus Millhouse Seneca tumbled to the stone flags of the chamber floor.

Paul nodded to Tony and stepped back amid a general sigh from the Senators.

Cicero raised an eyebrow. "I yield the floor to the president," he said calmly.

## A.G. Claymore

The president stepped forward. "Does anyone *else* wish to speak against Mr. Nathaniel's proposal?" He let his gaze drift dramatically toward the undignified heap on the floor below.

Chuckles punctuated the silence. Seneca had been a less than popular presence in the chamber. He'd never been reluctant to employ threats, coercion or outright blackmail and few were sorry to see his seat empty.

The president opened a large holo-screen. "I call for a vote." He waited until a few hundred ballots had already been cast before entering his own.

In less than a minute, Tony's fate had been decided. The president turned to him. "Please take your seat, Grand Senator Nathaniel."

Rebels and Patriots

# *Ganges*

**P**aul stopped halfway down the back ramp of the shuttle and shivered despite the heat. The equatorial weather on Ganges was quite warm – too warm, in fact. He stared up at the massive sea wall holding back the waters of the Black Pontic.

The capital, Bhavnagar, had been built at the head of the Munnar river delta twelve centuries ago. Back then, it had been an ideal site. The river had carried goods from the interior to the spaceport for centuries.

The factories of the interior also produced carbon dioxide in vast quantities. In the last few centuries, the average global temperature had steadily increased, shrinking the polar ice caps.

New rivers had sprung into life on the polar continents, carving their muddy way out to the network of seas that dotted the world.

The Black Pontic, in fact, was no longer a sea. Having joined its waters with the Palakad and the Parcha more than a century ago, it now formed part of the planet's first ocean.

As the decades slipped by, the wall around Bhavnagar grew, meter by meter, resulting in the current fifteen-meter-high barrier. The water levels were still on the rise and the planetary council had been debating the latest extension for more than five years.

As it was, any decent-sized cyclone required emergency shielding to prevent the storm surge from washing over the top.

He stepped down into the oppressive heat radiating up from the tarmac.

A sweat-glazed ground crew wrestled a new fuel core into the underside of the small craft. Their grimy orange coveralls marking them as class 4 indents.

They were little better than slaves and Paul's own father had been barely a step above these men. He'd taken the family to

# A.G. Claymore

Hardisty in a desperate attempt to better their lives but the mining consortium there had been a den of law-abiding thieves.

The company city was the only shelter on the planet. Employees had no choice but to rent company accommodation, buy company food and clothing and pay company taxes. Nobody lasted more than five years without falling into debt.

It was perfectly legal, of course, because it was good for business. Debtors became indentured laborers and 'indents' almost never earned enough to buy their freedom back.

If you couldn't stay afloat as a free worker, what chance did you have as an indent on quarter pay?

Paul's old revulsion for the class system threatened to bubble back to the surface again. He'd just fought to preserve this society but it was still one he hated.

His family had been a heartbeat away from becoming indentured on Hardisty when his father fell down that shaft. Not for the first time, Paul wondered whether his dad had sacrificed himself to give his family a chance.

The company had packed the small family off to the nearest gate station with a small accidental-death bounty. Paul had left his mother and sister there in the hopes that their meager funds might get them somewhere decent.

He'd lied about his age, claiming to be ten years old, and joined the Imperial Marines as a ceremonial drummer boy. He never saw his family again.

He walked to the area marked off for ground vehicles and handed his bag to a man standing under a holographic 'Inspector Grimm' sign. He sighed as he realized the open top vehicle was his ride.

# Rebels and Patriots

Despite the oppressive heat, open-top ground cars were still the traditional mode of transport here on Ganges. He climbed into the back and the driver eased them around to head for the spaceport exit.

The spice market was immediately outside the gates, filling the air with the pungent scents of local products. An overpowering wave of spice-pine seeds was accompanied by a variety of more subtle notes.

They rode between the rows of inter-connected high-rises. Ganges had been colonized before the advent of standardized arcology specifications but the buildings very nearly constituted an arcology already.

A maze of enclosed pedways connected the various buildings. Light monorail transit lines provided high-speed transport at various elevations.

Dark clouds were beginning to roll in as they pulled up to the gate of a white stone mansion at the south end of the city's central green-space. A black-clad private security agent confirmed his identity and waved them through.

A dozen native Gangians were out tending to the grounds. The climate change had affected them the worst. They were technically marsupials, carrying their young in a pouch for several months after birth, but their skin was scaly, an adaptation to the planet's originally dry climate.

With their planet changing so rapidly, the natives were in decline. They suffered from a host of problems ranging from respiratory diseases to a debilitating, scale-rotting fungus.

He caught the looks they threw his way, part curiosity, part hatred. Having grown up near the bottom of the heap himself, he couldn't blame them. Still, something seemed odd. The looks they gave him were more openly malevolent than usual.

He shivered again, despite the heat.

## A.G. Claymore

He'd been noticing it more, since his return from the Rim. He didn't know if it was just his imagination, but he certainly didn't feel as safe as he used to where native alien species were concerned.

He climbed out of the vehicle and walked up to the door, the driver following with his bag. Taking a deep breath, Paul reached out and pulled on the bell-cord.

The door opened and Paul was mildly disappointed to find a liveried servant inside. He knew it was frowned upon for the upper classes to answer their own door, but he'd forgotten.

"This way, Inspector," the elderly gentleman said, gesturing Paul inside the door and waving a servant over to collect the bag.

He led Paul down a broad central hallway and turned left, entering a study at the back of the building. "Inspector Paul Grimm," he announced.

Paul walked in to find a man in his sixties rising from his chair. He was in decent shape but with snowy white hair. He held out a hand. "Welcome to Ganges, Inspector."

Paul shook hands, noting the firm grip. "Thank you, Governor Urbica. I've never had the chance to come here before."

"It seems to be more *reason* than chance that brought you here," the old man chuckled. He waved to the chairs and led the way, dropping into his seat with a contented sigh.

Paul was starting to think this meeting was going well. Perhaps Julia's warnings were colored by her own difficult relationship with her father.

"Y'know," Governor Urbica began as he waved a servant over, "a few weeks ago, I would have refused to let you in the front door. Whiskey." The last word was barked at the servant who nodded and slipped away.

Paul started to think he'd been a little hasty in getting his hopes up. He fought the impulse to speak into the silence. The old man

Rebels and Patriots

seemed lost in his thoughts and, frankly, it might be the best place for him, at least until Julia could come to his rescue.

The governor of Ganges let out a silent snort of laughter before looking back at his guest. "I once started putting together a run for the senate," he told Paul. "Our family may not be one of the most important, but we'd spent decades building up political capital and I thought the time was right.

"It was looking good, damned good, and I knew our family's fortunes were about to take an upturn, but then I lost a major backer." He shook his head slightly.

"Seneca pulled his support, which he damned well owed me, and threw it behind some minor relative of his, a real dark horse. The silly twit got a big head, stopped being discreet about his bribes and such. It cost him the election and I lost all of my backers when that rat, Seneca, pulled out on me.

"He exiled us to this back-water ball of fungus when I complained a little too loudly." He accepted a tumbler of whiskey from the servant and carried on while the servant brought the tray to Paul.

"This is not a planet for an up and coming politician, Inspector. It's a place where families go to die." Governor Urbica stared moodily down into the amber liquid of his drink.

"But how did you end up on Ganges?" Paul asked. "This world is represented by Senator Nathaniel."

"We got re-sectored shortly after I got shafted," the old man explained. He looked up at Paul.

"I watched your appearance in the senate," he said. "How did it feel to squeeze the life out of that traitorous *húndàn*?"

Paul took his time with the answer. He looked down at the richly woven silk carpet for a few moments. "I know you're not supposed to enjoy something like that," he began, "but he'd killed two good friends and his idiotic plan would have destroyed us all." He looked up at the governor of Ganges.

"It felt good, strangling the bastard while Tony held him in place."

"Call me Lazarus." The old man held out his drink.

After a moment of surprise, Paul reached out his own drink and Lazarus tapped their tumblers together.

He'd already known that his relationship with the Nathaniels would have made an impression on the old man, but it seemed to pale in comparison to his involvement with Seneca. Executing the man who'd betrayed Lazarus had turned out to be a good move for so many reasons.

Lazarus leaned closer to Paul. "If you should ever feel the need to come here on your own to ask me a question, it won't be necessary."

Paul frowned. "I'm not sure I understand."

Lazarus shook his head wearily. "I'm through with fooling myself," he said. "I know my daughter will never accept any suitor that I find for her. She's already blown off dozens and the police are still searching for one of them.

"I've come to accept that neither Julia nor her husband are likely to ever take a seat in the Grand Senate. She doesn't want one and she won't marry a man who *does*."

Paul was back to thinking this was going well.

Lazarus jabbed a finger at him. "You'll probably never sit in the Senate but your children might, if they have Julia for a mother. The Grimm-Urbicas might just restore our family's fortunes."

Well, there it was. Paul wasn't an ideal candidate, but the old man seemed willing to cut his losses where Paul was concerned. The only question now was how Julia herself felt about the idea.

# Rebels and Patriots

He took it as a good sign that she'd invited him to Ganges. If she simply wanted to fool around, she could have picked any of a hundred more suitable places.

Only Ganges offered the chance to meet her parents.

It was surreal to realize the ten-year-old who'd left his mother on that station so long ago might see his own child join the ruling body of the Imperium. He was suddenly more conscious than ever of the weakness represented by oversights like Santa Clara and its dominance of the circuitry market.

"Now look," the old man said forcefully. "If she ever even *hints* at the idea of marrying you, sweep her off her feet and carry her to the nearest ship's captain. I don't care if it happens out in that hallway," he added, pointing at the door.

"I'd like to see the ceremony but I'd rather you get it done before she changes her mind."

Paul wasn't quite sure what to say to that. "I'll do my best…"

"You'll never succeed with that attitude," Lazarus declared. "Don't hand me that 'best' garbage. You just do whatever it takes. *Dong ma?*"

"Do whatever *what* takes, Laz?" a woman's voice asked.

Paul turned to look at the two women standing by the double doors leading from the study to one of the front rooms. Xene Urbica had the same face as her daughter, but her long graying hair was Paul's first hint at how Julia must look when not shaving her head.

Xene was a lovely woman. Her features might seem ordinary when considered in isolation, but the spirit that animated them made all the difference.

Paul was surprised to find that he liked the look. He was accustomed to Julia's shaved head and it had been hard to imagine her with flowing tresses.

## A.G. Claymore

The other surprise was Julia herself. He'd never seen her out of uniform or, more accurately, he'd never seen her in civilian clothing.

Julia stood next to her mother wearing a long linen dress.

"Finding our weaknesses on the Rim, my dear," Lazarus told her.

"Well, we found one that involves Ganges," Paul said.

"Ganges?" Lazarus turned back to Paul. "What weakness have you found here?"

"We haven't been getting enough circuit orders," Julia told him. "Worlds like Ganges need to start ramping up production.

"If you offer grants to the Bhavnagar Optical Data Group, Tony will get it matched by the Imperial Exchequer. It's vital that we get circuit production spread out again."

"If we invest public funds in the data industry," Xene cut in, "what assurances do we have regarding orders?"

"Tony is committed to getting this done," Paul told her. "If anyone tries to slow the process, they'll find the press on their doorstep. It's a matter of Imperial security."

"The people of Ganges," Lazarus enthused, "will be pleased to do their part for His Grace, just as our Julia will be doing her part out on the Rim."

Julia tilted her head, squinting at her father. "What are you playing at, Old Man?" He was being entirely too agreeable.

Lazarus tried to look affronted, but it wasn't very convincing. "Can't a father show pride in his daughter?" he asked. "Our family has produced only four colonels in three hundred years, and now we have a brigadier?"

"Maybe," she corrected. "The Emperor nominated me, but the Senate still has to confirm the promotion."

"They will," Lazarus insisted, "or Irricana might just rebel for real this time. They want you back as soon as possible."

273

# Rebels and Patriots

"Enough work talk," Julia declared. "I'm going to show Paul the grounds."

Lazarus frowned. "I'm not sure that's wise," he cautioned. "The 'scalers' are still out there, working on the hedges."

"They know I'm always armed," she replied. "As long as you don't get too close, they're no problem."

She led Paul back to the main hall and out a set of tall doors that opened onto a stone-paved surface overlooking several acres of trees and various exotic plants. The sky was growing darker, but it seemed to have no effect on the heat.

"So what did he do," she asked him, "offer to pay you off if you leave me alone?" She angled to the left, taking them down a tree-shaded pathway.

"Uhhh…" Paul was worried this might actually hurt his chances, but he knew he couldn't keep it from her. "He kind of told me he's given up on finding you a husband." He grinned. "Are the cops *really* looking for one of your old suitors?"

She laughed. "Technically, I suppose. He fled the planet after the hospital released him."

"You put him there?" Paul asked. "Let me guess, he wasn't quite as charming as your father thought?"

"And then some," she said, stopping to tease out a venus-magnolia flower. "He thought he could 'seal the deal' by force. I gave him a chance to back off, but when he ripped my shirt I broke one of his arms and most of his face."

"So now he has to rely on his winning personality?" Paul grinned again, taking a deep breath of the cool fragrant air.

Cool was a relative term on Ganges. It was certainly better than standing out on the stone terrace where the air was still shimmering with heat accumulated from the recently-obscured sun. Still, he'd be looking for the environmental controls if it were this warm on a ship.

# A.G. Claymore

She resumed walking. "So the old man's given up, has he? What was he *really* harping about when we came in then?"

"He's decided to pin his hopes on *me*. Told me not to waste time asking him for your hand if you ever showed an interest in getting married – just find a captain and get it done."

"Are you seriously telling me he's got no objections to having you as his son-in-law?"

Paul spread his hands. "Why do you have to put it like that?" He affected a hurt tone but his grin took off the edge. "I've got prospects, y'know…"

That won him a treasured giggle.

"I know," she said. "I'm just surprised the old bastard is willing to consider *any* man who can't trace his lineage back to Montgomery himself."

They reached the west edge of the garden, rounding the corner to find flashing orange lights on a red utility vehicle. Two police officers were sipping bags of coffee while a technician loaded a dead Gangian native into the vehicle.

"Afternoon, Officers." Urbica the Marine was back suddenly.

Polite nods. "Miss Urbica," the slightly older officer replied. "We'll get this cleared up right away."

The younger officer frowned. "Ma'am, have you heard of any disturbance, anything that might help explain what happened here?"

His partner shot him an angry look. "Don't trouble yourself, ma'am; we'll sort it out."

"It's no trouble, Officers," Urbica assured them. "I shot him this morning."

Paul stared at her. "You what?"

"He came at me with that hedge trimmer over there," she pointed to a long implement that looked like an old-fashioned bow, except

# Rebels and Patriots

it had a plasma arc instead of a draw string. It lay crackling on the dirt beside the path.

"No hedges anywhere near here," Paul mused, "and yet it was turned on."

The younger cop ran a scanner over it before reaching down to turn it off. "His prints are all over it but no evidence that Miss Urbica even touched it. Not even any dead skin cells from handling it while wearing gloves."

"Salazar!" the older man growled, "of course she wouldn't plant evidence; she's the governor's own daughter, you idiot!"

"Officer..." Paul waited for the older man to look in his direction. "You should let him do a proper investigation. Any number of vile stories can be cooked up about this if we don't have all the facts available."

"And you," the older man retorted, "should stay out of police business, Mr. ...?" He knew who the local elite were, and Paul wasn't one of them. He might have had the sense to consider the fact that Paul had just arrived on the scene in Julia's company, but his blood was up.

Paul activated his transponder, the standard response of any citizen when being questioned by a cop.

The older man's face seemed to lose some of his Gangian tan. "Inspector, I meant no disrespect. I..."

Paul waved off the apology. "Never mind about that," he insisted. "Have you had an increase in native trouble lately?"

The man looked relieved to talk business. "As a matter of fact, we've been seeing a lot more lately. The last week or so, they've been acting like there's a double full moon or something.

"Not like a planned thing, though," the younger cop added, "more like they've hit a boiling point and the frustration's just gotten out of control."

## A.G. Claymore

The older man nodded. "That's about it. Mouthing off to the cops, property damage, substance abuse. Hells, they've even assaulted a few Humans, but this is the first time one of em's gone after anybody important."

Paul looked at Julia and she raised an eyebrow.

"There's no such thing as coincidence," she said.

He nodded. "They're acting like you'd expect them to, assuming they had high expectations. Expectations that were shattered."

Julia's eyes flickered over to the cops.

"The local cops need to know," Paul insisted. It would help if they understood why the native aliens were causing trouble but, more importantly, it would lead to another bump in the media cycle, pushing the Imperium toward taking action.

The angrier the public was about the Grays, the better it was for the Imperium. It might even lead to another war.

The economy had been in a steady, slow decline since shortly after the end of the Warlord Era. Empires either grew or shrank. The Imperium, with no new aliens to subjugate, had turned to subjugating its own people.

That was a formula that led to disaster.

"I think aliens throughout the Imperium may have known that something big was coming," Paul told the two cops. "The Grays thought their time had come to bring us to our knees, so they probably had agents on every world to prepare for the big day."

"*Jiàn ta de gui*," the older man muttered in shock. "They might have all sorts of weapons stashed away on Ganges."

"And they might just decide to use them anyway," Paul told him. "They're pissed and they don't have much to lose. It's a dangerous combination. Tell your boss. Say you got it straight from the *Eye*."

They continued their walk while the cops climbed back into their vehicle.

Rebels and Patriots

"Things are going to get ugly," Urbica remarked.

Paul shrugged. "Things were *always* ugly for most Imperial citizens," he said. "The only difference is that now the rich will be affected along with the poor."

The first drops of a Gangian rainstorm slapped wetly against the foliage above and she led him toward the shelter of a broad-leafed tree.

"I suppose I've had a privileged childhood – especially compared to what you had to go through." She perched herself on a well-worn low-hanging tree branch. "I'm amazed you don't hate me for it."

Paul sat next to her gazing out at the lawn where the first drops were already on their way back up in the form of a fine mist. "You left all of this behind for the hardship of military service. If anything, I respect you even more because of the choices you've made." He nodded out toward the lawn.

Tendrils of water vapor snaked their way into their leafy sanctuary, teasing out moisture collectors on the red lichen covering the trunks.

"I left my life behind for the relative step *up* in living standards when I joined the military," he told her.

She hopped off the branch, brushing fragments of bark from the back of her dress. "Let's go back to the house and see if a messenger from the Grand Senate is waiting for me."

It was time for General Urbica and Inspector Grimm to get back out on the Rim and keep the newly augmented 1st Gliesan Dragoons busy.

The *Eye* had finally agreed with CentCom on something. It was useful to embed an inspector with troops on the Rim.

Paul's role in finding the lost citizens had not gone unnoticed and he was being sent back out to work with the recently decorated

## A.G. Claymore

dragoons. He'd even been included in the list for the Emperor's unit-citation.

1GD would continue to aggressively patrol the border regions and seek out trouble. It was small, as Imperial responses went, but it was a start.

Both the Imperium and the Grays had been dealt a shock. It was only a matter of time before someone decided it was an ideal time for something daring and unexpected.

Julia intended to be that someone.

When you sign up for my new-release mail list!
Follow or scan the link below to get started!

# http://eepurl.com/ZCP-z

A.G. Claymore

# FROM THE AUTHOR

First off, many thanks to Chris Nuttall for offering me a work visa in the *Empire of Ashes*. Quite a few of the folks reading my stories have also read Mr. Nuttall (though there are far more who read his than mine, of course) and I'd already read my way through his excellent *Outside Context* series before hearing of this project.

He's put a great deal of thought into the structure and rules of this universe and I've enjoyed the time I've spent in it (hopefully you have as well).

I figure a posting to the Rim would cause a curious guy like Paul to start thinking about the *beyonder* colonies.

He'd been to the Rim before, as a military cop, and he's heard the rumors. He's watched desperate Humans take ship for the enigmatic colonies where the Imperium doesn't regulate your every thought or tax you into an early grave. Most cops on the rim assumed émigrés were following a fool's dream and would end up in an alien lab or on a dinner table, but Paul had always been one of those who believed the rumors of the Magi. A secretive group, if they really exist, the Magi guard the beyonder worlds against Imperial discovery, preserving sectors where Humans can do and think as they please and where the oppressive weight of the Imperial economy is nothing but a fading memory.

Seems to me, a lot can happen on planets like that.

It also sounds like the kind of place the Imperium might look if they were shopping around for a short war of expansion to bolster a flagging economy.

There's also the Grays.

I doubt that Brigadier Urbica (You don't really think the senate would refuse to confirm her, do you?) would sit quietly

281

on the Imperial side of the border. She'll want to probe Gray space and find out what new schemes they might be hatching and she'll need to watch her back. Her recent success has made her and Paul into targets.

When you're a target, sitting still is the last thing you want to do.

As always, thanks for reading this story and if you enjoyed it, please consider leaving a review. Word of mouth makes a huge difference and even a simple word or two helps to get a story discovered by new readers.

Thanks for taking the time to read this book!

Andrew.

Made in United States
Troutdale, OR
05/17/2024

19953233R00174